# Praise for the Knitting Mysterie[...]

## Dyer Consequences

## A Killer Stitch

*continued . . .*

# Dyer Consequences

## Maggie Sefton

BERKLEY PRIME CRIME, NEW YORK

**THE BERKLEY PUBLISHING GROUP**
**Published by the Penguin Group**
**Penguin Group (USA) Inc.**
**375 Hudson Street, New York, New York 10014, USA**
Penguin Group (Canada), 90 Eglinton Avenue East, Suite 700, Toronto, Ontario M4P 2Y3, Canada
(a division of Pearson Penguin Canada Inc.)
Penguin Books Ltd., 80 Strand, London WC2R 0RL, England
Penguin Group Ireland, 25 St. Stephen's Green, Dublin 2, Ireland (a division of Penguin Books Ltd.)
Penguin Group (Australia), 250 Camberwell Road, Camberwell, Victoria 3124, Australia
(a division of Pearson Australia Group Pty. Ltd.)
Penguin Books India Pvt. Ltd., 11 Community Centre, Panchsheel Park, New Delhi—110 017, India
Penguin Group (NZ), 67 Apollo Drive, Rosedale, North Shore 0632, New Zealand
(a division of Pearson New Zealand Ltd.)
Penguin Books (South Africa) (Pty.) Ltd., 24 Sturdee Avenue, Rosebank, Johannesburg 2196,
South Africa

Penguin Books Ltd., Registered Offices: 80 Strand, London WC2R 0RL, England

This is a work of fiction. Names, characters, places, and incidents either are the product of the author's
imagination or are used fictitiously, and any resemblance to actual persons, living or dead, business
establishments, events, or locales is entirely coincidental. The publisher does not have any control over
and does not assume any responsibility for author or third-party websites or their content.

PUBLISHER'S NOTE: The recipes contained in this book are to be followed exactly as written.
The publisher is not responsible for your specific health or allergy needs that may require medical
supervision. The publisher is not responsible for any adverse reactions to the recipes contained in
this book.

DYER CONSEQUENCES

A Berkley Prime Crime Book / published by arrangement with the author

PRINTING HISTORY
Berkley Prime Crime hardcover edition / June 2008
Berkley Prime Crime mass-market edition / June 2009

Copyright © 2008 by Margaret Conlan Aunon.
Cover illustration by Chris O'Leary.
Cover design by Rita Frangie.

ISBN: 978-0-425-22836-4

BERKLEY® PRIME CRIME
Berkley Prime Crime Books are published by The Berkley Publishing Group,
a division of Penguin Group (USA) Inc.,
375 Hudson Street, New York, New York 10014.
BERKLEY® PRIME CRIME and the PRIME CRIME logo are trademarks of Penguin Group
(USA) Inc.

PRINTED IN THE UNITED STATES OF AMERICA

10  9  8  7  6  5  4  3  2  1

# Acknowledgments

First, I want to thank Jill Koenig, one of the Lambspun regulars, who suggested the title for this, the fifth book in the Knitting Mystery series, *Dyer Consequences*. Jill's a great gal who knits and spins in addition to breeding llamas and Navajo-Churro sheep.

Next, I want to thank the owner of Lambspun, Shirley Ellsworth, for giving me a private lesson on how she creates her gorgeous custom-dyed yarns. It was fascinating to watch as she mixed powdered crystals and liquids, creating entirely new colors, then allowed the yarns to absorb those colors. Each finished skein was unique in its patterns.

Finally, I want to add a note about a character I referenced briefly in *A Killer Stitch*, but who went on to play a much bigger role in *Dyer Consequences*: the Larimer County policeman who patrols the canyon areas—Deputy Don.

I took the inspiration for this character from my dear friend and neighbor Ann Gouin. Her late husband, Don, had spent many years as a deputy sheriff for Larimer County, here in Northern Colorado. Don Gouin was a career Air Force officer, a navigator, who served several tours flying in Vietnam during the 1960s and 1970s, and finally flew home safe and sound to his wife, Ann, and their two daughters, Lee Ann and Sherry. After retiring from the Air Force, Don entered law enforcement and patrolled the mountain areas near Fort Collins, including our beautiful Cache La Poudre Canyon and Red Feather Lakes. Ann and Don spent a great deal of their spare time fishing in the canyon. A pastime they both loved.

I never had the pleasure of knowing Don Gouin because he died much earlier than he should have. But I've grown to appreciate him by way of the wonderful stories his wife, Ann, has shared over the years I've known her. So—when the fictional deputy sheriff made his first appearance in my mysteries, I knew immediately what his name was—Deputy Don. This fictional "Don" has gone on to develop quite a personality of his own, as all my characters do once they're allowed on the page. I hope you enjoy reading his scenes as much as I enjoyed writing them.

# One

**Kelly** Flynn angled toward the clearing, her skis slicing through the new-fallen snow. Colorado Powder. She slid to a stop and took in the view of the Continental Divide—all 360 degrees of it. Turning in a slow circle, Kelly gazed at the mountain peaks—glazed white with winter—surrounding her. On this early February afternoon, the sky was a brilliant blue, and sunshine reflected off the glaciers in a blinding glare. She'd forgotten how beautiful it was up here on the slopes. Had it really been five years since she'd last skied?

She heard an adrenaline-soaked yell, and a flash of yellow streaked by as a snowboarder descended the lower portion of the ski run, his posse of friends trailing in his wake.

Beautiful *and* crowded, Kelly thought as she scanned the slopes above and below. Fully half the people negotiating down this moderate-level ski run were riding snowboards rather than skis. Snowboarding had exploded in popularity. She also noticed that—like her—most of the people coming down the slope were now wearing helmets. That was definitely new.

Kelly tried to inch her scarf up higher to cover her cold nose. She'd also forgotten how frigid it was up on the slopes. Her nose and cheeks were freezing. Even her fingers felt frozen inside her insulated ski gloves, especially after her last tumble down the slope. And her goggles were fogging up again. Steve had joined her on the chairlift earlier and reminded Kelly how to clean her goggles. Kelly felt like she'd forgotten almost everything she ever knew about skiing.

But it was slowly coming back. Memories of shifting her weight as she descended the slope, remembering to use the edges of her skis, balancing—it was all coming back. Kelly just wished it would come faster. Moguls on this moderate blue run were still causing her problems.

A flash of red and black caught Kelly's attention as her boyfriend, Steve Townsend, swooshed to a stop beside her. "Ready to try a black diamond run?" he said after he pulled down his ski mask. "I'll ski with you."

"Not yet. I want to be able to make it over all these moguls without falling before I tackle an advanced run."

"Then I'll see you at the lodge below. Greg's hungry again, and I could use some hot chocolate." Pushing away with his poles, Steve shot down the slope in a low crouch.

Kelly stared after the streak of red and black, watching Steve deftly zoom in and around boarders and skiers alike, while visions of hot liquids danced before her eyes. Hot chocolate. With marshmallows. Kelly could almost taste it. And where there was hot chocolate, there was bound to be coffee. Hot coffee. The caffeine lobe in Kelly's brain began to throb. Even lukewarm coffee would taste good right now.

That settled it. Kelly snuggled into her newly knitted alpaca wool scarf and took off at a more modest pace down the slope. The moguls between her and the promise of caffeine were getting smaller by the second.

**Carefully** balancing her cup of hot chocolate, Kelly clomped her way to the cozy corner where she and her friends had claimed two comfy sofas in the spacious wood-beamed ski lodge. She'd also forgotten how clumsy she felt walking around in ski boots sans skis.

Awkwardly maneuvering around relaxing skiers and riders in the crowded slope-side lodge, Kelly finally managed to reach the corner sofas, hot chocolate intact.

"Aren't you warm yet?" Greg teased. "That's the fifth chocolate."

"Wrong." Kelly's friend Lisa spoke up beside her boyfriend. "The first three were coffee. This is Kelly, remember? The Queen of Caffeine."

"Hey, leave me alone. I'm just starting to thaw out," Kelly said as she settled on the sofa beside Steve.

"Reflexes coming back online?" Greg asked. "You looked like you were doing okay on the slopes."

Kelly took a sip of the sweet chocolate. "I wish they'd come back faster. Moguls are still throwing me, literally."

"You're doing great," Steve said, his hand tousling her dark hair before settling on the back of her neck. "I predict you'll be zooming over those moguls the next time we come."

"I keep forgetting how gorgeous it is up here," Lisa said, sweeping her long blonde hair into a ponytail as she stared through the windows.

"We should schedule a whole weekend next time," Greg suggested before draining his cup.

Kelly caught the devilish grin Lisa sent her way and decided to ignore it. A weekend trip meant she and Steve would share a room. Kelly didn't know if she was ready to go there yet. She was getting close, but . . .

"I'm game, but you'll have to run it past Miss Work-aholic here," Steve said as he stroked the back of Kelly's neck. His hand was warm on her skin.

"Hey, isn't that the pot calling the kettle black?" Kelly retorted. "You've been buried since the holidays with plans for your new site in Old Town."

Greg leaned back into the sofa beside Lisa. "I thought your schedule was getting better, Kelly. What's up?"

"That ranch property in Bellevue Canyon is what's up," Lisa replied before Kelly could. "She's been working more than usual ever since she bought the canyon ranch last month."

Kelly drained her hot chocolate. "Remember, I didn't have enough money to buy the ranch. That's why I took out a short-term investor loan, and it's due in June. By then, Cousin Martha's house in Wyoming should be sold, so I can pay off that loan. But I also want to make extra money for all the ranch repairs that'll be needed before I can move in."

"Meanwhile, Kelly's staying in her cottage. Right where we can keep an eye on her," Lisa said with an affectionate smile. "Who knows how much trouble she'd get into in the canyon all by herself."

Kelly joined in her friends' laughter, but Lisa's comment did bring up a thought that had nibbled around the edges of her mind for the last month. Would she be happy living in the mountains all by herself? Would she miss walking across the driveway every morning to visit with her friends at the knitting shop? Would those beautiful mountain views keep her from being lonely?

"Have you had any more trouble around the cottage?" Steve asked, his face revealing concern.

Kelly crushed the foam cup in her hands as she pictured the recent vandalism that had occurred at her cottage across from the knitting shop, House of Lamb-spun. "No, thank goodness. Those outside lights your guys installed must have done the trick." Frowning, she tossed the crushed cup to the pine tabletop.

Steve's warm hand stroked her neck. "Gus and the guys did a good job of cleaning off the paint, too, considering it's still the middle of winter."

Greg shook his head. "Man, stucco is hard to clean, too. And red paint . . . whoa. That's just plain mean."

"It's more than mean," Lisa countered, frown puckering her face. "It's damn vindictive. They smashed Kelly's windshield the week before, remember?"

"Do the police have any leads on those jerks?" Greg asked.

"Unfortunately, no," Kelly said as she pictured her smashed windshield. Remembered anger chased away the mellowing effect of hot chocolate. "Bastards."

Lisa peered over her cup. "You're keeping your car in the garage now, aren't you?"

"Oh, yeah. With a bolt and key lock, too. I'm not leaving anything outside that's valuable anymore."

Kelly tried to relax into the sofa again, but the comfortable feeling was gone—chased away by the frustration and resentment that flooded through her whenever she remembered the acts of vandalism that had started with the slashing of her tires right before Christmas.

Steve's warm hand rested on her shoulder. "Don't worry. The cops will get them. Vandals always slip up and make a mistake sooner or later."

"Boy, I hope so," Kelly said. "I want to see them go to jail."

"Hey, I checked my schedule, and I can drive up into the canyon with you this week if you're free," Steve said, clearly trying to change the subject. "We can start getting ideas where you'd like to put the new ranch house."

"What's wrong with the old one?" Greg asked, leaning his head back on his hands.

"Well, it's kind of old and run-down. Plus . . ." Kelly hesitated.

"Two women were murdered there, remember?" Lisa said. "I don't blame you, Kelly. I'd want a new house, too." She gave an exaggerated shudder.

"Now that the snowstorms have let up, I can go and check things out. I haven't been into the canyon since New Year's. Jayleen said she'll come with me tomorrow, so we can take a look around."

Steve reached for his coffee cup. "How many alpaca do you have again?"

"Fifteen."

"Wait a minute," Greg interrupted. "When did you buy livestock?"

"When I bought the ranch. The seller was from out of town, so she wanted to get rid of everything at once. Ranch, barn, alpaca, the whole thing. Kind of a package deal. I even hired the same caretaker she was using for the animals. Bobby Smith. He's a college student and has been taking care of the herd ever since the bank took over the property last summer."

"Is he still working out?" Steve asked.

"Oh, yeah, Bobby's great. He comes twice a day." A smile darted across Kelly's face. "That's another reason I need to go up there. Jayleen says I have to bond with my livestock. She and Bobby are the only people the animals have seen for months. Jayleen swears the alpaca think I'm just a tourist."

"The only thing I know about alpaca is they make great warm scarves," Greg said.

"The alpaca didn't make that scarf, I did." Lisa gave him a playful swat.

"Boy, I sure could use one of those scarves. It's pretty cold outside on those building sites, Kelly." Steve sent her a sly smile. "When's that curse gonna be over?"

"You mean the 'Don't knit for your boyfriend, or you'll scare him away' curse?" Greg teased.

"It's still too soon," Lisa admonished, schoolmarm fashion. "You should wait another few months."

"It'll be summer by then. I won't need it."

Kelly laughed. "I'll check with the Knitting Sages next fall and see what their considered wisdom is regarding our relationship."

Greg snorted. "Considered wisdom, my ass. Who's up for another run before we leave?"

Lisa grabbed her jacket. "I'm game, and I think I can take you on that double black diamond."

"In your dreams," Greg taunted as he sprang from the sofa. "You coming, Steve?"

"Absolutely. Ready to hit the slopes one more time before we head home, Kelly?"

Kelly screwed up her nose. "Sure, providing I can convince my legs to cooperate."


"Hang on, it's gonna get rough," Jayleen Swinson said as she steered her truck onto the snow-covered driveway leading to Kelly's canyon ranch house.

Tire tracks had already sliced through the deep snow, creating icy ruts. There was at least two feet of snow, Kelly observed, as she braced herself between the truck's door and its frayed rooftop padding.

"Wow, the snow's much deeper here," she said, scanning the expanse of white pastures. "Thanks so much for driving me, Jayleen. I never would have made it up here in my car."

"You got that right. Your pretty little car would've been high-centered for sure," Jayleen said as she jerked the truck to a stop in the center of a cleared area between the ranch house and the barn. "Looks like Bobby had to shovel this out himself. The plow service is really running behind this week."

Kelly spotted Bobby's old gray pickup truck parked beside the barn and searched for signs of the caretaker. Several alpaca were clustered in the corral outside the barn. "I feel sorry for the animals having to be outside in this cold," she said as she pushed the truck door open. Jayleen had already jumped to the ground. Kelly felt her boots slide as she stepped onto the slippery packed snow.

Brilliant blue sky, blazingly bright sunshine, and cold as hell. Colorado Winter. Kelly had forgotten those winters.

Jayleen adjusted her Stetson against the chill wind. "You forget where alpaca come from, Kelly. Way high up in those South American mountains. That's why they have such thick coats."

"Well, I'm glad I don't have to be outside all day," Kelly said, waving at the lanky, denim-clad young man who approached from the barn door. "Hey, Bobby, did you have to shovel this clearing yourself?"

"Yes, ma'am," Bobby said. "That plow guy told me he might be late sometimes. He's swamped." He pushed his hat back, revealing a mop of curly blond hair. "I wish the university would plow better. I had to pull three folks outta the snow yesterday. I expect today will be worse."

"How many classes you takin' this semester?" Jayleen asked, hands shoved in her back jeans pockets in her usual pose.

"Can't afford more than two, Miss Jayleen. Plus the homework is getting harder." A boyish grin appeared. "Ranch management and ecology. If I pass those, I can take more."

"Well, you're a hard worker, Bobby. I'm sure you'll do well," Kelly reassured him with a big smile. "Meanwhile, you keep track of how many times a month you have to shovel, and I'll pay you extra. I really appreciate your doing that."

"Hey, thank you, Miss Kelly, that's real nice of you," he said. "By the way, I'm glad you let Miss Jayleen bring you up here in her truck. Your car looks exactly like the ones I've been pullin' outta snowdrifts in town."

"Bobby, didn't I tell you to call me Jayleen? I don't know about Kelly, but I get an itch whenever anyone acts too polite around me."

"Same goes for me, Bobby. Kelly and Jayleen are just fine."

Bobby grinned. "Yes, ma'am. I'll try to remember. Did you wanta check out the livestock while you're here? They're doing real well. I've changed their feed like Miss—uh, like Jayleen told me. Since they can't graze and all."

Kelly glanced toward the corral where more alpaca appeared, clustering about, clearly interested in their visitors. Then she caught a glimpse of the Rocky Mountains shimmering in the distance. The View To Die For. Not as stunning as yesterday's view on the slopes, but still beautiful.

"The animals look great, Bobby. But today, Jayleen and I want to walk through the barn and stable and take stock of what needs to be done. I'll be coming again tomorrow with an architect to give me ideas about where to build a new ranch house."

"Why're you gonna build a new one?" Bobby asked, clearly surprised. "The old house looks pretty good."

Jayleen shook her head. "Looks can be deceiving, Bobby. That ranch house has some rotted timbers, and the roof's bad, so it'll hav'ta be torn down." She stared at the ramshackle barn in front of them. "Barn's in bad shape, too. So it'll hav'ta go."

"I can be here if you need me," Bobby offered.

Kelly shook her head. "That's okay, Bobby. We'll only have time for a walk around before we both have to get back into town. Steve's got a meeting, and I have a class later."

Jayleen stared at Kelly with surprise. "What kind of tomfool class are you taking? I thought you said you were up to your ears in client work. You need me to help out?"

"Thanks, Jayleen, but I think I'll be okay. Mimi's giving one of her classes on dyeing fibers at Lambspun, and I've signed up. Jennifer talked me into it to get me away from the computer. To tell the truth, it didn't take much persuading. I love those gorgeous colors Mimi comes up with. Apparently she's been creating them ever since she started Lambspun. They're her specialties. I want to learn how she does it."

"Well, let me know if you need help with the accounts," Jayleen said as she headed toward the barn.

Bobby glanced over his shoulder at the ranch house as he followed behind her. "Are you sure they both have to go, ma'am? They look like they still have some life left."

"Sometimes, Bobby, we just have to start fresh. And Kelly here deserves a newer place," Jayleen said with a grin. "Besides, she's got an architect and builder for a boyfriend, so it's an easy decision to make, right, Kelly?"

"Ask me that when the bills come in," Kelly joked as she fell in step behind them.

# Two

Kelly stomped snow from her boots before yanking open the door to the House of Lambspun knitting shop. "*Brrrrr!*" she said, spotting her friend Jennifer, who was standing beside some baskets that overflowed with plump skeins of yarn. "I swear, it's as cold here as it was up in the canyon this morning."

"You've been complaining about the cold ever since the snows started in December," Jennifer said, stroking the yarns that spilled across a maple table. Lemon yellow, cranberry red, pumpkin orange, and rich browns that ran from light caramel to deep chocolate.

Kelly couldn't resist touching and sank her hands into another basket filled with luscious alpaca yarns. Black, brown, and gray alpaca combined in one skein to create a tweed. Kelly had used a similar color combination to make the luxurious scarf that protected her neck from the wind's wintry blasts.

"That's because I've been *cold* ever since December. The cottage must need more insulation or something. I have to wear a thick sweater inside even when I turn up the heat."

Jennifer brushed her auburn hair away from her face and gave Kelly a sly smile. "If you let Steve stay over some night, I bet you wouldn't have to turn up the heat."

*Here we go again.* Jennifer had stepped up her teasing lately. Kelly shifted the knitting bag over her shoulder and headed for the shop's inviting main room. "Okay, okay. You can stop now."

"Just making a suggestion," Jennifer said as she followed. "You don't hear me complaining about the cold because I do something about it at night. Last night, it was Eddie. Tonight, it'll be John. I think. Or maybe Ken."

Spying another friend sitting across the library table, Kelly smiled. "Hi, Megan. Jennifer's telling me how she stays warm at night."

"I'm trying to be helpful," Jennifer said as she plopped her knitting bag on the table and pulled out a chair. "Kelly's always complaining about the cold, and I told her Steve would be more than happy to raise the heat at her place. If she'd let him."

Megan's busy needles slowed as she looked up from the Valentine red yarn in her lap. Her fair complexion stained pink with a faint blush as she grinned. "I'm sure he would."

Kelly noticed Megan wasn't blushing as intensely as she used to whenever Jennifer's conversations got descriptive. "Okay, you can both stop now," Kelly countered as she settled into a chair. "Why don't you concentrate on one of those guys, Jennifer? Then you can stop snooping on Steve and me."

"I've told you, I don't do permanent. Besides, there's safety in numbers," Jennifer said as she pulled a royal blue sweater from her bag and resumed knitting.

"Hey, Kelly, can I convince you and Steve to sign up for another mixed doubles tennis tournament at the club? You two did great last December." Megan glanced up from the bloodred yarn, stitches quickly forming on the needles.

*Is that a scarf taking shape?* Kelly wondered if she'd ever be able to knit without paying attention like her friends could. She pulled out the variegated wool scarf she'd started. After the serious tweed alpaca yarns, Kelly needed color. These new yarns were a promise of spring for her eyes. The reds ran from bold strawberry to soft raspberry all the way to zinfandel pink and back again. She examined the last stitches. They were neater, and—sure enough—there were fewer mistakes. Despite all her doubts, she was getting better. *Wonder of wonders.* Her friends were right.

"Megan, you're being way too kind. Steve and I had our butts kicked in that tournament."

"But you made it halfway through. That's saying a

lot. Marty and I both think you and Steve could be dynamite if you played more."

Kelly laughed softly. "That would take a lot of practice, Megan, which means a lot of time. And that's what neither Steve nor I have right now. He's buried in that new building site in Old Town, and I'm up to my neck trying to earn money to start repairs on the canyon ranch."

"See? There's another reason to play," Megan said, her blue eyes bright with enthusiasm. "You *both* work too much. Tennis will help you relax."

"I know something that would relax them even more," Jennifer offered, not looking up from her needles.

Kelly studiously ignored her. "You and Marty still wiping up the tennis courts with your opponents?" she asked Megan.

"We try our best."

Kelly marveled again at how the supershy Megan had "backed into" dating without even knowing it. Clever Marty had slowly escalated from tennis matches to tennis-plus-dinner or tennis-plus-a-movie. Kelly wondered if Megan even realized she was dating Marty. She was clearly enjoying their time together.

"How's Marty doing? I haven't seen him for a while."

"We haven't seen him because we haven't had a potluck since the holidays. Bring out the food, and I guarantee, old Marty will show up," Jennifer said.

Megan laughed. "You're right about that. He really

puts it away. I swear, he eats way more than I do, and you guys know my appetite."

"Unfortunately I do," Jennifer said with a sigh. "Why is it that skinny people can eat like it's their last meal and not get fat? Me . . . all it takes are a couple of doughnuts, and I see it on my hips the next day." She shook her head.

"If you'd run a little, you wouldn't gain weight," Kelly teased good-naturedly. "Just think how many doughnuts you could eat then."

"Or you could learn to play tennis at our club," Megan offered.

Jennifer sent Megan a jaundiced look. "I told you two, I prefer indoor sports."

"Tennis is indoors," Kelly said.

"It would be good for *both* of you," Megan continued, a righteous fire of conviction shining forth. "Jennifer needs the exercise, and Kelly needs to relax from work."

"Maybe in the summer, Megan. I'll have to wait and see how my schedule is by June. After I've paid off that loan for the property, maybe I can cut back on my workload then."

"The girls are right, Kelly. You *do* work too much," another voice chimed in. Kelly turned to see the motherly shop owner, Mimi Shafer, smiling at them while she arranged knitting books on the surrounding shelves.

The warm, welcoming knitting room was lined on two sides with floor-to-ceiling bookshelves crammed with books on knitting, crocheting, spinning, weaving, dyeing, felting, and garment patterns. If it had to do with fiber, there was a book on it. The sheer enormity of the topics always amazed Kelly. She was still stumbling through her stitches. Well, maybe not stumbling, but certainly not "tripping lightly" through them. Knitting still required her concentration.

Kelly returned Mimi's smile. "I can't help it, Mimi. I've gotta earn lots of money to fix up that ranch. This morning, Jayleen confirmed what I suspected. In addition to the ranch house, both the barn and stable have to go. Steve and I will be going up tomorrow to decide where to build."

"Well, now, that's exciting," Mimi said. "Aren't you lucky to have Steve design your house. I'm sure he'll put his heart and soul into those plans."

"Steve could put his heart and soul into a whole lot more if she'd let him," Jennifer teased.

"I'm sure he could," Mimi said, clearly trying to contain her laughter as she headed toward the classroom doorway.

Kelly gave in to the inevitable. Once Jennifer started teasing, there was no stopping her.

"How's Carl liking all the snow?" Megan asked Kelly, changing the subject. "I don't see him outside in the yard chasing squirrels."

"Believe me, Carl doesn't spend more time outside in the cold than he has to. Even the squirrels don't tempt him. He watches them from his doggie bed inside. I think we're both adjusting to Colorado winters."

"Is Carl doing his Rottweiler duty at night to scare

away those creeps who've been causing trouble?" Jennifer asked. "I haven't heard anything new, and I figure the Lambspun network would be the first to know."

Kelly held up crossed fingers as she spied Lambspun regular Burt Parker enter the room, carrying a large fleece-filled plastic bag. "So far, so good. Those new outside lights must have done the job because nothing else has happened."

"I'm glad to hear that, Kelly," Burt said as he pulled out a spinning wheel from the corner and sat down. "You be sure to let me know if you see or hear anything suspicious, okay?"

Kelly watched Burt, a retired cop turned spinner, place a hunk of creamy white wool fleece in his lap and start pulling the fibers apart gently, creating batten. "Count on it, Burt. Have you heard anything from your old partner?"

Burt's fingers worked the batten as his feet worked the treadle, yarn feeding onto the wheel. "He said there were reports of one bunch that tore up someone's garage north of town a couple of weeks ago. Stole some electronic equipment then painted their slogan in red on the side of the garage."

Kelly sat up at that. "Whoa! Red paint? That may be them! Any leads on that one?"

The soft hum of the wheel continued as yarn slowly filled the spindle. "Not yet. Unfortunately vandalism has gotten much more common over the years as more people have moved to Fort Connor. Problem is, there's only so much manpower to go around, and other crimes have increased, too. Like burglaries and assaults. Those take a lot of time to investigate."

"That could be the same bunch, Burt," Kelly offered, pulse racing despite the meditative hum of the wheel.

Most of the time Kelly found it soothing to sit beside Burt or the other spinners. She liked to let the hum of the wheel and the peacefulness of knitting quiet her mind, arrange her thoughts, and bring new ideas. But not this time. Right now, all peaceful sensations of knitting were wiped away by ugly memories.

"Maybe so, Kelly. Meanwhile, Dan's keeping an eye out and checking all reports of vandalism that come in. We'll find them eventually."

Kelly released a frustrated sigh, feeling the tension in her shoulders relax. "I know, I know. Everyone says that, Burt, and I know you're all right. It's the eventually part that bothers me."

**"Thanks** for the refill, Sarah," Kelly called to the waitress as she left the café located at the rear of the knitting shop. Balancing her coffee mug and knitting bag, Kelly headed down the hallway. She had worked all afternoon and now she needed a break badly. This particular client's accounts were testing her patience. Despite her instructions, this guy refused to enter all his expenses and sales receipts. Kelly was about to send him to someone with more patience—a lot more patience.

She started to rush around a corner, but this time she stopped and paused. Good thing, too, because Jennifer was standing on the other side checking the cones of novelty yarns stacked on the wall.

"Hey, Jen, you have time for coffee? The café is hosting a banquet, so they're still open. I'm taking a break from a nightmare client." Kelly headed through the arched doorway to the main room.

"Don't mention nightmare clients," Jennifer replied, following after. "That's why I left the office early. Both of my young client couples left me voice mails saying they plan to buy new homes *and* they've already signed with builder sales reps." She dumped her large knitting bag on the library table. "I swear I've been taking them around for over a month now. *I* could have taken them to the building sites, but they didn't even ask. It's *so* frustrating when this happens."

Kelly plopped her things on the table and pulled out a chair. "It'll get better, Jennifer. It always does. I've watched you sell real estate for nearly a year now, and it seems to come and go."

"Feast or famine." Jennifer nodded resignedly. "But tell that to my landlord."

"Hey, you can always bunk in with me if times get really tough," Kelly said, bringing out the variegated pink and red yarn. Chunky wool, too, like her very first winter scarf. Kelly wanted to play with the huge needles again. "The sofa's comfortable. Carl sneaks up there all the time."

"Thanks, but I wouldn't think of it. I wouldn't want

to cramp Steve's style. Just in case you have one martini too many some night and your defenses are down." Jennifer smiled as she withdrew the sweater she was knitting. "But then, Steve is such a gentleman, he would never take advantage like that."

"It's a good thing, too," Kelly said, playing along this time. *If you can't lick 'em, join 'em.* "If Steve tried anything, Carl would probably bite him in the butt."

Jennifer laughed out loud. "You're right, he probably would. . . . Hey, look who's here. *Tracy!* It's about time you showed up," she called into the next yarn room. "I've been telling you about this shop for weeks now."

Kelly glanced up and spotted a slender blonde, who looked to be in her early twenties, standing in the midst of the yarns with that glazed expression she witnessed on most newcomers' faces. Kelly remembered the first time she entered the Lambspun shop . . . and promptly fell down the rabbit hole. She hadn't come out since. "Friend of yours?" she asked.

"Yeah, she's a student at the university who also works part-time in our real estate office." Jennifer beckoned Tracy over. "Come meet my friend Kelly. You've heard me talk about everyone here in the shop."

Tracy slowly approached the table, her eyes scanning the walls in obvious wonder. "Wow, you didn't exaggerate, Jennifer. This place is fabulous. All these yarns . . . wow . . ." Her voice trailed off as she gazed.

"Lambspun has that effect on people," Kelly said, offering her hand. "I'm Kelly Flynn, Tracy. Glad you dropped in."

Tracy seemed to snap out of the yarn trance long enough to shake Kelly's hand. "Hi, Kelly. I'm Tracy Putnam. Jennifer's been tempting me with descriptions of the yarn at Lambspun ever since I told her I was a knitter."

"Now you know why I did," Jennifer said. "Knitters who haven't been here are seriously deprived. Did you leave the office early today?"

Tracy reached into a nearby bin filled with tidy coils of variegated yarns—brown merging from chocolate into mahogany and russet, then burnt umber into pumpkin orange. "Susan sent me on an errand and said I didn't need to return if I finished early."

"Susan's one of our superstars," Jennifer explained. "You know, the ones with such huge client lists they never have to bunk in with their friends and wind up sleeping on the sofa with a Rottweiler."

Kelly laughed softly, as did Tracy. "Well, I'm glad you decided to drop by for a visit. Jennifer says you're taking classes at the university. What are you studying?"

"Chemistry. I'm one of those science geeks, I guess. I can only afford two courses a semester, so it's taking forever. But I'm finally into my major courses now."

"Good for you. It's worth it, Tracy. Hang in there," Kelly advised. "It sounds like you need knitting to relax like the rest of us do. I'm a CPA, and I escape over here regularly. Whenever the numbers start crossing in front of my eyes."

Mimi bustled into the room then, her arms filled

with fluffy billowing bunches of yarns. Fuschia, cherry red, and bubblegum pink. "Hello, girls," she greeted. "Don't forget the class tomorrow night."

Kelly reached out and sank her hand into a frothy pink billow. *Soft, soft.* "Are you kidding, Mimi? This is the reason I'm taking the class. I want to see how you create such gorgeous colors."

"Mimi, meet Tracy. She's a knitter from my office, and I've been telling her about the shop for weeks," Jennifer said, gesturing to her friend. "Tracy . . . uh, Tracy? . . . Uh-oh. I think we've lost her. Fiber trance."

Kelly chuckled, watching Tracy stare wide-eyed at the seductive billows of froth in Mimi's arms. "Mimi, this is Tracy, and she's under the spell."

"Welcome, Tracy, I'm so glad you came to see us," Mimi said, holding the froth closer. "Go ahead and touch if you want."

Tracy sank both hands deep into the billows, delight registering on her face. "Wow . . . this is so . . . so gorgeous. Do you make this yourself?"

"Well, we buy the fleeces and often spin them ourselves, but yes, we do a lot of the dyeing. That's how we get such yummy colors." Mimi beamed with pride. "I think I'll call this one 'Christmas Candy.' What do you think, girls?"

"Please don't remind me of the holidays. I'm still losing weight from that party," Jennifer complained, fingering the fibers.

"You dyed this?" Tracy peered into Mimi's face. "How? I mean, what chemicals do you use?"

Mimi laughed lightly. "Oh, we use lots of chemicals, trust me. That's what I'm teaching in that class tomorrow night."

"Hey, Tracy, you should join us," Kelly suggested. "I mean, you're a chemistry major, after all. This stuff will be right up your alley."

Tracy stared into the billowing fibers as her hands caressed the froth. "Boy, I wish I could."

"C'mon, join us," Jennifer said.

"It would be wonderful to have a real chemist in the class," Mimi added. "You could teach us a lot, I'm sure."

Tracy looked up with a shy smile. "I'm far from a chemist, believe me. You'd be teaching *me*." She stroked the candy colors again. "I sure wish I could."

Kelly noticed a wistful expression crossing Tracy's face and sensed that her hesitation stemmed from a common condition of college students—lack of funds. An inspired suggestion came to mind, and Kelly spoke without thinking.

"Tracy, I can tell you'd like to take the class, and you'd enjoy it even more than we would. If it's money that's holding you back, don't worry about it. The shop has scholarships for special cases. Right, Mimi?" Kelly deliberately caught Mimi's gaze.

Mimi quickly followed her lead. "That's right, Tracy. And you're definitely a special person, what with your chemistry background and all. Why, you would bring a lot to our class. Please come."

Tracy looked to Mimi in surprise. "Really?" she

exclaimed softly, almost as if she didn't believe it. "Oh . . . oh, that's wonderful! Thank you! Thank you! You are so sweet to do that, Mimi."

"You're welcome, dear," Mimi said with her maternal smile. "I'll see you tomorrow, then. Five o'clock. We'll look forward to creating new colors together."

"Oh, yes," Tracy breathed, clearly still excited, face flushed with pleasure. "I can't wait. In fact, I'd better run back to my apartment right now and do all my homework tonight, so I'll have tomorrow night completely free. See you then." Tracy turned and sped from the shop without waiting for their good-byes.

"I didn't know the shop had scholarships," Jennifer said.

Mimi smiled as she headed toward her office. "We didn't until now."

"That was my bright idea," Kelly confessed. "I remember being a broke college student. By the way, Mimi, since I thought it up, put Tracy's fee on my bill, okay?"

"I wouldn't dream of it," Mimi said over her shoulder. "This is my treat."

# Three

Kelly stood by her patio door and sipped her second cup of morning coffee while she stared out into the backyard, watching Carl galumph through the crusty snow. Good thing she had extra rugs waiting by the door. Four big wet dog feet made quite a mess.

Carl ran to the fence and began to bark, little white puffs of frozen dog breath floating upward in the frigid air. Squirrels were probably taunting him from the treetops, Kelly figured, as she glanced into the cottonwood trees that bordered the adjacent golf course and shaded her backyard. Sure enough, Carl's nemesis, Saucy Squirrel, clung to one of the overhanging branches.

Kelly was about to turn away when a movement

beside the trees caught her eye. What was that? Was someone standing there? She didn't see anything, just the trees. Then she saw the outline of someone in a dark jacket edge slowly from behind a tree. He stood still, staring into the backyard.

*Who the hell is that?*

Kelly yanked open the glass door and raced out onto the patio. "Hey, what do you want?" she yelled at the intruder. Carl's barking had turned furious now.

The black-hooded figure took one look at Kelly, then turned and broke into a run across the frozen golf course. All Kelly could tell in that brief glimpse was that he was tall and slender and apparently in good shape because he was running fast. She watched him glance over his shoulder once, then head for the busy street and traffic.

Her heart raced as she watched the man disappear in the distance. Was that one of the vandals? Had he come back? *Why?* Was he looking for something else to damage? *Damn it!* Why was he targeting her place? What would he do now that she had confronted him?

Carl paced back and forth atop the crusty snow, barking doggie threats into the icy air. Still agitated and frustrated, Kelly started pacing, too, ignoring the freezing cold. From the corner of her eye, she spied Steve's big red truck heading down the Lambspun driveway and pulling to a stop beside her cottage. The huge engine's throaty rumble silenced even Carl's barks. It was a monster truck, not your average go-to-the-mall, haul-around-garden-supplies, handyman kind of truck. Out west, trucks were serious vehicles.

Steve stepped out and slammed the door. "Hey, there," he yelled. "Ready to head up into the canyon?"

Carl had raced to the fence the moment he saw Steve. Playmate Steve. Provider-of-golf-balls-and-toys Steve. Roll-on-the-grass-in-the-summer Steve. This time, Carl's bark was welcoming as he stood, paws on fence, waiting for a head scratch.

Steve obliged. "Hey, boy, whatcha been doin'? Chasin' squirrels?"

"No, he's being a good watchdog. He was barking, and I saw a guy standing over there beside the trees." Kelly pointed.

Steve's smile disappeared. "You're kidding."

"I wish I were. Now I'm wondering if it was one of those vandals checking out the place again. *Damn!*"

"What did he look like? Did you get a good look at him?"

"Just a glimpse. He was standing beside the trees, staring into the yard. I came out and yelled at him, and he took off over the golf course, heading toward the street." Kelly rubbed her arms, feeling the cold at last.

Steve stared toward the snowy greens. "You know, he could have just been some kid cutting across the course, Kelly. Maybe he came over to see Carl, that's all."

"I don't know. Maybe." She stamped her feet as she stood beside the door. "This whole vandal thing has really gotten to me. Maybe he was just a kid, but maybe he was one of those jerks coming back to see what else he could do."

"Go in and grab your coat. Let's get some coffee from Pete's and head to the canyon. We can talk about it on the way."

Kelly stared at the empty frigid greens and let out a frustrated sigh. "Okay, here's my mug. Tell Pete to fill 'er up. High octane." She tossed the mug across the fence.

Steve caught it with one hand. "Hey, what's with the underhand girly throw? Where's that first baseman's arm?"

"It's frozen along with the rest of me. You won't see it until the spring thaw."

**Kelly** grasped the banister and hastened down the steps to the shop basement, following after the rest of the students in Mimi's evening dye class. Tracy was at the front of the line.

"This is where we store everything. Forgive the chaos," Mimi called out as she led her students around piles of large plastic bags filled with colorful yarns.

"I'm amazed they can find anything down here. Stuff is piled all over," Jennifer said over her shoulder to Kelly.

That was putting it mildly, Kelly thought as Mimi led them through a rabbit warren of rooms leading to the back of the basement and the dye tubs. Since the house had been built in the 1930s, its basement was typical of that period, with a maze of small, low-ceilinged rooms opening one into another, and a huge, noisy ancient furnace. In other words—dark, spooky, and scary. Since she'd grown up in Fort Connor, Kelly remembered playing in this basement many times as a child. That was when Uncle Jim and Aunt Helen still owned the farmhouse—and were still alive.

"I'd forgotten how many rooms were down here. I haven't been in the basement since I was a kid," Kelly said as she peered into room after cluttered room.

Everywhere she looked, Kelly saw bags of yarn in every color imaginable. Metal shelves were stacked high with bags of fibers, fleeces, and spun yarns. Bags were on the floor, piles on top of piles. Floor-to-ceiling storage in every room.

"All right, everyone, gather around and we'll get started. Watch your heads in the doorway," Mimi said as she led her little troupe into the small room next door to the furnace.

Kelly ducked her head and found a spot beside Jennifer in the semicircle around Mimi. "Boy, Mimi, it's a good thing you're here. We need a guide to get back to the shop. I'm lost already."

"Well, it's certainly out of the way, I'll say that. But that makes it really peaceful and quiet. It's a nice place to work," Mimi said.

"If you're a ghost, yeah," Jennifer said, glancing around the low-ceilinged room. "This is creepy down here. I almost expect that character from the *Halloween* movies to show up."

"Thanks for creeping us all out, Jennifer," Tracy said as laughter and nervous squeals rippled around the group. "If we have nightmares tonight, it's your fault."

"Hey, just making an observation."

"O-kay!" Mimi announced in a clear voice, taking control of the class again. "Now, your handouts have all these steps in detail. Right now, I simply want you to watch what I'm doing, so you'll remember what each step looks like." She lifted a large billowy skein of creamy yarn and held it up. "We always start with a cleaned fleece, which has been washed, carded, then spun like this one." She offered it around for the class to touch.

"Soft," Kelly observed as she caressed the fibers.

"It should be. This skein is made up of fifty percent merino wool and fifty percent silk." Turning toward the laundry tubs attached to the walls, Mimi dabbed her fingers into the water. "This skein has also been prewet and spun dry. That's the first step. You have to prewet the yarn with a wetting agent. That's a chemical solution we put in the water to help remove anything which would keep the yarn from taking the dye. Then we drain it, and spin it dry in the washing machine." She dropped the skein into the water and poked at it with a metal rod beside the tub.

"What kinds of things get on the yarn?" Tracy asked.

"All sorts of things can inhibit the process. For example, sometimes commercial spinners use spinning oils. That's why we prewet first." Mimi poked at the skein again. "This is good and soaked, so now we can start with the dyeing." She stirred a measuring cup of clear liquid into the dye tub. "First, we add white vinegar. Next, we dissolve the powdered dye crystals in water before adding them."

She pulled on thick rubber gloves before opening two plastic containers. "We'll use pink and blue for this first demonstration."

Scooping from both containers, she sprinkled them into separate water-filled bottles, coloring the waters bright pink and vivid blue. Mimi proceeded to pour each bottle into the dye tub.

"We're looking for variegated colors, so each skein will have pinks and blues and purples distributed throughout."

"You don't mix it?" Jennifer asked, watching Mimi gently poke the skein in the tub with the metal rod.

"No, because you'd lose the variegated colors we're looking for. Instead, you'd have one solid color. It all depends on what colors you want."

Kelly peered into the tub, noticing the skein taking color differently throughout its length. Robin's egg blue, light pink, lavender, periwinkle. "Wow, look at the colors," she observed. "It's doing exactly what you said, Mimi."

"Well, let's hope so." Mimi poked the skein again.

"Fascinating," Tracy said, staring wide-eyed at the process, clearly captivated by the chemistry experiment taking place before her eyes.

"Now, we'll let this set for thirty minutes or so. It would be longer if you wanted a darker color, but we're going after light springtime colors. Once you've got the colors you want, then you would drain the tub and refill to rinse the yarn thoroughly."

"You drain all that dye water out then refill the tub?" Jennifer asked. "How hot is the water?"

"Hot enough to burn," Mimi warned. "About one hundred seventy degrees."

"Ouch." Jennifer flinched.

"After you rinse the yarn, you'll spin it to remove the excess water." She pointed to the doorway leading into the darkened furnace room. "Then you'll spread out the yarns on frames so the commercial fans can blow the yarn dry. There's yarn on the frames right now. Go take a look."

Tracy and the others headed for the room next door. Kelly followed, but noticed that Jennifer stayed put. "Don't you want to take a look?"

"Nope. That looks too much like horror movie territory to me."

Kelly gave her a playful punch in the arm, then glanced into the furnace room from the doorway. There were the frames with freshly dyed dark blue fibers spread out. Two large fans sat on the floor. "Those are big fans, Mimi," she said as she returned to the dye tubs.

"And they make a *big* noise, too. That's why they're turned off right now."

"Can you use a hair dryer?" Jennifer asked.

"Sure, if you've only dyed a small amount. But you'd want to use the big fans for a lot of yarn." Mimi removed a large skein of pink yarn from a nearby shelf. "But now, I want to show you something else we do before we even rinse the yarn." She dropped the skein of yarn into the dye tub.

"Whoa, did you mean to do that?" Kelly asked.

"I bet I know why," Tracy said.

"I bet you do," Mimi said with a smile.

"You're trying to use up all the dye, right?"

"You're right, Tracy. We always put another skein into the water in order to exhaust the dye, soak it all up. It's also ecologically the right thing to do."

"Give chemistry major Tracy an A," Jennifer teased.

Kelly watched the pink yarn take the dye. Different colors were emerging. "Look at that. Rose pink and violet and deep lavender. New colors, entirely. That's cool, Mimi."

Mimi laughed softly. "We think so. Now, let's get you girls up to your elbows in the tubs, okay?"

# Four

"C'mon in, Carl. You can't stay outside while I run. It's too cold," Kelly said as she held the patio door open.

Carl hesitated on the patio, staring toward the yard, as if weighing his decision. Inside and warm or outside and frozen.

Kelly zipped up her insulated running jacket and pulled her knitted hat down over her ears. "Get inside, Carl. You'll turn into a doggie popsicle if you stay out there." She patted her thermalwear-clad leg, beckoning him inside. Carl hurried through the door before it slammed shut.

Tugging on her guaranteed-to-twenty-below-zero gloves, Kelly headed out into the bitter cold morning. The sky was a brilliant blue, Colorado Blue, as blue as a summer's day. Only it wasn't. She skipped down the front steps, her breath frosting up the moment the warm air left her lips.

*How can it be so pretty and still be so cold?* Kelly thought as she rounded the front yard and set off for the river trail bordering the golf course. The Cache La Poudre River sliced through the city diagonally as it flowed out of the Rocky Mountains down toward the South Platte River and the flatlands of Kansas.

Sunshine reflected off the snow-covered greens. The sun was rising earlier, Kelly observed, and she was counting down the days until the vernal equinox in March. The first day of spring. She could hardly wait.

She was about to pick up her stride as she aimed for the golf course, noticing how the sun bathed the beige stucco of her cottage and garage in a reddish orange glow. In fact, the sun's rays turned the garage sunset red, bright red, almost. . . .

Kelly jerked to a stop and stared at the garage nestled beside two tall evergreens edging the golf course. Its red-tiled roof and beige stucco matched the Spanish colonial style of the cottage and the sprawling farmhouse turned knitting shop across the driveway. Except now, the small square structure was covered in red paint.

Fire engine red. Exactly the same color of paint that was thrown on her cottage last month. Quickly racing around the garage, she confirmed her fears. The front and both sides were splashed with red paint.

*Damn it!* She knew the guy she saw yesterday morning was up to no good. He was probably one of those bastards come back to check out his handiwork. Pulling off a glove, Kelly touched a finger to the paint, frozen now in the cold. Little ice crystals sparkled, catching the early morning sunlight, mocking her with the beauty of the reflected colors.

A shaft of anger shot through Kelly as she glared at her vandalized garage. Thank goodness for the heavy-duty lock—otherwise those jerks would have smashed her windshield again, or worse. *How come she didn't hear anything last night?*

Thinking back, Kelly recalled Carl waking her up once in the night, barking. But she had seen nothing when she'd looked out the windows into the back and side yards. She'd even opened the front door and checked the front and the driveway. Nothing.

*"Damn it!"* Kelly swore out loud this time as she raced back to the cottage and her cell phone.

How could a bunch of vandals be so stealthy? Was it a bunch? Or was it just that one guy? Kelly's mind raced as fast as her pulse as she tossed her gloves and hat to the sofa. She shrugged off her jacket and punched in Burt's phone number.

Burt answered on the fifth ring. "Hey, Kelly, why so early? Everything okay?"

"No, everything's not okay, Burt," she complained. "Those bastards came back and threw paint on my garage this time. Red paint again. Thick red paint."

"Ahhhh, Kelly, I'm sorry to hear that." Burt's friendly baritone turned serious. "Have you called it in yet?"

"I'm about to. I've still got the card of the officer I spoke to last time." Kelly exhaled in exasperation. "Damn it, Burt, why are these guys targeting me? They've slashed my tires, smashed my windshield, thrown paint on my house . . . now they're at it again!"

"I know, Kelly, it's frustrating. Let me give Dan a call, too. I'll see if he's gotten any more information on the group that was spotted on the north side of town. I'll get back to you, okay?"

"Please do, Burt," Kelly said, pacing from her small living room into the dining room and back again. "I'll be here making phone calls. I'm hoping Steve's cleanup crew can come out before that paint is frozen solid on the stucco. It's colder now than it was in January when it first happened."

"Talk to you later. And, Kelly . . ."

"Yeah?"

"It'll be okay."

"I don't know, Burt. I've got a baaaad feeling in my gut about all this. It's almost like a . . . a vendetta or something."

"I know you want an answer, but vandalism almost never makes sense, Kelly. It's usually just random. I'll call you later."

Kelly clicked off as she searched her desk for the card of the police officer who had investigated January's damage. She punched in the number as she started another lap around her living room.

"Random," Burt had said. *Uh-huh.* Right now, Kelly

felt anything but random. She felt singled out and targeted. Definitely targeted.

The drone of power equipment rose and fell in an insistent whine. Normally the sound would be annoying, but this whine was music to Kelly's ears.

She took another deep drink of the café's rich coffee while she watched Steve's cleanup crew work to remove the thick red paint. Large power brushes spun in blurred circles as their bristles sliced away red paint. Unfortunately, the stucco was sometimes sliced off, too. Kelly could see unsightly splotches of cracked, broken, and missing stucco on both sides of her garage.

*Well, at least it matches the cottage now,* she thought with a dejected sigh. Whole sections of stucco had come off the cottage last month when it was being cleaned. Dollar signs danced in front of Kelly's eyes as she estimated the cost of repairing two stucco buildings this spring. In addition to saving for repairs to the canyon property, of course.

Her cell phone jangled in the pocket of her ski jacket, and Kelly recognized the number of her friend, mentor, and ranch adviser, Curt Stackhouse. She flipped it open while she drained the last of the coffee.

"Kelly, this is Curt." His voice was a deep, resonant bass. "I just heard the bad news. I sure am sorry you're having to put up with that mess again."

"I couldn't believe it, either, Curt. I feel like these

guys are targeting me or something. And I don't like it."

"Don't you worry, Kelly girl. The police will find 'em. Just you wait."

"How'd you hear about it so fast? The Lambspun network must be even better than I thought." The whine of the power brushes rose in pitch, and Kelly could see a dusty cloud of disintegrated stucco floating above both men's heads as they cleaned. Stucco was disappearing before her eyes.

"Jayleen told me you called her this morning. She's over here helping me sort through Ruthie's fleeces in the storage shed. I don't wanta tell you how many bags are in there."

"Probably as many as I saw stored at the Wyoming ranch. It sounds like my cousin Martha was a lot like Ruth," Kelly said, picturing Curt's late wife, Ruth. "The last time I was up there checking out the place, I counted over a hundred bags of fleece. Both sheep and alpaca."

Curt's chuckle warmed her. "Well, I gotcha beat, Kelly. Ruthie had a whole lot more than a hundred. Jayleen suggested I pay to get them cleaned and carded then hire that little gal over at Lambspun to spin them for me. You know, Lucy, the one who's expecting a baby."

"Good idea, Curt. Lucy could use the work. She's trying to build her spinning business so it'll support her and the baby. I promised I'd bring my fleeces to her next summer. That is, providing I can afford to build a new barn by then. There's nowhere else to store those bags."

"How's it going with the canyon property? You and Steve decided where to build the new ranch house yet?"

"As a matter of fact, yes. We drove up there yesterday and took more pictures. And we both agreed that we'll put the new ranch house where the old one is now. Whoever did the first place wasn't much of a builder, but he sure picked the right spot. The views are best from that location. The barn and stable—"

"What in Sam Hill is that noise in the background? Is Steve's crew there already?"

"Yes, thank goodness. And they're having to work twice as hard to get the paint off this time because it's frozen solid. In January, we were having a warm spell when the cottage was damaged."

"From the sound of those brushes, I suspect you'll have to restucco both the cottage and the garage come spring. Hate to say it, but stucco doesn't hold up real well under the best of circumstances."

Kelly gave a derisive snort. "Don't I know it. You should see the clouds of stucco floating away as we speak." Now that her trusty ranch adviser had opened the door, Kelly rushed through it, bringing her worries with her. "Curt, how am I going to pay for all these extra repairs? I've been saving all I can to start work on the canyon ranch in the spring, and now this. . . ." She sighed dramatically. "Damn, it's so frustrating."

"Take it easy, Kelly. It'll all work out. We can always

sell off the rest of the cattle you've got on that Wyoming land this winter instead of waiting for spring. You may get a lower price, but if you need the money we'll do it. Don't worry. There's always a way."

The coffee's warmth had evaporated from her veins, and Kelly could feel the cold penetrating her jacket as she stood in the sunshine. She hadn't noticed it before. The cold must have shaken loose the rest of her anxieties because they tumbled out now as she stamped her feet on the icy driveway, which wound around the knitting shop and the cottage.

"What if that Wyoming property doesn't sell, Curt?" she asked, worry filling her voice. "Those investors want their loan paid back in June. What if that land doesn't sell by then? Where will I get the money to repay the canyon loan? I don't have anything left to sell."

"I've told you not to worry, Kelly. Those investors will be more than happy to extend the loan," Curt reassured her.

Kelly refused to be consoled. "Yeah, at that awful interest rate, too."

Curt's soft laughter sounded. "Kelly, all this stuff going on with your cottage has got you spooked. You know everything will work out just like we planned. You gotta trust me."

"I trust you, Curt, and you're right, this vandalism is getting to me."

"Tell you what. Why don't you and Steve go out to that fancy café in Old Town you two like so much and listen to your jazz music or whatever. Sounds like you need it. I'm getting another call, Kelly, so I'll talk to you later." He clicked off.

Kelly shoved her phone in her pocket and headed for Pete's café in the back of Lambspun. She needed more coffee. The afternoon sun had warmed her for a while, but the cold finally won out. Steve's crew was still working and would be for another couple of hours at least. Racing up the wooden steps behind the café, Kelly escaped into the warmth.

Julie, one of the waitresses, gave her a friendly wave. "I wondered when you'd be in here. Weren't you freezing, standing outside all that time?"

"I was too aggravated to be cold," Kelly said, accepting the large mug of black coffee she offered. Drinking deep, Kelly felt the dark brew rush down her throat, bringing its familiar burn. "Ahhhh, thanks, Julie. I can feel my toes thawing out now."

Tracy Putnam rounded the corner into the café then, and her face lit up when she saw Kelly. "Hey, Kelly. Did you come back to work on the yarns? I rushed through my homework today, so I could go downstairs and try that Aztec Blue again."

Kelly had to smile at Tracy's enthusiasm. Tracy had taken to the dyeing class like a duck to water. Considering how much time was spent with your hands in the big dye tubs, it was like *being* a duck in water. "Actually, I'm here to warm up with another shot of Eduardo's coffee." Kelly lifted her mug, saluting the smiling cook beside the grill. "I'll gladly leave the extra time in the dye tubs to you. It took me forever to get that magenta color off my hands last night."

Tracy laughed. "You weren't the only one. I swear I still have blue arms." She held up the looped skein of Aztec Blue yarn and gazed into the shimmering depths. "This may not make sense, but I simply have to see if I can match Mimi's shade of blue. I got so close last night, remember?"

"Yes, you were the only one who knew what to do with those colors. And that pink shade you came up with was scrumptious, too. Mimi ought to use it, for sure."

"Thanks, Kelly. That's sweet of you," Tracy said, her cheeks revealing a faint blush. "Mimi said I could come back and practice anytime and stay as late as I want. That's why I thought I'd try this blue again. I really, really want to see if I can match it."

"Tracy, you may have found your perfect part-time job. You know Mimi can always use a smart, talented person like you in the shop. Think about it."

Tracy's head came up, and Kelly saw excitement flash through her eyes. "Do you really think she'd hire me? I mean, the real estate office is okay, but working here would be . . ."

"Heaven for you, probably," Kelly said with a laugh. "Think about it. Personally I think you'd be a great asset to the shop. And Jennifer can vouch for you, too." The sight of a familiar car pulling into the parking lot caught Kelly's attention then. "Excuse me, Tracy. I see

Burt outside and I need to speak with him. Good luck with your Aztec Blue, okay?" she said as she headed for the café's back door.

Bounding down the steps, Kelly waved to Burt as she called out his name. The whine of the power equipment, however, drowned out her voice. Burt was obviously checking the crew's results on the side of the garage they'd finished.

"How's it look, Burt?" Kelly asked as she strode up beside him. "This one side took them nearly two hours."

Burt shook his head. "That paint was a son of a gun to clean, I bet. Especially on stucco."

If Kelly heard the words "paint" or "stucco" one more time today, she thought she'd scream. So, she changed the subject. "Did your old partner Dan have any new information? Anything about that bunch in the north of town?"

"There was another garage break-in near Wellesley last night, and a car was stolen. And whoever did it left their calling card on the fence in red spray paint just like last time. We think it may be the same bunch that stole the electronics gear a couple of weeks ago. But this time, they beat up a guy. It was his car, and apparently he caught them breaking into it." Burt shook his head. "He says he didn't recognize anybody, but you can tell he knows them and is afraid to say anything."

A chill ran over Kelly that had nothing to do with the cold afternoon air surrounding her. "Whoa, Burt, that's scary."

"Yeah, it is. The problem with these gang wannabes is they scare the hell out of the neighbors. Everyone's afraid, so no one will identify the culprits."

"How will you catch them?" It was impossible to keep the anxiety from her voice.

"Dan and the guys are working on it. Don't worry, Kelly. Someone will slip up and say something. And Dan will find them." Burt's careworn face drew into what she recognized as a fatherly smile. A former cop's fatherly smile.

Kelly managed a sardonic smile in return. "Everyone tells me not to worry. Curt says don't worry about all the extra expenses. You tell me not to worry about a bunch of gang wannabes who like to break into places around town and who may have targeted *me* now. I gotta tell you, Burt. Everyone's asking a helluva lot."

# Five

Kelly zipped her running jacket to her chin as she left the cottage and walked over to the square post by the corner of her front yard. It was her favorite place to stretch before setting off on a morning run—when it wasn't covered with snow.

Thanks to the warmer temperatures over the last two days, most of the snow had melted into slushy piles. Since the early morning February sun was fairly weak, those slush piles were ice-covered now and would be until noon.

She stretched one long leg behind her as she leaned against the post. A flash of movement across the driveway caught her attention, and Kelly saw Pete race down

the café's back steps and through the outside patio behind the shop.

"What's up, Pete?" she yelled as she stretched her
other leg. "I thought I was the only one who went running this early."

Pete came to a stop as he rounded the corner of the
patio and spotted Kelly. He quickly changed direction
and headed her way.

Kelly wondered why Pete was outside on a busy
Saturday morning, until she glanced toward the park-
ing lot. No cars were in sight except Pete's old beige
Volvo and Eduardo's new green pickup. *That's strange.
Saturday is their busiest day of the week.*

"Hey, where are your customers, Pete? I've never
seen this parking lot empty on a Saturday morning."

Pete panted as he came to a stop, his normally smiling face filled with concern. "I . . . I told Eduardo . . .
to wave them off. The café and the shop were hit last
night by vandals." He drew in a breath as he brushed a
stray lock of blond hair off his forehead.

Kelly's heart sank. The vandals had come back,
and this time they'd found bigger targets. "Ohhhh, no!
Pete, I'm *so* sorry." She reached out and gave his arm
a squeeze. He'd run outside without his coat and was
standing in his shirtsleeves, shivering. "Let's go back
inside. Have you called the police yet?" She beckoned
Pete toward the café.

"Y-yeah, I called them first thing. And Mimi. Sh-
she's on her way," he said through chattering teeth.

"R-Rosa should be here, too. She works Saturdays in the shop."

Kelly raced through the patio, her feet barely touching the flagstones, and up the back steps, Pete trailing behind. Afraid of what she'd see, Kelly shoved open the glass door and stepped inside. She sucked in her breath.

Broken glass and bottles were scattered all over the wooden floor, beer and wine pooling into puddles. Piles of what looked like flour or sugar were dumped everywhere. Napkins, silverware, dishes, candles, and jelly jars were jumbled all together beneath overturned tables and chairs.

"Oh, no . . . " Kelly whispered. "This is awful."

"Wait'll you see the kitchen. It's worse," Pete said sadly, walking through the destruction. "They left the refrigerator doors open and pulled everything to the floor. Spaghetti sauce is all over. All the food is ruined."

Kelly followed him to the kitchen and flinched when she saw the damage. Pete wasn't kidding. Spaghetti sauce smeared the counters, dripped down the grill, and splashed onto the walls. The smell of oregano and basil hung in the air. Wilting vegetables were scattered across the floor. Cheese balls lay where they'd rolled into corners, and chef's knives and cleavers were standing on end, dug into the wooden chopping block as if they'd been thrown there.

"What a mess," Kelly said, feeling guilty somehow.

The vandals had targeted her, and she'd led them to their new targets. "We'll help you clean up, Pete. Everyone will pitch in, and the sooner we do it, the sooner you can open the doors again." She spied Eduardo still standing outside the front door, explaining to customers what had happened as they arrived.

Pete gazed wistfully out the window at his disappointed and disappearing customers. "I don't know how soon that will be, Kelly. Wait till you see the shop. That will take quite a while to fix. Mimi and the others will have their hands full."

Kelly grimaced. The sight of the trashed café made her momentarily forget the knitting shop. "How bad is it?" she asked, heading down the hallway that led to the interior of the shop.

"Pretty bad. I didn't see much stuff broken, but everything's in huge piles," he said, following her.

Kelly turned the corner into one of the yarn rooms and stared. Pete didn't exaggerate. The shelves that lined the walls and were usually filled with colorful fat cones of novelty yarns sat empty. Everything was on the floor. A huge multicolored pile of yarn. Cones of yarn, skeins of yarn, spools of yarn. All mixed together. Scattered on top were various knitted items—shawls, long fringed scarves, fluffy eyelash scarves, mittens, hats.

"Oh, what a mess." Glancing to the large loom in the corner of the room, Kelly didn't see any obvious damage. Neither did she see any bottles or liquids poured on the floors or over the yarns. "At least they didn't pour wine over it." She tiptoed around the pile and through the doorway into the next room, trying not to step on the gorgeous fibers.

This time, she saw no discernible pile. Instead, skeins of yarns and knitted garments were scattered everywhere, covering the floor entirely. At least a foot deep in yarns. The baskets and bins lining these walls gaped at her—empty. She could see through the arched doorway ahead into the main room and the library table—the gathering place. The table and floors were now filled with books, which the vandals had swept from the shelves.

She tried to step carefully through the foot-deep blanket of yarn covering the floor. "This will take days for them to sort through. You and Mimi both have insurance, don't you?"

Pete didn't answer, because Mimi burst through the front door into the foyer, her coat open and red knitted scarf dangling. She came to a halt. "Oh, *no*!" she wailed, hands to her face. "Look at this . . . it's . . . it's *awful*!"

"I don't think the yarns are hurt, Mimi, just thrown on the floor," Kelly offered, picking up several fluffy bundles of sherbet colors.

"Why would anyone do this?" Mimi said as she bent to pick up skeins that littered the foyer. "I never have understood vandals. Pete, did they hurt the café?"

Pete nodded dolefully and Mimi sucked in her breath, hand to her mouth. "Ohhhh, noooo! What did they do?"

"Threw food and wine all over the place," Kelly

said. "It's a mess. Spaghetti sauce, wine, beer, smeared over everything. It's nasty."

"Yeah," Pete said, releasing a discouraged sigh as he turned toward the café. "I'd better go and call that insurance agent. I'll see you later."

"Ohhhh, Kelly, this will take forever to clean up." Mimi shook her head, staring balefully as she surveyed the rooms. "Oh, look at all the books on the floor. And patterns, too. I hope they're not torn."

Rosa charged through the door then, and her eyes popped wide at the scene. *"Madre de Dios,"* she said softly, scanning the wreckage. "This is terrible!"

Kelly started clearing a path through the yarns, picking up skeins and tossing them into the corners, creating a walkway. "How'd they get in, Mimi? Did they break the lock on the front door?" she asked, as she watched Rosa start clearing another pathway.

Mimi checked the heavy walnut door. "No, they didn't," she said, peering at the door handle and lock. "There're no marks. Oh, my word, was the door left unlocked?"

"No way, Mimi," Rosa protested, her arms filled with bunches of fat cotton chenille. "We *always* lock that door. And Connie was working at closing last night, and she's a bear about that, remember? Her house was broken into once."

"Well, the back door to the café was okay, too," Kelly added. "No signs of a break-in. And Pete always locks that front door when he leaves in the afternoon. I know, because I searched for a way to get inside the shop one night when I left my bag here with my cell phone. All those doors were locked tight."

Mimi let go of the front door, and it closed with a solid thud. She stood, staring out into the shop, both hands at her breast now. "Ohhhh, no . . ." she whispered. "Tracy has been staying late working with the dyes. Could she have forgotten to lock the door when she left last night?"

Rosa looked surprised. "I don't think so. Tracy stayed late on Wednesday and Thursday nights, too, and she remembered to lock the doors. I showed her how to do it. Why would she forget on Friday?"

"That doesn't make sense," Mimi said, worrying her lower lip. "Tracy's such a conscientious girl. I can't imagine it slipping her mind."

Kelly pondered for a second. "I noticed the lights on late last night when Steve brought me home after dinner. I didn't think anything of it because I knew Tracy was probably downstairs and up to her arms in the dye tubs again. She's gone crazy for it. You've got a devoted pupil, Mimi. But I agree with Rosa, I can't see Tracy forgetting something as important as locking the door. She impresses me as being very careful."

Rosa started arranging the chenille yarns inside the antique cabinet where they'd been previously displayed. "Speaking of downstairs, I'd better go check the basement to see if they trashed it as well." She started picking her way through the room, clearing a path as she did.

"Please, God, not the basement," Mimi prayed as

she closed her eyes. "All those bags of fleece and dyed yarns . . . I don't want to think about what they could do down there."

Following Rosa's lead, Kelly started filling empty yarn bins and shelves. Sorting could come later. Right now, they had to find the floor again. "Maybe they didn't even get to the basement, Mimi. It was hard enough for us to get around down there when we were working over the tubs." She pictured the rabbit warren of rooms below.

"Lord, I hope so," Mimi said, stuffing springy balls of eyelash yarn into the antique cabinet. "I hope they found what little money we had in the cash box and ran off—"

A muffled scream cut through the air, silencing Mimi. She stared at Kelly, mouth open. "Oh, my God! Was that Rosa?"

"I think it was," Kelly said, dumping the rest of the yarn onto the floor. This time she stomped through the fibers, not caring what she stepped on, as she hurried toward the back of the shop and the basement stairway.

"What happened?" Mimi cried out as she followed behind Kelly.

Racing through the hallway, Kelly rounded the corner and charged down the steps. Pete was already ahead of her.

"Rosa, are you all right?" Pete yelled as he disappeared into the maze of rooms below.

"*Madre de Dios, no!* Please, no!" Rosa's voice cried from the back room.

Kelly raced after Pete, her heart in her throat. Bursting into the tub room, she stopped short, almost tripping over a metal rod on the floor. The air was sucked out of Kelly's lungs in an instant. She felt like she'd been punched in the gut.

Rosa stood weeping, her face in her hands, shoulders heaving. Pete was leaning over the laundry tub. A woman's body hung over the tub. Her face and chest were submerged in the dark blue dye water. The woman's blonde hair floated on the water, spread out in a fan around her submerged head. Blonde, no more. Now the hair was blue, as were the woman's arms, which floated beside her. Dark blue. Aztec Blue. Tracy Putnam's favorite color.

Kelly felt sick to her stomach. She barely heard Mimi's piercing scream behind her.

# Six

**Steam** wafted off Kelly's mug of coffee as she stood in the middle of the driveway's melting slush. Mimi and Pete stood beside her, sipping her home-brewed coffee from an assortment of travel mugs. Kelly and her friends were huddled together outside the knitting shop as they had been most of the morning—watching Fort Connor police officers and investigators run in and out of the building, carrying bags, carrying cameras, conferring with one another.

Kelly and the others had watched sadly as the medics arrived and carried Tracy Putnam's sheet-shrouded body to the ambulance. Mimi and Rosa wept softly. Kelly recalled a similar scene last summer, when she and her friend Megan had discovered Allison Dubois dead in her apartment. That same tight feeling was in Kelly's gut now.

A young police officer—no more than a kid, Kelly thought—had questioned each of them separately, writing their answers on a small notepad. After that, the investigating detective in charge, Lieutenant Morrison, wanted to question them all again individually. Kelly offered her cottage as a place for interviews, hoping to soften the crusty Morrison. She still sensed he hadn't forgiven her for solving her aunt Helen's murder before he did last spring.

Watching Rosa come down the steps now, Kelly figured that Morrison would call her last.

"Oooo, that man is so, so . . . gruff," Rosa said as she joined them, accepting a coffee mug from Pete.

"Don't let Lieutenant Morrison scare you, Rosa. He's not mean, just intimidating," Kelly said. "What did he ask?"

"He wanted me to tell him everything I remembered when I went downstairs and found . . . Tracy." She closed her eyes. "I don't want to remember all that. I'm trying to forget." She shuddered.

Mimi squeezed Rosa's shoulders. "I know, Rosa. I'm trying to forget, too."

"Why would those guys kill Tracy?" Pete asked as he stared at the clusters of uniformed officers and investigators who continued to stream into and out of the building. "I mean, if all they wanted to do was grab money and trash the place, they could have just locked her in the basement."

Kelly spotted Burt emerge from the shop's front door, engrossed in conversation with his old partner, Dan. Burt had arrived within minutes of Mimi's phone call this morning, right after the police, and had shadowed his old partner ever since.

"I don't know, Pete," Kelly mused out loud. "Maybe they panicked." She remembered the metal rod she'd spied on the basement floor earlier. *Did they hit Tracy, meaning to just knock her out? Is that what happened? Did she accidentally fall into the dye tub?*

"Ms. Flynn, could you come in, please?" Lieutenant Morrison called from the cottage doorway.

"You bet," Kelly replied brightly as she crossed the muddy path her walkway had become and raced up the front steps. "Mind if I refresh my coffee before we start, Lieutenant?" she said as she held up her mug and headed for the kitchen.

Morrison nodded, then perched on the edge of her black leather sofa. "I wouldn't mind a cup myself. Black."

"The only civilized way to drink it," Kelly replied, hiding her smile as she filled another mug. If this was Morrison's way of smoothing over their earlier relationship, it worked for her.

"How well did you know Tracy Putnam?" Morrison asked as he accepted the mug.

Kelly took a deep drink before answering. "Not too

well. I just met her about a week ago when my friend Jennifer introduced us at the shop."

Morrison scribbled in his notepad. "Did you see her after that? Or have a chance to speak with her?"

"Actually, I saw Tracy several times after that. We were in the same class Mimi taught on dyeing fibers, and Tracy started coming to the shop every afternoon to work on her projects." Kelly gave him a sad smile. "She loved working with fibers and creating colors."

"Did she ever share any details of her personal life? Mention any friends or coworkers?"

Kelly shook her head. "I'm afraid not. We only talked about the yarns or the shop. Unfortunately, I never got the chance to learn more about her." She sipped her coffee while Morrison scribbled away. "Let me ask *you* a question, Lieutenant. Why would those guys stop trashing the shop and café and kill our friend downstairs? That doesn't sound like random vandalism to me."

Morrison looked up from his notepad. "It's still early in our investigation, but it appears Ms. Putnam's death may have been the result of a burglary gone bad."

A "burglary gone bad." She'd heard that reason once before and from Morrison himself. When her aunt Helen was strangled in the cottage nearly a year ago, police had chalked it up to a burglary gone bad, a tragic accident. In Aunt Helen's case, however, Kelly had gone on to prove her aunt's death was no accident but deliberate murder.

"Do you think they panicked? I mean, it makes no sense to kill Tracy if they're only trashing the place."

"That's one possibility," Morrison replied, clearly unwilling to provide more details.

Kelly continued to probe anyway. "What if they were high on drugs or something? Maybe that's what happened."

Morrison eyed her over his coffee mug. "Believe me, Ms. Flynn, we're looking into every possibility. Now, why don't you tell me about these instances of vandalism you've experienced recently."

Kelly heard the tone of finality in Morrison's voice. He wasn't about to speculate on Tracy's death. She also knew Morrison's investigative style. He would make her repeat everything she'd told the officer earlier when she was questioned.

"It started right before Christmas. My tires were slashed when I was inside the shop at a party. Then in January, red paint was thrown on my house, then my windshield was smashed."

"And you never heard or saw anyone when these incidents occurred?"

"Nope. I was away from home each time." Kelly drained her coffee.

Morrison flipped through his notepad. "But you told Officer Grebs that you were home for this last incident when paint was thrown on your garage. And you still didn't hear anything?"

Kelly recognized Morrison's skeptical tone, so she leveled her gaze and dropped her voice. She might have left corporate behavior behind, but it hadn't left her. "No, Lieutenant, I did not. However, my dog started barking in the middle of the night, so I got up and checked outside. I saw nothing, and I heard nothing. The lights had gone on, but I've noticed that animals can set them off. So I thought Carl had heard a fox or a raccoon. But I did see a guy hiding in the trees at the edge of my backyard one morning. He ran off when I spotted him."

"Did you get a good look at him?"

"Not really. He was wearing a dark hooded jacket and pants and took off like a rocket when I yelled at him." Kelly headed for the kitchen and more coffee.

Morrison scribbled again. "Tell me, Ms. Flynn, have you had any altercations with other people these last few months? Any sharp or violent disagreements or incidents where you might have made enemies?" He peered over his mug at her before drinking.

Kelly took her time pouring the black stream into her mug as four faces suddenly flashed before her eyes. *Enemies? Oh, yeah.* She shook them away then took a large drink of coffee.

"I'm an accountant, Lieutenant. We try not to make enemies. We just do their accounts."

"So, there's no one you've met in Fort Connor who might hold a grudge against you or harbor a strong dislike for any reason?" He set his mug aside and rose.

"Well . . . I wouldn't say that exactly," Kelly admitted with a wry smile as she strolled back into the living room.

Morrison's bushy eyebrows arched. "Nor would I, Ms. Flynn. If memory serves me, I recall you've played a role in helping police investigate several murders. Consequently, you've been in situations that have brought you into conflict with other people. In fact, there are four people either in jail right now or awaiting trial because of you."

Kelly's smile disappeared. Morrison was right. If not for her, those people would have gotten away with murder. And they would be free today. "You're exaggerating, Lieutenant. I simply helped the process along, that's all."

Morrison smiled slightly. "All the same, Ms. Flynn. There are some people in town who probably don't think of you too fondly."

Kelly stared through the dining room windows at the snow-covered golf course while she sipped her coffee. She didn't like the picture Morrison painted, so she shook it away as well. "I don't know, Lieutenant. I still think it was a bunch of violent scumbags looking for trouble that damaged my place. And that's how they found the shop." She started to pace the small living room. "If it was someone who hated me personally, then they would have no reason to trash the shop. That doesn't make sense."

Morrison shoved his notepad into the front pocket of his gray suit and headed to the front door. "You're probably right, Ms. Flynn, but we plan to look into every angle."

Kelly followed Morrison, who was obviously eager to leave and escape any further discussion. She was about to ask him another question anyway when he turned in the open doorway and fixed her with a level gaze.

"Take care of yourself, Ms. Flynn. And try to stay out of trouble, okay?"

Kelly couldn't resist being her usual contrarian self. She grinned. "I'll do my best, Lieutenant. But I make no promises."

"I figured as much," Morrison said before he strode down the steps.

Kelly spied her friends still standing in the slushy driveway, huddled around Burt and deep in conversation. She headed their way.

"Hey, Burt, I wondered when you'd be free to fill us in," Kelly said as she joined them. "Morrison just told me they think it was a burglary gone bad and that Tracy's death was accidental. What can *you* tell us?"

Burt zipped his jacket snug to his neck as the breeze ruffled his gray hair. "That's exactly what Dan told me a while ago. They think the vandalism was unplanned. A hasty crime of opportunity. The shop was all lit up and unlocked in a secluded setting. They were probably looking for money or anything valuable. Mimi's cash box was emptied, and they broke into both registers and grabbed whatever cash was there. All three were dusted for prints. They'll check, just in case there's someone with a record of burglary and assault."

His expression saddened. "Tracy's death was probably a tragic accident. They must have surprised her downstairs, and maybe she started screaming. Who knows? Anyway, Dan thinks she was hit on the head to knock her out. Tracy must have slumped into the tub and drowned while they went back to trashing the upstairs."

"How awful . . ." Mimi whispered, pulling a wad of tissues from her pocket to wipe her eyes.

Pete shook his head sadly. "Much too young to die."

"I want to see those guys caught and sent to jail!" Rosa's dark eyes sparked.

"Believe me, folks, the police will catch the guys who did this. I can promise you that," Burt said with an emphatic nod. "Meanwhile, Mimi, you and Pete have to get an alarm system installed as soon as possible. You've got to have some security in place or none of us will sleep at night."

Mimi nodded. "I know. Lieutenant Morrison told me the same thing. I admit, I was thinking about it."

"Me, too, Mimi," Pete said. "I'll check into what's available."

"I'll help you folks pay for it, too," Burt added. "No arguments—"

"Absolutely, not," Mimi interrupted.

"Not necessary, Burt. I've been saving for it," Pete said.

Kelly waited for Mimi and Pete to silence all Burt's repeated offers to help before she spoke up. "Well, I'm definitely going to contribute to the security system. It's my fault those guys trashed the place. If they hadn't been coming to my place to cause trouble, they never would have discovered the shop."

Both Mimi and Pete countered with refusals, but

Kelly ignored them both. Then Burt looked at her sternly. "This was *not* your fault, Kelly."

Mimi and Pete both nodded, offering vigorous denials. Kelly wished she could believe them. But no matter what anyone said or how much they tried to reassure her, deep inside she couldn't. She still felt guilty.

"Okay, okay," she acquiesced. "At least I can help you clean up the shop and café, can't I? I'll show up with a bucket and sponge, anyway. So you might as well put me to work. I won't be able to sleep at night unless I can do *something*."

Pete laughed, his round face softening for the first time this morning. "That's a deal, Kelly."

"And after you finish at Pete's you can help us," Mimi added. "I'm sure the Lambspun network will spread the word, and we'll have plenty of worker bees to help clean. You could help Rosa go through the office. I certainly hope they didn't trash the files—" Suddenly a look of horror crossed her face. "*Oh, no!* My new laptop computer. I left it in the office!"

Kelly flinched. That laptop was probably in Denver by now. Stolen for sure. "I'm sorry, Mimi. I'll help you find another one online." She reached over to give her friend a sympathetic pat on the shoulder.

"Why didn't I bring it home last night?" Mimi berated herself, shaking her head. "I just bought it three months ago."

Burt reached over and gave Mimi a hug, which she returned. "I'll call Dan and ask him to check your office again, Mimi. I only glanced in there. I was so relieved it wasn't trashed like the yarn rooms, I didn't even notice a laptop."

"Don't worry, Mimi," Kelly reassured her. "Megan knows great computer websites. She'll find you a deal."

"Meanwhile, let me take all of you to lunch," Burt offered. "You've been here the entire morning. Morrison is finished with you. No need to hang around anymore. The police will probably be here the rest of the day."

Pete drained the last of his coffee. "Good idea, Burt. I'd like to try someone else's food for a change."

**Kelly** stared at her computer screen as she tabbed through the spreadsheet, entering figures, calculating numbers, column after column, row after row. There was something soothing about working with numbers. When they added up, that is. When the amounts at the bottom of the spreadsheet columns didn't make sense, it was annoying, but it was still easily solved. Not like working with people. People did things that didn't make sense all the time.

Her cell phone jangled, and she flipped it open. "Kelly here."

"No, *I'm* here. You're there." Jayleen's familiar laughter came over the phone.

"Hey, Jayleen, how're you doing?" Kelly asked, glancing at her watch as she pushed away from the sunny corner desk. Had she really been working for three hours straight? Checking the angle of the late afternoon sun confirmed it.

"I'm fine. Gettin' tired of shoveling snow, that's for sure. I declare, I'll be ready for spring whenever it wants to mosey along. What're you up to? Slaving over those damn accounts, I bet."

"Well, I wouldn't say slaving exactly, but I am trying to work ahead so I can take a day or two off to help Pete and Mimi clean up when the police say it's okay." She leaned against the kitchen counter while she refilled her coffee mug. "I spent all morning standing outside watching the cops run around."

Jayleen made a sympathetic sound. "I sure am sorry Mimi and Pete got hit by those no-goods. And to think they'd kill that young girl downstairs. Lord-a-mercy. Jail's too good for that bunch."

Kelly heard the hint of old-fashioned vigilante justice in Jayleen's voice. "I agree, Jayleen. They had to be a bunch of vicious scumbags to kill Tracy. It kind of makes you wish for the days when you could round up a posse and go find 'em. But according to Burt, those guys are hard to catch. They scatter into holes like rats."

"The cops will catch 'em, don't you worry. Listen, Kelly, there's another reason I called. Do you want me to keep an ear out and see if any of the other breeders are looking to expand their herds? What with all those extra expenses you've had recently to clean up and repair your place, I figured you might need some extra cash."

Kelly paused, pondering what Jayleen said. "Hmmm. Let me think about that, Jayleen."

"Okay. You just let me know. Meanwhile, I'll keep an ear out. Talk to you later."

Kelly clicked off her phone and sipped coffee as she watched the pale winter sun head toward the mountains. She could feel the drop in temperature already, even though she was inside.

The familiar loud rumble of an engine caught her attention. *That sounds like Steve's truck.* Carl was already at the front door, dancing in place. His best buddy was outside. Could playtime be far away?

She grabbed her jacket and escaped outdoors, where the cold air bit her face and cheeks. The wind had picked up, blowing over the mountains of the Front Range. The foothills, the locals called them.

"Hey, I didn't expect to see you until later tonight. Aren't we going to dinner?" she called to Steve, who was already out of the cab and opening boxes in the back of his truck.

"We're not going to dinner until I install these outdoor lights for the garage, Kelly," Steve said as he pulled some oval-shaped lights from a box. "And I've got extra ones for the cottage, too. Dinner can wait."

"Did you drive all the way over to Greeley to get these yourself? You shouldn't have. A couple of days wouldn't—"

Steve shot her an "I don't believe you said that" look. "Kelly, a girl was killed here last night. Maybe *you're* not concerned for your safety, but the rest of us are worried as hell. So don't even think about arguing with me." He opened an onboard toolbox and grabbed a portable electric drill.

"*Me?* Argue?" Kelly teased with a grin. "So what can I do to help?"

"You can make a mug of that black tar of yours. That'll last me until we get to the restaurant. This won't take long." He slid a ladder from the flatbed of his truck.

"Coming up," Kelly acquiesced, heading toward the cottage while Steve carried the ladder to the garage. "I'm gonna let Carl out in the backyard to see you. He's going crazy inside."

She stopped in the middle of the fast-freezing mud of her walkway when she saw a police officer exit the knitting shop. Were they still poking around in there? Watching him duck beneath the yellow police tape wrapped around the front entry, Kelly was surprised to see the young man, who wore a buzz cut, stride toward her, a large plastic bag in his hand.

"Excuse me, miss. Are you Kelly Flynn?" he asked as he approached.

"Yes, I am. Were you looking for me, Officer?" Kelly met him at the driveway's edge. She spied Steve leave the ladder and head their way.

"Yes, ma'am. Lieutenant Morrison asked me to bring this over to you for safekeeping. We found it in the knitting shop. I believe it belongs to the shop owner, Mrs. Shafer." He held out toward Kelly the plastic bag, which was holding something heavy, from the looks of it.

"Thank you, Officer. I'll be glad to keep it for her. What is it?"

"Looks like a laptop, ma'am," the young officer said as he turned away. "Have a good evening."

"What's that?" Steve asked as he approached.

Kelly stared into the plastic bag. Sure enough, there was Mimi's laptop computer. "I don't believe it," she said, pulling off the plastic, checking for signs of damage. "Those guys must have missed this last night. Why else would they leave something they could sell so easily?"

"I'd say Mimi got lucky," Steve said before returning to the garage.

*I'd say.* Kelly wondered what kind of vandals would steal a few dollars from a cash box and leave a new laptop worth several hundred dollars. Maybe it was in a drawer or hidden under stuff.

Spotting the young officer back his cruiser away from the shop, she waved at him and hurried over.

"Yes, ma'am?" He looked up at her politely.

*Why am I always a "ma'am"? Do I look that old?*

"Officer, I'm curious. You and I both know those guys could get a lot of money for this laptop. Was it hidden in the office or buried under yarn so they couldn't see it?"

He grinned at her, revealing how young he really was. Probably former military, judging by his look and bearing.

"No, ma'am. It was sitting right on top of her desk.

Plain as day. Take care, now," he said before nosing his cruiser down the driveway.

Kelly watched him drive away as the whine of Steve's drill cut through the fast-disappearing daylight.

# Seven

"I still can't believe it happened," Megan said, her fingers anxiously working a shamrock green yarn, stitches gathering quickly on her knitting needles.

Kelly glanced at her friend across the table in a sunny corner of Mimi's kitchen. The more Megan worried, the faster she knitted. Kelly had seen Megan worry many times before, and always watched in amazement at the speed with which the knitted garments took shape. From froth to finished right before her eyes. Megan could finish a scarf in hours. Worrying about her friends, worrying about Kelly's sleuthing, worrying about her computer consulting clients.

But this was worse. Lambspun was a second home for all of them. Not only had it been vandalized, but someone who wanted to join the "shop family" had died as a result. None of them knew Tracy very well, but they had looked forward to learning more about the shy student. And Mimi had taken a motherly interest in her as well.

"I know, Megan. It still feels unreal, like a bad dream." Kelly worked the variegated red and pink yarn piled in her lap. Unlike Megan's project, Kelly's new scarf was far from finished. She had at least three feet to go. Her knitting times disappeared when Lambspun was vandalized.

Mimi leaned back in a rounded maple chair and held her teacup tightly. Sunshine from the window behind brought out the reddish highlights in her hair. "A nightmare, you mean. I barely slept at all last night. These awful dreams kept waking me up."

Lisa spoke up from across the table. "What does Burt say? Are the police searching for these guys? There's got to be someone who knows them." A turquoise and gray sweater bundled on her swift-moving needles.

"Yeah, they're searching, all right. But finding is the problem, according to Burt. These guys scatter when they hear the cops are looking," Kelly said.

Kelly watched her needles work the stitches. *Slip. Wrap. Slide. Slip the needle under the stitch, wrap the yarn, slide the stitch off the needle.* Kelly still remembered the cadence someone around the table had recited once. Remembered how she'd struggled to capture the rhythm when she first learned to knit. Now the movements felt natural, almost automatic. And her stitches looked more even and smooth, row after row. Not as many holes or dropped stitches, either.

"Have you heard from Burt today?" Megan asked, glancing toward Mimi.

"I called him this morning and invited him to join us for breakfast. He said he'd come as soon as he had a chance to talk with Dan. They're hoping the medical examiner will have a report today—"

A brief knock was followed by Burt's voice as Mimi's kitchen door suddenly opened. "Good morning. I was hoping to find you folks here."

"Hey, Burt, glad you could join us," Lisa called in greeting as he stomped snow from his boots onto the floor mat.

"Looks like we'll be gathering here at Mimi's until we can get the shop back up to speed," Kelly added as she pulled out a chair beside her. "Have a seat."

Mimi greeted Burt with a hug. "We've saved eggs and bacon and biscuits for you. Why don't you sit down, and I'll fix you a plate."

"Just coffee for now, thanks," he said before giving her a light kiss on the cheek.

"When do you think we'll be able to go into the shop and clean up?" Megan asked. "Mimi says it's a mess."

Burt settled into the chair. "You folks can probably start this afternoon. I've already talked with Dan."

Kelly caught Burt's subdued tone, and her needles paused. "Are the police still checking the shop?"

Burt nodded as Mimi poured a dark stream of coffee into a ceramic sunflower mug in front of him. "They went back this morning. They should be finished pretty soon."

"But I thought they had finished yesterday," Mimi said, looking concerned. "Why'd they go back?"

Burt took a large sip before answering. "They wanted to take another look, because the situation has changed. The medical examiner decided that Tracy's death was not caused by accidental drowning. He found bruising on the middle of her back and on one wrist, leading him to conclude that she was held under the water until she drowned. That would also explain the blue dye splattered on the wall behind the tub. Splashed there, no doubt by Tracy." Burt took another drink, then stared into his cup.

*Oh—my—God.* Kelly felt the cold creep back to her gut. It hadn't gone far. Someone murdered Tracy Putnam in the basement of Lambspun. How could that happen? Lambspun was a safe place, another home.

"*What?* That's . . . that's crazy," Lisa protested, her hands gesturing, no longer knitting.

Megan's eyes went huge, her face ashen. "That's *horrible*! Why would anyone deliberately kill Tracy?"

Mimi clutched the back of a kitchen chair. "I'm going to be sick."

Burt rose to his feet, but Mimi had already sprinted for the bathroom, hand to her mouth.

Kelly stared at her friends, her own shock registering in their eyes. They said nothing. The only sounds were Mimi's German cuckoo clock ticking on the wall and her retching in the bathroom.

Kelly could tell the sun had already gone beneath the clouds without looking out the window. She could feel the chill.

**"This** refrigerator is clean, Pete. I'm starting on the one in the corner," Kelly called from the café's kitchen. Scooping up sponges and towels and cleaning spray, she knelt in front of another undercounter fridge and started in. Dribbles of spaghetti sauce had dried hard and crusty across the polished metal surface. Kelly substituted elbow grease with the sponge for a scrubbing brush so as not to mar the surface.

Across the kitchen, Jennifer sat cross-legged, washing out cabinets. "I think we're finally beginning to see daylight. How're you coming with the grill, Eduardo?"

"Ask me later, when I'm not so angry," the normally genial cook replied before muttering something in Spanish.

"We're getting there, folks." Pete's voice sounded from the dining room. "I've almost finished the floors, and Julie's done the walls. You guys have the scut work. The kitchen was the worst."

"You know, I'm amazed we've gotten so much done," Kelly said, concentrating on a stubborn drop of tomato sauce. "With luck, we'll be finished by dinnertime."

"That's because Pete was lucky," Jennifer said as she wiped a towel across shelves and cabinet doors. "I've worked in other restaurants that were vandalized, and those places were completely trashed. I mean, windows broken, furniture smashed, walls gouged out, glasses and dishes shattered, everything. Some of those places had to shut down, as I recall."

Kelly rubbed the last fleck of sauce from the shiny metal while she considered what Jennifer said. "That's something else that doesn't add up. Like Mimi's laptop." She stopped her scrubbing and sat back on her heels, wiping her plastic-gloved hand on her jeans.

Jennifer glanced over her shoulder. "What do you mean?"

"Most vandals would have done a lot more damage, and they would have stolen Mimi's laptop for sure. That's easy money. But that didn't happen here, and I'm wondering why."

"I told you. Pete was lucky."

"Maybe it wasn't luck." Kelly reached in and removed the wire racks from the fridge and sprayed inside. "What if there weren't any vandals? What if one person did all this? That would explain the smaller amount of damage and overlooking Mimi's computer."

"You think someone killed Tracy then did all this to make it look like vandalism?"

"Maybe. Maybe the killer didn't figure anyone could tell Tracy had been held underwater."

"I don't know, Kelly. I'm not sure I can buy into that. I still can't understand why someone would deliberately kill Tracy Putnam. An accidental death is awful and tragic, but murder? It's horrible." Jennifer finished wiping the end cabinet then stared off into space. "I wish I'd never told her about the shop."

"Jen, you can't blame yourself for what happened to Tracy. It sounds as if there was a lot more going on in Tracy's life than anyone knew." Kelly paused. "Did she ever let on that she was having trouble with anyone? You know, a classmate or a boyfriend?"

"If she was having trouble with anyone, she never said a word. But I remember her mentioning a guy once."

"Oh, really? Was he her boyfriend, you think?"

Jennifer shook her head. "I don't know. She just said she was seeing someone. Didn't mention his name."

"Was he another student? Or maybe even someone from the office?"

"She never said. In fact, when I asked about him, she clammed up. I figured she was super private, so I never asked again."

"Hmmmm. A mysterious boyfriend with no name," Kelly said, replacing the wire racks onto the cleaned fridge shelves. "Did she talk about her family at all? Maybe they know something."

Jennifer gave the last cabinet a parting swipe with her towel before she pulled herself off the floor. "I think she was pretty close to her older sister. I remember her saying how much she missed their phone calls. Apparently her sister works abroad. I can't remember her name, either. But she seemed to get along with her family all right. She didn't have any horror stories to tell."

"Why don't you check if your office has her family's phone number," Kelly suggested as she closed the fridge door and stood up. "Maybe you can call them and—"

"And maybe we should let the *police* do their jobs," Jennifer said with a smile, leaning against the now-clean counter. "I'm sure they'll be all over that office first thing tomorrow morning asking questions. And the university will have all Tracy's personal family information on record."

"You're right, you're right," Kelly admitted with a sigh. "The cops will be on it. I can't help it. I go on automatic sometimes."

"Sometimes?" Jennifer arched an amused brow.

"Maybe that guy she mentioned is the killer."

"And maybe he's not," Jennifer said quietly. "Maybe that gang of vandals freaked out when they saw Tracy. If they were high on drugs, anything's possible. Maybe it really happened exactly like the police said. A burglary gone bad."

Kelly stared at her friend. What Jennifer said made sense. Why, then, did she have trouble accepting that explanation? "That's true, Jen, but the police still need to hear about the boyfriend. I'm calling Burt." She dug her cell phone out of her jeans pocket.

"I'm getting some coffee. I assume you'll want some."

"You assume right," Kelly said as she headed out of the kitchen and into the hallway leading to the knitting shop. She could hear voices coming from the yarn rooms.

Punching in Burt's number, Kelly stood in the doorway and watched the Lambspun network try to bring order to chaos. They were definitely making progress.

The floors appeared clear of fiber and the yarn bins and shelves were filling up with brightly colored yarns—twisted coils, fluffy balls, and plump skeins. There was only one thing missing from the picture. *Mimi.*

"How're you doing, Kelly?" Burt sounded tired.

"I'm okay, Burt. We're practically finished at Pete's, believe it or not, and Megan and the others are making great progress here in the shop. The floors are cleared and they're sorting everything now. How's Mimi?"

"She's resting. The doctor gave her a sedative, so she's sleeping right now."

Kelly could hear the fatigue in his voice and began to worry. "Sounds like you need to do the same thing, Burt. Why don't you stretch out on the sofa and take a snooze? You've gotta take care of yourself, too."

"I can't sleep, Kelly. I already tried. I keep seeing Tracy." She heard the sound of whistled breath. "You'd think I'd be immune to that stuff by now. But you never get used to it. I keep thinking how she died. Struggling in the water. Hot water, too, according to Mimi. Hot enough to burn. *Damn.*"

That new image caused Kelly's stomach to churn. *What an awful death.* "My God, Burt, who would do such a thing?"

"I don't know, Kelly, but I can promise you that Dan and the others are making this their priority. Dan's reaching out to his informants to see if any have ties to the bunch that's been working the north of town."

"Okay, well, here's another lead, I think. Jennifer told me that Tracy mentioned she was seeing a guy.

Maybe he was her boyfriend. Unfortunately she never told Jennifer his name."

"Was he a student in one of her classes?"

"Tracy never said."

"Okay, Kelly, I'll pass that along to Dan."

"I know it's not much, but it's something."

"Every little bit helps, Kelly. We build a case piece by piece. Tell Jennifer thanks for remembering, okay?"

"Will do. And you remember to rest. You had a heart attack once, Burt. Remember that."

"I'll rest, I promise. After I call Dan."

"Why don'tcha call while you're lying on the sofa?" she suggested with a laugh. "Either you take care of yourself or we'll be forced to send Lisa over there to ride herd on you. If you think I'm overbearing, you haven't seen Lisa in action. She's positively scary."

# Eight

**Kelly** lengthened her stride as she rounded a turn on the river trail, picking up her pace. She'd cut her run short this morning, and she wasn't sure why. An unexplained uneasiness suddenly surfaced, tugging at her inside. Whether it concerned her clients or her friends, she didn't know. But something was bothering her.

A flutter of wings above caused Kelly to glance upward, and she saw a raven fly off a nearby branch, ebony wings outstretched. Kelly figured she must have been the first runner to disturb the bird this morning. Early sun peeked between the bare limbs but brought no warmth. Icy temperatures had forced Kelly to slather her face in protective cream before running.

Her breath frosted in cloudy puffs as she left the trail and edged around the golf course, still crusty with snow. Heading toward her cottage, Kelly ran the ugly images of the previous day through her mind. The news of Tracy's horrible death. No wonder she was feeling spooked. Mimi was still at home, unable or unwilling to return to her beloved shop.

Megan and Lisa would be at Mimi's this morning, Kelly thought as she approached her backyard. Maybe she could finish her client work early and visit this afternoon. The shop was almost back to normal. Maybe that good news would cheer up Mimi.

As Kelly neared the back fence, she came to a halt. Carl was across the yard, his head down, face in the grass. He appeared to be vomiting. She'd seen Carl do this at other times, but it only took a few seconds and he stopped. This time, Carl didn't stop. He kept heaving and choking into the grass.

"Carl? You all right, boy?" Kelly called out as she walked around the fence, getting closer.

Carl didn't respond to her voice. He didn't even raise his head. Kelly spotted something shiny on the snow-covered yard. *Is that foil lying on the ground?*

Kelly swung her long legs over the fence in one fast movement then raced over to Carl. On the ground a few feet away was an opened foil package with what looked like hamburger meat inside. She picked it up and sniffed a sickly sweet smell, and her heart sank. She'd read about dogs being poisoned with antifreeze mixed into meat, and that it was recognizable by its sweet smell.

*Is that antifreeze? Who would do such a hateful, cruel thing?* The answer surfaced immediately. The vandals. It had to be them.

"Carl? *Carl?*" she cried as she knelt beside him, her heart racing with fear. Carl turned toward her, his eyes red, spittle drooling from his mouth. She had to get him to the vet's right away.

Kelly sped into her cottage and grabbed her cell, anxiously searching the directory for the vet's number. Snatching her keys and bag, she tore out the front door to her car. She could call the vet while she drove. Every minute counted. Carl needed help *now*. She'd heard how quickly poison could kill a dog.

Tossing the package of meat onto the passenger seat, Kelly revved the engine and backed her car as close to the fence gate as she could. Just then, Rosa drove up and parked in front of the shop.

Jerking her car to a stop, Kelly leaned out the window and yelled, "*Rosa! Rosa!* Carl's been poisoned! I need help getting him in the car. *Please!*"

Rosa paused as she exited her car and stared for a second before racing over. "Oh, no, Kelly, now they're after your dog!"

**Kelly** edged around the waiting room of the university's veterinary hospital. Completing another lap of the perimeter, she began again. She'd lost track of how many laps she'd done. Circling the rows of chairs in the middle of the large reception area, past the coffee bar, past the oncology doorway, past the long admissions desk filled with hospital staff, past the television, past the kiddie playroom, and past the double doors that led to the emergency room. Where Carl was.

She glanced at her watch. It had been over an hour since she watched the vet triage team wheel Carl into the ER. Kelly's frantic call to Carl's vet while she drove wound up sending her in another direction entirely. The vet agreed that the meat was probably tainted with antifreeze and urged Kelly to get Carl to the vet school—"immediately!" The antifreeze poison destroyed liver cells, and it acted fast. Catching it in time was the only way to save a dog's life.

Kelly was so frantic, she ran a red light racing through Fort Connor toward the sprawling vet school campus near the foothills. The ER triage team was waiting outside as she pulled up. Carl staggered like a drunken man when he tried to stand up. Kelly's heart wrenched, watching the vets carefully lift her big strong Rottweiler onto a metal cart and quickly roll him inside the hospital.

Kelly shoved her hands into the pockets of her running jacket and started another lap, trying to forget the scary images of her stricken dog. Passing the coffee bar again, she hesitated but kept going. She'd had three cups of the dismally weak coffee already. Vending machine candy bars had been breakfast.

*Where was the vet?* she wondered. *They said they'd let me know how it was going. It's been over an hour. How come they haven't come out?* A cold thought crept from the back of her mind. *Maybe Carl's dead. Maybe they just don't want to tell me. Maybe . . . maybe . . .*

The admissions double doors swung open, and a woman walked in with a shaggy sheepdog. Or, rather, the dog walked in with her. Dragged her, actually. An elderly man entered next, daintily holding the lead of a miniature dachshund as he approached the front desk. The shiny little brown dog took one look at the shaggy sheepdog and started to yap. Playtime.

Kelly distracted herself with the various animals and owners who entered and left. At ten fifteen in the morning, the waiting room was already filled with people. All of them waiting, like her, for word about their beloved pets.

After another three laps around the waiting room, Kelly spotted one of the vet team members coming through the emergency room doors. Kelly hurried over to the woman, who appeared to be in her late twenties or early thirties. "How's Carl?" she asked anxiously. "Is he going to be all right?"

"We won't know that for a while yet," the doctor said, tucking a clipboard under her arm as she swept away strands of reddish hair that escaped her ponytail. "We're still flushing his system with IV fluids, trying to get the poison out before it kills too many liver cells. Then we'll inject him with the antidote medication.

Carl's lucky you got him here so fast." She exhaled a long sigh then shoved her hands into the pockets of her white coat.

"When . . . when will you know? If he'll be all right, I mean?" Kelly asked, her voice softer than normal.

"We'll know from his blood work. We'll keep checking his liver values. If we see the liver enzyme stay elevated, that won't be good news. It means more cells are being destroyed."

The cold fist in Kelly's gut squeezed tighter. "When will you test them again?"

"In a couple of hours. You can go home if you want. We've got your cell phone number. I promise I'll call you as soon as I see the blood work."

"No, no. I want to stay here," Kelly said. "I'll be right here. Please come out and tell me as soon as you learn something."

The doctor gave her a little smile as she checked the clipboard. "Okay, Kelly. I know where to find you. I'm Dr. Barber." She handed Kelly a card. "By the way, there's a snack bar on the third floor, if you're tired of candy bars. The coffee's better up there, too. I'll see you later."

"Thanks, doctor," Kelly said as the young woman walked back toward the ER doors. Staring around the busy waiting area, filled with adults of all ages and children, Kelly headed toward the stairwell. She'd follow up on the vet's suggestion. Real food and better coffee could help her wait this out.

\* \* \*

**Kelly** spied Jennifer walking toward her across the waiting room, a familiar fast-food bag in her hand. "Boy, am I glad to see you. The snack bar is closed, and I don't think I can eat another candy bar."

Jennifer dropped the bag into Kelly's outstretched hands then shed her coat and sat down. "Greasy Burger to the rescue. I ate one on the way over. Couldn't help myself."

Kelly had already torn off the packaging and taken a huge bite. "Ummmm!" was all she could manage.

"My sentiments exactly. I tell you, Kelly, if things don't settle down pretty soon, I won't be able to fit into my jeans. I've gained ten pounds this week just worrying about everyone." She reached into her oversized bag, withdrew the royal blue sweater, and began to knit.

"Mummph," Kelly tried, then swallowed. "Just like Megan."

"With one big difference. When Megan worries, she knits faster. When I worry, I eat."

Kelly polished off the huge drippy burger and sipped the soft drink Jennifer had kindly provided. "That was delicious. Thanks, Jen. That'll last me for a while."

"Any word since those last tests?" Jennifer's needles picked up speed.

"Nope. The doc said they'd check the blood work again around six. I'm just praying that liver enzyme starts dropping soon. It went down a little the last time, but not enough." She ran her hand through her dark shoulder-length hair. Freed of the scrunchy rubber band she wore to run, her hair fell across her face and forehead. Normally, Kelly couldn't stand that. She barely noticed now.

"I'd join you in a prayer, but we wouldn't want the walls to shake," Jennifer teased.

Kelly managed a small smile. "I appreciate it, Jennifer. So does Carl."

"How much longer are you going to stay? You're not going to sleep here, are you?"

"If I have to. I'm not leaving until Carl starts to improve." She stared at the tiled floor as she willed herself not to think about the alternative. "And . . . and when he gets better and comes home, he'll have to stay inside the house during the day. He can only go out when I'm there and can watch him. I . . . I can't risk anything happening to him again."

Jennifer knitted quietly for a few moments. "You know, Kelly, I've been thinking about this . . . what happened to Carl and all, and—"

"I know, I know," Kelly interrupted as she rubbed her hand across her forehead. A headache was starting right between her eyes. "It's gotten worse. This isn't just vandalism anymore. It's a vendetta, I swear it is. I only wish I knew who could be behind it."

Jennifer went quiet again. "I agree with you, Kelly. It has gotten worse. And you're right, it is a vendetta . . . of sorts." She emphasized the last two words.

That caught Kelly's attention. "What do you mean?"

"I think there's a connection between all these things that have been happening at your place. You know, the damage to your house and your car, and even today with Carl. I think it's related to your purchase of the canyon ranch."

Kelly stared at Jennifer. "*What?* That doesn't make sense, Jen," she protested. "What possible connection could there be? Everything's happened right here."

Jennifer released a long sigh before answering. "Bear with me for a moment, okay? Let's take a look. The first time anything happened was a few days after you started to buy the property. Your tires were slashed. After you signed the contract in January and the place was officially yours, then more stuff started to happen. Worse each time. And now, it's Carl."

Kelly wagged her head. "Sorry, Jennifer. I don't see the connection at all. I know you're trying to help, but I really think you're out in left field with that. Far left field."

"Okay, let me bring it closer to home." Jennifer dropped the needles to her lap and looked up at Kelly. "After I heard about Carl this morning, I contacted the real estate agent in our office who listed the canyon ranch last December. I remembered her saying something happened in the canyon that spooked the client and scared her into selling."

Kelly sat on a plastic chair beside her friend. "Did she say what it was?"

"Ohhhh, yeah." Jennifer nodded. "I pulled her aside

when she came into the office and told her what's been happening at your place. Then I told her about Carl, and she went white as a sheet. She told me her client's dog was killed while the woman was up in the canyon touring the ranch last December. That's what scared the woman off. Apparently she came back to her car and found her little pekeapoo lying in a bloody pile on the seat, his throat cut."

The cold hand inside Kelly's gut squeezed. "Oh, no!"

"Oh, yes. The woman totally freaked after that and dumped the property. Understandably."

Kelly stared at the pattern on the tile floor. Could Jennifer be right? Was there a connection between her buying the canyon ranch and all these attacks? Her analytical side weighed in with an emphatic no, but her intuitive side wasn't as easily placated. That little alarm in the back of her head kept ringing.

"Any chance a mountain lion got into the car?" she suggested, trying to find some other explanation for the chilling picture Jennifer had painted.

Jennifer shook her head. "According to the agent, there was no sign of entry by man or beast. The woman swore she locked her car door when she left her little dog. And get this: the door was locked when she came back and found him inside the car, dead."

"Who would do such a vicious thing?"

"I think it's the same person who poisoned Carl."

Kelly stared into Jennifer's dark brown eyes and saw the concern there. "You really think all this is related to the canyon ranch?"

"Yes, I do. Think about it. Go back to the first time the ranch went on the market. The real estate developer bought it to build a mega mansion up there. Remember what happened to him? His condo project in town was torched and a gas can was left on the ranch porch as a warning."

Kelly nodded, a little shiver running over her skin. "I remember."

"With him, it started with vandalism, just like at your place. The next buyer didn't live here, so whoever's doing this simply waited until the woman was in town to check out the property. Then they killed her dog." Jennifer glanced away as she shook her head. "I swear, Kelly, it's all connected. I know it is. I can feel it. Someone doesn't want you to have that ranch."

"But why?" Kelly protested. "Who would want to keep me or anyone else from owning the ranch?"

"That's what I'm going to find out. At least I'm gonna try." Jennifer shoved her knitting back into the bag. "I'll start with a records search back at the office and see what pops up on all these transactions." She slung the bag over her shoulder as she rose. "You know, I really hate leaving you here to worry about Carl all alone. Do you want me to stay?"

"Naw, that's okay. Steve said he'd come out as soon as he finished at the Old Town site. With any luck, he'll bring food, too." She grinned, hoping to ease her friend's concern.

"More food always helps. That's my motto. Anything I can get you before I head to the office?"

An idea inched from the back of Kelly's brain. "Yeah. You can get that out-of-town buyer's name and phone number for me. I want to give her a call."

**Kelly** leaned against her car door and drew Steve closer, their embrace warm in the frigid night. His kiss lingered before he lifted his mouth from hers.

"You okay now?" he whispered. "Promise you won't drive over here in the middle of the night?"

"I promise," Kelly said as she leaned out of the embrace. "I'm going straight home and falling into bed. Turn off my cell and sleep late." She fished her car keys from her jacket pocket.

"Carl's going to be okay, Kelly. Those last liver tests showed his levels dropping. You can stop worrying now."

Kelly opened the car and tossed her bag inside. "I won't stop worrying until Carl's back at home and acting like himself again." She draped an arm across the car door and stared up at the ink black sky. Cloudless and clear and brilliant with stars. And bitter cold. No cloud cover to warm the nighttime temperatures. "He looked so pathetic and helpless lying there," she said, recalling the glass oxygen-filled intensive care unit where Carl lay.

"He's going to be okay, Kelly. The big guy is gonna be back in the yard before you know it." Steve reached over and zipped up Kelly's half-open jacket. "You need to knit yourself a hat," he said before he turned away. "I'll call you in the morning."

Kelly waved goodbye as she climbed into her car and revved the engine. A blast of icy air poured from the heating vents.

She heard the throaty roar of Steve's truck engine come to life behind her. His blinding headlight beams cut through the darkened veterinary school hospital's parking lot. Kelly nosed her car out of the lot and into the diminished nighttime traffic flow.

Heading toward the streets that led home, Kelly dug in her jacket pocket again and withdrew a slip of paper. She held it up, catching Steve's headlights through the back window to quickly scan the number. Flipping open her cell phone, she punched it in.

The phone rang five times before the call was answered, and Kelly began to regret calling so late. Suddenly, the phone picked up. "Is this Jacquie Weeden?" Kelly asked when a woman answered.

"Yes, it is. Who's this, please?"

"My name's Kelly Flynn, Ms. Weeden. I'm the one who bought your Colorado ranch in December. I'm sorry to be calling so late, but I had a question about the property."

The woman paused for a few seconds. "Oh, oh, yes . . . I'm sorry, I didn't recognize your name. An attorney acted on my behalf at the closing. I don't know if I can help you or not, Ms. Flynn. I confess I don't remember much about the ranch."

Kelly pulled to a stop at a traffic light and watched Steve give her a goodbye wave as he turned onto another street. "I understand, Ms. Weeden, and I appreciate anything you can tell me."

She paused, wondering how to phrase what she was about to say. Kelly sensed that Jacquie Weeden had deliberately closed off certain memories concerning her Colorado real estate experience.

"Actually, Ms. Weeden, I'm hoping you can tell me about the last time you visited the ranch and . . . and the attack on your dog."

There was a long pause before the woman answered, and her voice was noticeably softer. "I . . . I would rather not, Ms. Flynn. I've been trying to forget that awful day."

"I can understand, Ms. Weeden, and believe me, I would never mention something so painful to you except that my dog was attacked early this morning."

Ms. Weeden sucked in her breath. *"No!"*

"I'm afraid so. Someone tried to poison him by throwing hamburger that had been mixed with antifreeze into the yard. Carl ate most of it, of course. Thankfully, I got him to the vet school hospital before his liver was destroyed."

"Oh, no . . . that's awful!"

"My friend Jennifer works in the same real estate firm as your agent, and she told me what had happened to your pet last December, and I was wondering if you had any idea at all who could be behind these vicious attacks."

"I'm afraid not, Ms. Flynn. Believe me, if I did, I

would press charges. I . . . I wish I could help you. I cannot understand why anyone would target me and now you. It makes no sense."

Part of Kelly agreed with Ms. Weeden, but she continued. "Were you at the ranch alone that day? There's a caretaker, Bobby. Was he there?"

"No, I was there alone. I met Bobby the day before when he was feeding the animals."

"Did you notice anyone else in the vicinity? A parked truck or car near the driveway? Anyone walking around near the pastures?"

"I don't recall seeing anyone lurking about, if that's what you mean. As for parked trucks or cars, well . . . I remember seeing trucks parked everywhere along that canyon road." She exhaled a sigh. "I'm sorry, Ms. Flynn. I wish I could be more helpful, but I have really tried to forget everything about that horrible experience. In fact, I have trouble even remembering what the ranch looked like. And . . . and I think that's a blessing. If you know what I mean."

Kelly knew exactly what Jacquie Weeden meant. "I understand completely, Ms. Weeden. If it had been Carl that had been killed like that, I'm sure I'd want to block it out of my mind, too. Please forgive me for disturbing you. I was simply searching for answers. I want to find the person who's responsible."

"I wish you good luck, Ms. Flynn. And let me know if you do. Although, I'm not holding out much hope."

"I promise I will. Good night, Ms. Weeden, and thanks again."

Kelly clicked off her phone and tossed it onto the seat beside her as she steered around a darkened corner.

She'd find the culprit. Kelly swore she would.

# Nine

**Kelly** reached across her corner desk and grabbed the ringing cell phone, her eyes still on the computer screen. "Kelly here."

"Hey, Kelly." Burt's voice came over the line. "I hope you haven't burrowed into your accounts yet, because I need you to spread the word. I'm throwing a little get-together for Mimi and Pete tonight after the shop closes. Just the shop family and all you guys, of course. We're keeping it kind of quiet and low-key."

Kelly took a sip from her coffee mug. "That's a great idea, Burt. Mimi's coming, right?"

"Oh, yeah. I think she really wants to go back." He paused. "But I can tell she's a little scared, too. And that's understandable, considering what happened to poor Tracy. Mimi's still haunted by that. But coming back to see the shop all put together again will help Mimi a lot. At least, I hope it will."

"I think you're right, Burt. Okay, I'll start spreading the word. What do you want us to bring?"

"Just yourselves. This is my treat. I'm bringing pizza and beer. I want to get Pete out of the kitchen so he can relax and celebrate with the rest of us."

"Burt, you're a sweetie to do this. It should definitely help Mimi."

"I sure hope so. I'll see you tonight after the shop closes, okay?"

"Sure thing. By the way, what's happening with the investigation into Tracy's death? Any leads on that boyfriend she told Jennifer about?"

Burt sighed. "Dan said they haven't learned anything new, I'm afraid. They've interviewed all of Tracy's classmates who knew her and the staff at Jennifer's real estate firm. Everyone said she was a quiet, hardworking student who kept to herself. No indication of trouble with anyone and no enemies, either. And nobody could recall Tracy ever mentioning a boyfriend or anyone else who was 'special' in her life. Apparently she only told Jennifer and didn't give any name or details."

"Not much to go on."

"I'm afraid not. But they're working all the angles they can. Dan is contacting some of his informants who've been useful in the past. Maybe one of them knows something about those guys who vandalized the shop. It still looks more likely that they committed the murder."

Something about that still bothered Kelly. She wasn't sure why. "Maybe so, Burt. I don't know. . . ."

"Neither do I, Kelly," Burt admitted. "But somebody killed that poor girl. She sure didn't fall in the tub and drown herself. Not with those bruise marks on the middle of her back. Someone held Tracy under that hot water until she died, and I promise you, Dan and the guys are gonna find out who."

Kelly heard the frustration in his voice and switched subjects. "Did you learn anything about dogs being poisoned in town?"

"Thanks for reminding me, Kelly. I'm going in so many different directions, I forgot about Carl. The animal and humane officer said we haven't had an instance of dog poisoning like that for two years. I guess this was an isolated act of cruelty."

"I don't know, Burt. I used to think all these incidents were random, but now I'm not so sure. Did Jennifer talk with you?"

"Yeah, she did, but I think it's a stretch to try to connect what happened to those other people who bought the ranch with what's happened to you."

Kelly frowned into her little phone. "Three days ago I would have agreed with you, Burt. But that was before Carl was poisoned. And before learning that this other woman's dog was killed at the ranch. Now

I'm worried that Jennifer may be right. Somebody doesn't want me to have that ranch, and they're hoping to scare me off. First, by trashing my place, and now, by trying to kill Carl."

Burt paused for a moment. "I wish I had something to say that would reassure you, Kelly, but I don't. Just trust that the police are looking into everything, okay? Meanwhile, come on over tonight and have some pizza and beer with us. It'll make you feel better. See you later."

Kelly listened to the click of his phone and wished pizza and beer could chase away the cold feeling in her gut, but she doubted it.

"**Have** you heard from the vet this morning?" Megan asked, looking across the long library table.

Kelly could see the worry in her friend's face. And the nearly-completed Shamrock green sweater was a dead giveaway. Megan had been knitting furiously.

Between keeping Mimi company and worrying about Carl, Megan was in danger of depleting her wool stash. And Megan's stash was bigger than anyone's except Mimi's. Most knitters had bags and bags of gorgeous yarns they bought because they couldn't resist the luscious fibers. Unfortunately, the amount of knitting time available did not increase in proportion to the size of the larger stashes. There weren't that many hours in the day.

"I saw the vet early this morning when I went to

check on Carl. His liver values continue to drop. Thank God. I saw him through the window and he's drinking water, but he still looks weak. The vet said I can come inside and pat him this afternoon if he continues to improve."

Megan closed her eyes. "Oh, thank goodness. We were all so worried. Lisa and Mimi and I must have gone through a basket of yarn yesterday morning, we worried so much."

Kelly glanced around the room, now restored to its former organized layout of full yarn bins and bookshelves. "Maybe that's what helped Mimi return to the shop. She needed more yarn," Kelly joked softly.

Megan leaned back in her chair. "So many awful things have happened lately. Tracy's been killed, the shop and café vandalized. And now, Carl has been poisoned. Do you think there's any connection, Kelly?"

Kelly pulled her scarf from the knitting bag, mulling over what Megan said. Vandalism at her cottage. Vandalism at the shop. Tracy killed, most probably by the vandals. Police had found no one else who could be responsible. Their searches had turned up no boyfriends and no enemies. No one. It seemed her death was a tragic accident, just like the police said. A horrible act of random violence. But random was hardly the word Kelly would use to describe the incidents that had happened to her.

"No, Megan, I don't," she answered at last. "I used to think the vandals that hit my place were the same ones who trashed the shop. But now, I don't. Not after talking to Jennifer. She's convinced me that someone is after the canyon ranch, and they're trying to scare me into selling."

Megan looked up, wide-eyed. "You're kidding?"

"No, I'm not. The first buyer was scared off when his building site was torched last year. The second buyer dumped the property when her little dog was killed in her car while she was checking out the ranch."

Megan cringed. "Oh, how awful!"

"Yeah. Whoever is after the ranch must like to kill dogs. That's why Carl was attacked. So, you can see that I'm definitely being targeted. Just like the other buyers." She picked up her needles and resumed knitting. "Tracy's death appears to be accidental. A horrible, brutal act of random violence, just like the police said."

"Kelly, what are you going to do? To protect yourself, I mean . . . and Carl?"

"Well, Carl won't be in the yard unless I'm there to watch him. And, there are lights everywhere now. Maybe we can catch the bastard who's doing this if he comes creeping around again."

From the corner of her eye, Kelly saw Mimi walking through the next room, staring into yarn bins, touching, stroking fibers, as if reassuring herself that her beloved Lambspun was intact. The ugly murder that had happened in the basement hadn't touched what was good and beautiful above.

Megan lowered her voice. "Mimi is much better. She's still not herself yet, but she's better."

"I couldn't help but notice how quiet and subdued she is. She's not talking much. When I came in this morning, she rushed over and gave me a huge hug, but all she said was that she was praying for Carl." Kelly watched Mimi assisting a customer pick out yarn. "I just hope we get the old Mimi back. Burt thinks getting together tonight should help."

Megan leaned forward over the table. "Did Burt say anything about Tracy's murder?" she whispered. "I've been afraid to mention it anywhere near Mimi. Have the police learned anything new about those vandals?"

Kelly glanced over her shoulder to check, but Mimi was deep into yarn talk. Even so, Kelly lowered her voice. "When Burt called this morning, he said the police were targeting some informants they've worked with before, to see if they know anything. So keep your fingers crossed."

The shop doorbell jangled then, and Lisa strode into the room. "Kelly, I got your message on my cell. The big guy is on the mend, right?"

"Yep. He's officially off the critical list."

"That's good news. And seeing Mimi back in the shop is even better news." Lisa plopped her knitting bag on the table beside Megan and withdrew a skein of variegated yarn—scarlet red, royal blue, and emerald green—and circular needles with only a few rows of stitches. Clearly, a new project.

Too small to be a sweater, Kelly noticed. "What are you working on?" She pointed to the small circlet of vibrant yarns.

"I'm making a hat for one of the therapists at the fitness center. It's her birthday next week. The big five-oh." Lisa's fingers picked up speed. "It's easy, Kelly. You should try it. Aren't you getting bored with scarves?"

"Not yet. Besides, it's winter. You can never have too many scarves," Kelly said, slipping another finished stitch off her needle.

"Yeah, you can."

"You should try a hat, Kelly. It'll be easy," Megan promised as she continued working the bright green yarn.

Kelly laughed. "That's what you always say whenever I try a new project. And invariably, I get all tangled up and make a million mistakes."

"It's yarn, what do you expect?" Lisa teased.

"Why don't you start a hat while it's still winter?" Megan suggested.

Kelly watched the colorful stitches fill her needle. Maybe she should try making a hat after she finished this scarf. She certainly could use one. Hadn't Steve mentioned that she needed a hat last night?

Besides, the green knit hat Megan made for her had accidentally fallen into the washing machine and shrunk. It was now suitable for dolls. Hot water and knitted wools—not a good combination unless you were felting.

"You know, I just might give hats a try after I finish this scarf."

"Well, it's either a hat or socks, Kelly. Which one?"

Lisa asked. "I was here when you made that promise to Hilda in December, remember?"

"What promise?" Kelly searched her memory, but no hat or sock discussions surfaced.

"I remember it, too," Megan added with a big grin. "You promised Hilda you'd learn to knit socks when she learned to spin. Well, I sat in on one of the spinning classes last week, and Hilda's coming along fine. A little slower than the others, but she's spinning."

"That does it, Kelly. You don't want Hilda to start ragging on you. She's relentless," Lisa warned.

"And you're not?"

"Consider it encouragement."

"Okay, okay, I'll do it when I finish the scarf," Kelly agreed in surrender as she slipped another stitch off her needle. "I'll try the hat. It looks easier than socks."

Lisa shook her head. "Hilda will give you hell. You promised socks."

"That had to be a moment of temporary insanity. There's no way I could manage those skinny little double-point needles you have to use for socks. And not just two needles, but three of them, for Pete's sake. Why the heck do you need three needles?"

"Just because," Lisa intoned in a deep voice, which made Megan giggle.

"I hate it when you say that."

"Somebody has to give you a hard time, Kelly. No one else will. Except Jennifer and me. So it's up to us to kick your butt."

"Excuse me?"

Lisa pinned Kelly with a laser look. "About Steve. He's waaaay too patient. When are you going to get serious? He's not seeing anyone else, and neither are you. It's time for some commitment here."

Kelly released a huge sigh and reached for her ever-present coffee mug. Empty. *Damn.* She'd have to endure one of "those conversations" without caffeine.

"How'd we get from socks to Steve? I swear, you're as bad as Jennifer."

"Did I hear my name taken in vain?" Jennifer's voice floated from the yarn room behind them.

Kelly watched her friend approach the table and settle into a chair beside her. *Oh, boy. Stereo teasing.* She braced herself.

"I take my reputation seriously, you know," Jennifer said as she pulled the royal blue sweater from her bag. "Lisa's not even on the radar screen of bad."

Megan laughed over her yarn, glancing slyly at Kelly. "Lisa was giving Kelly a hard time about Steve."

Kelly stared at Megan. Supergeek, too-shy-to-date-until-recently Megan was teasing Kelly about moving slowly. Something was definitely wrong with this picture. Kelly resisted the urge to tease back, however, because she and her friends were afraid of spoiling the blossoming relationship between Megan and Marty. Superjocks, both. Marty was brilliantly moving the relationship forward inch by inch.

*Kind of like Steve*, the little voice in the back of her head whispered. That caught Kelly's attention. Hmmmm.

"Oh, good. I came at just the right time. Where'd you leave off, Lisa?"

"I asked Kelly when she was going to kick that relationship up to the next level. She's been dithering about it for months now. What's the matter with you, Kelly?"

Kelly stared at her friend, incredulous. *Dithering?* She'd never dithered in her life. How could they say that? She was just . . . taking her time.

"*What?*" she protested, indignant. "I do *not* dither."

"Do, too," Jennifer said, not looking up from her needles.

"Do not."

"Yeah, you do," Lisa chimed in.

"I'm just . . . moving slowly, that's all."

Lisa snorted, her fingers working the colorful yarn. "Slowly? Glaciers move faster."

Megan burst out laughing, then clamped her hand over her mouth, shoulders shaking.

"Kelly's got 'issues,' " Jennifer said in a theatrical voice.

Kelly rolled her eyes. "Oh, *please.*" She didn't think she could get through any more of this without coffee. Noticing Rosa around the corner filling yarn bins, Kelly caught her eye. "Hey, Rosa, could you ask someone in the café to bring me some coffee, please? I can't take this aggravation without caffeine."

Lisa peered over at Kelly. "*Issues,* my ass. So your old boyfriend was a sleaze and dumped you. That happens to lots of people. Get over it."

Lisa's and Jennifer's well-aimed barbs were hitting

home. Kelly could feel their words penetrate inside. She'd already said these same things to herself. *Why, then, am I still hesitating?* She hadn't figured that out yet, but she was working on it.

"I'm getting there, guys, believe me, I am—"

Jennifer dropped her needles in her lap and turned to her. "You know, Kelly, I've known you for nearly a year now. You are scary brave. You quit your corporate job and started a business here, you took on that Wyoming ranch, bought a place in the canyon. Even all those murders you've gotten involved in, sleuthing. You don't back down. I've watched you. You'll get right in a killer's face if you have to. You're a risk taker in every aspect of your life, except one. Relationships. Why is that?"

Kelly stared into her friend's earnest dark brown gaze. She felt Jennifer's question resonate within. *Whoa.* Why was that? she wondered. She didn't have an answer.

"Uhhhh," was all Kelly could manage at the moment.

"Just something to think about, Kelly." Jennifer returned to her knitting. So like Jennifer. She would joke and tease, then she'd zero in and hit the target.

"Good advice, Kelly," Lisa added. "I'd be curious—"

Kelly was saved from further interrogation or perceptive analysis by the jangle of her cell phone. She flipped it open while a café waitress placed a large mug of black coffee in front of her. Saved at last. Kelly took a big sip, ignoring the burn, as Jayleen's voice came on the line.

"Kelly, I've got a question for you." Jayleen jumped right to the point in her usual no-nonsense style. "A rancher friend of mine is looking to expand his herd, and he remembered that Geri Norbert had some fine alpaca females. I told him you bought her herd, and he's wondering if you'd be interested in selling any of them. I told him I'd ask and take him up there for a look-see if you agree."

It took only a second for Kelly to switch into accounting mode, grateful for the diversion. "You know, Jayleen, if you'd asked me that a month ago, my answer would have been an automatic no. But now I've got way too many expenses and not enough money to pay them. I checked with the business office at the veterinary hospital this morning, and Carl's vet bills are two thousand dollars and still climbing." She noticed her friends' shocked expressions and nodded.

"I kinda figured that," Jayleen said. "That's why I called. When life throws you those curveballs, it kinda changes your perspective."

"It sure does," Kelly said, leaning back into the curved wooden chair. "I'm getting pretty tired of catching them, too. How many females does he want to buy? I don't want to lose them all."

"I can drive him up there tomorrow morning. Let's see which ones he's interested in, and then you and I can talk, okay?"

"Sounds like a plan, Jayleen. Call me tomorrow. Oh, by the way, Burt's throwing a little get-together here tonight, to celebrate the reopening of the café and the shop. He's just inviting close friends, and that means you. I think Curt's coming, too."

"Awwww, I sure wish I could come, Kelly, but I've scheduled tonight to start sorting through tax stuff. I've gotta get everything in order before I dump it all on your desk. I don't want you to drop me as a client the first time out." Her warm chuckle sounded.

"No hurry, Jayleen, it's still February," Kelly said, glancing at her watch. It was time to leave if she wanted to see Carl during visiting hours. "Give me a call after you and the guy take a look in the canyon. I'll let Bobby know you folks will be there."

"Will do. I think we've got a couple of days yet before the next snowstorm hits. Talk to you later."

Kelly shoved the colorful scarf into her bag. More snow, huh? Boy, she definitely wasn't used to these Colorado winters. It had been snowing nearly every week since before Christmas. Sounded like she'd need that knitted hat after all.

**"What?** Pepperoni is gone, again?" Steve cried as he reached toward the open pizza boxes scattered across the littered library table.

"Marty ate it all. I saw him," Greg said before demolishing the last bite of a pepperoni-laden slice. Removing the evidence.

"Naw. I only ate half," Marty replied with his good-natured grin as he leaned back in his chair. "Besides, what's that you're shoving into your mouth?"

Kelly noticed the casual way Marty draped his arm on the back of Megan's chair as she sat beside him. *Atta boy, Marty,* Kelly thought with a grin. Earlier in the evening, Marty caught her eye and winked. Kelly gave the amiable redhead a surreptitious thumbs-up in encouragement.

"Folks, there are four more boxes of pizza, so not to worry," Burt said from his spot at the end of the table next to Mimi.

Kelly was relieved to see Mimi relaxing around the crowded knitting table with shop family and friends. Burt was right. This was exactly what Mimi needed. She had even laughed out loud when tall, skinny Marty grabbed the first pizza box and started racing around the shop, Greg in hot pursuit.

"How many pizzas did you bring?" Lisa asked.

"Ten. Two for Marty, and the rest for us."

"Two? That's just an appetizer," Marty said, playing along.

"Dude, you make a move toward those boxes, and I'm gonna pound you," Greg threatened, reaching for a slice of double cheese.

Marty cackled, arms behind his head in a trade-mark pose. "Gotta catch me first."

"You couldn't catch him before you started eating, Greg. What makes you think you can catch him now?" Megan said with a laugh, cheeks flushed.

"Hey, I'm gaining my strength," Greg replied, before gobbling the cheesy slice.

"Boy, I hope you guys saved some for Pete," Jennifer said as she returned to the table.

Mimi glanced over her shoulder. "Where is Pete, anyway? Oh, dear, is he still working?"

Jennifer nibbled her half-eaten pizza before answering. "He kept promising to come and then he'd find something else to do. So I finally enlisted 'Sheriff' Curt's help."

Kelly sipped her soda and leaned back against Steve's arm, which was draped around her chair. "What's Curt going to do, lasso Pete and drag him in?"

"Whatever it takes . . . hey, here he is," Jennifer said, pointing toward the archway leading to the main room. Pete approached, Curt Stackhouse close behind. "You can remand him into my custody, Sheriff Curt. I'll keep an eye on him." She pulled out the chair beside her.

"Sorry, folks. It's hard for me to get away sometimes," Pete said with a sheepish grin as he sat down.

"Did you have to lasso him, Curt?" Kelly teased the silver-haired rancher.

"Nope, Pete was real cooperative. I told him everybody was waiting on him to start eating." He cast an appreciative eye about the empty pizza boxes. "Looks like you folks just made a liar out of me."

Pete laughed and reached for a slice. "I know this crew, Curt. When there's food around, they wait for each other like one pig waits for another."

"Hey, don't get personal," Jennifer said, giving Pete a gentle poke.

"Looks like we need more," Steve said as he retrieved two additional pizzas from a corner table that had been temporarily cleared of winter yarns.

"Pete, you've gotta learn to relax," Curt advised as he helped open the boxes. The heady aroma of oregano and cheese and pepperoni floated through the air.

"Well, I had promised myself I would, but that was before the chaos happened." Pete accepted a can of soda.

"*You*, relax?" Jennifer looked askance. "That'll be the day."

"Hey, I was going to, honest." Pete's genial grin spread across his face as he brushed that wayward lock of blond hair off his forehead. "Incidentally, I want to thank you two again for all your help cleaning the café." He held up his soda. "To Jennifer and Kelly. Cleaning supersquad. We couldn't have reopened as soon as we did without you."

"That's what friends are for, Pete," Kelly said, acknowledging the lifted soda cans.

"Kelly had even more incentive, Pete. The thought of doing without your coffee for another day struck sheer terror into her heart," Jennifer said.

"Well, I want to thank all of you, too. For everything you did to put the shop back together again," Mimi said when the laughter died down. "I cannot tell you how much it means to me."

Kelly listened to the outpouring of affection directed

toward Mimi, who sat, flushed with pleasure, as her friends spoke up. Draining the last of her soda, Kelly was about to ask Pete to hand her one from the box behind him, until she saw the look on his face.

Pete was watching Jennifer. But that wasn't what caught Kelly's attention. It was the expression on Pete's face. It didn't last long. Only an instant. But Kelly saw it. She'd seen that look on Pete's face before. She'd caught him staring at Jennifer before with that same look. An unmistakable look of longing.

Fleeting and camouflaged well, it was gone in a second. Pete turned his attention to someone else around the table, joining in the fun.

Kelly reached for another slice of cheesy pizza and smiled to herself. *Well, well, well.*

Burt's voice broke through. "I guess this is as good a time as any to bring in dessert."

"Please, no, I've gained enough already," Jennifer said, before taking another bite of pizza.

"Dessert? Where'd you put it? We only cleared off that table," Rosa said, pointing to the corner.

Steve grinned. "It's outside in my truck, staying safe."

"It's freezing outside," Kelly said, astonished. "What'd you bring, ice cream?"

"Nope. I brought our favorite. Chocolate raspberry torte from the French bakery." He gave her a wink.

"Hel-*lo*!" Marty said, springing from his chair. "I'll bring it in, Steve. Don't lift a finger."

"The hell you will," Greg countered, dropping the

pizza slice and scraping back his chair. "There's no way we're letting you within ten feet of that chocolate cake."

"Two cakes, actually," Steve said, egging them on for a second. "But since it's my truck, I pick who gets to go. And I pick Curt and Burt to guard the tortes."

"We're on it," Burt said as he and Curt headed from the room to the sound of laughter.

"Hey, Kelly, how's Carl?" Rosa asked.

"He's doing great. In fact, the doctor said I could bring him home tomorrow."

"Really? Are you going to keep him inside?" Lisa asked.

"Absolutely. In fact, you may not see me in the shop as much for a while. I want to keep a close eye on him."

"Why don't you bring Carl over here, Kelly?" Mimi suggested, arms folded on the table. "He'll be okay, I'm sure."

Kelly rolled her eyes. "I'm sure he won't. This is Carl, remember? He has no manners. He doesn't know how to behave. He'll be into the yarn bins, sniffing everything; he'll jump up on customers with those big Rottie feet. I'm used to it, but other people . . . no way."

Rosa leaned over the table and gave Kelly a warm smile. "Kelly, I can help you with Carl. I teach dog obedience classes, too. I'll be glad to help train Carl. Once he learns to behave, he'll be fine in the shop."

Kelly stared at Rosa as if she'd sprouted another head. "Oh, I don't know, Rosa . . . this is Carl we're talking about."

Rosa laughed indulgently. "Believe me, Kelly, I've trained some pretty difficult dogs. Carl is a sugar bear. He'll be an easy train."

"I don't know . . ." she hedged again, trying to picture Carl obeying commands. It wouldn't come into focus.

"Why don't you give it a try?" Steve suggested. "Can't hurt. Give the big guy a chance."

"Trust me, Kelly, he'll be fine," Rosa promised.

Kelly was spared from answering by the arrival of the chocolate raspberry tortes and the chocoholic chaos that ensued.

# Ten

"**The** squirrels have missed you, Carl. See, they're waving their tails," Kelly teased, watching the chorus line of squirrels scamper along the fence top, just out of reach.

Carl galumphed through the foot-deep snow in a valiant race to the fence, but the squirrels were quicker. They reached the ground and skittered across the snow, heading for the nearby cottonwood tree by the time Carl made it to the fence.

"It's hard to chase squirrels in the snow," Kelly commiserated as Carl stood barking at the cottonwood branches above. "Don't worry. Spring will come one of these days."

Kelly leaned her head back and let snowflakes fall

on her face. Big, fat flakes—falling thick and fast. The storm front had moved in overnight, and she awoke to see at least four inches of new snow accumulated on the glass patio table, which served as her measuring stick. Of course, that was on top of the six inches or so of snow already on the ground. And it was still snowing. Kelly's morning run had turned to a slog along the river trail.

She gazed about the golf course, the trees bordering the Poudre River, the buildings across the street—all blanketed in white. Smothered. She could barely make out the buildings along the edge of Old Town. The low ridge of mountains, or foothills, had disappeared completely. Swallowed up by the snow.

Standing on her patio, Kelly pulled her hood back and listened to the quiet. She barely heard the traffic from the surrounding streets. That was the most fascinating thing about snow. It smothered sound. Everything was suddenly peaceful.

Even Carl had stopped barking. Watching her dog sniff and poke his way around the snowy backyard, Kelly could tell he didn't have his usual go-go energy. It would take a while for him to get his strength back, the vet had said. Right now, Kelly was simply happy to have him home. And if that meant she'd be standing in the snow, in the rain, and in the freezing cold countless times a day while Carl went outside, it was a small price to pay to keep him safe.

The muffled sound of her cell phone ringing from

her coat pocket broke the blanket of silence. "Kelly here."

"Kelly, this is Bobby. I figured I'd better call right away. I just got here to feed the animals, and I spotted some smoke coming from the barn—"

"Smoke! Oh, no . . ." Kelly interrupted. "Is there a fire?"

"It wasn't a big one, so I was able to put it out. Looks like someone poured kerosene on hay inside the barn. It was mostly just smoking when I got there."

The peacefulness was gone. "Did they leave a gas can, by any chance?" she asked, remembering the developer's experience.

"Gas can? No, ma'am. Smelled like kerosene to me. There's some on the shelf for the lanterns."

The cold fist in her stomach tightened. She was right. All of this was linked to the canyon ranch. "Bobby, did you see anyone around when you came? Maybe parked along the road or something? Anyone walking along the road?"

"No, I sure didn't. You know, ma'am . . . uh, Kelly, I think you should tell the police. I mean, considering all that's been happening up here. What with that real estate fella and the nice lady from Ohio and her little dog. That liked to make me sick hearing about it. I . . . I don't know what to make of it all."

"Neither do I, Bobby," Kelly confessed. "Listen, would you consider moving into the ranch house for a few weeks until I can sort this out and figure out what's happening? That way you could keep an eye on the place. With this storm now, I won't be able to get up into the canyon for a couple of days."

"Sure, ma'am, I'd be glad to keep watch over the place for you. Matter of fact, it would save me on my rent. So it would help me out. I'd be able to get into town for my classes earlier, too."

Kelly exhaled a relieved sigh. "Thanks, Bobby. I really appreciate it. And if you hear or see anything or anyone suspicious, call me right away, will you?"

"Don't worry, I will. And don't you even think about driving up here until this storm's over and they've cleared the roads. It was slippery for me this morning, and I've got my truck."

"Don't worry. I know what those roads are like in the snow. The storm is supposed to be over by tomorrow morning, so I'll see what it looks like by the weekend. And Bobby, thanks so much for agreeing to stay at the ranch. That makes me feel much better."

"Glad to, ma'am. But I still think you should call the police."

"I will, Bobby. You bet I will."


Kelly sipped from her coffee mug, steam rising out of the small opening, as she stood by the edge of the snow-blanketed flower beds beside Lambspun's front steps. Rosa was walking Carl back and forth along the front patio and porch, stopping every twenty paces, instructing him to "sit."

At first, Carl seemed clueless as to the point of Rosa's behavior. But after a few times around the porch and some quick tugs on the training collar, Carl got it. He sat. Every time Rosa stopped, Carl sat. Kelly was shocked.

Not only did Carl obey Rosa's verbal commands, but he began watching her hand signals as well. He sat. And when Rosa began walking again, Carl was up and beside her left knee, whether Rosa had ordered him to "heel" or simply patted her left leg. He obeyed. Would wonders never cease? Carl was trainable.

Glancing up into the blue Colorado sky, Kelly was glad for the sunshine today. These outdoor sessions with Carl had convinced Kelly she really did have to start that knitted hat and soon. The sun might be shining but the temperatures were still in the single digits. She thought her ears would freeze and drop off during Carl's early morning bathroom break.

The crunch of tires through snow sounded as Burt pulled into the knitting shop's driveway. Kelly strolled over to his car. "Can you go in the back door, Burt? I've hired Rosa to give Carl obedience lessons, and it looks like it's working. I'm amazed."

Burt watched Carl go through his paces. "Well, look at that. Maybe our steaks will be safe on the grill from now on."

"I wouldn't go that far. These are 'sit' and 'stay' commands. I'm not sure there's a 'no steak for you' command."

Burt's smile faded. "Since we're out here, I'll update

you on what's happening with the investigation into Tracy's death. I'm trying not to say anything around Mimi. Not for a while yet."

"Have they learned anything new?"

"Well, they're working on it. Thanks to Dan's informant, they brought a guy in for questioning. He runs with the group that's been causing trouble up in the north side of town. Dan thinks they may be able to connect those guys with a couple of break-ins. That means he can start to put pressure on them. He'll round 'em up one by one if he has to. Squeeze until somebody spills something."

"Boy, I hope so, Burt. Somebody must have seen or heard something when they trashed the shop. Maybe they slipped up and said something in a bar, I don't know . . ." She stared out at the sunshine glinting off the alabaster golf course.

"They're working the bars, too. Don't worry. We'll get 'em."

Something nagged in the back of Kelly's mind. A persistent thought that wouldn't go away. "What if it wasn't a gang of guys that did this? What if it was only one vandal? That would explain why Mimi's laptop wasn't stolen and why there wasn't a huge amount of damage to the café and shop. Jennifer says she's seen vandalized cafés that have had to shut down they were trashed so badly."

"I think that's kind of unlikely, Kelly," Burt replied after a moment. "Why would one person trash a knitting shop and a café? And why on earth would a lone vandal kill Tracy? It doesn't make sense."

"No, it doesn't, Burt," she admitted. "But a lot of stuff bothers me about this whole thing. Blaming everything on these vandals. What if Tracy was killed before they got here? What if they discovered her body, got scared, and took off? That might explain why the damage was less."

"Believe it or not, Kelly, Dan has considered that theory. But without much of a clue as to who would want Tracy dead, it doesn't lead anywhere. The 'mysterious boyfriend' Tracy mentioned to Jennifer never turned up. Maybe Tracy made him up, who knows? No one else ever heard her talk about him. And as I've said before, no one else has shown up on the radar screen."

Kelly swirled the coffee in her mug in frustration. "I know. Just random violence. No leads. No nothing. It's so . . . so frustrating."

"Welcome to the realities of investigative work, Kelly," Burt said with a sardonic smile. "Frustration comes with the territory."

"Well, if you're used to frustration, then join me. There's been another incident at the canyon ranch. Bobby arrived yesterday morning and found a small fire smoking in the barn. No one in sight. Someone is definitely trying to scare off anyone who buys that ranch, Burt. And whoever it is will trash houses, kill dogs, and set fires to do it."

Burt frowned. "It's more likely that kids or squatters spent the night in the barn and set the fire."

"I don't think so, Burt. I've got a bad feeling about all this."

"I know you do, Kelly, but don't start imagining things, okay? Listen, I've got to teach a spinning class. See you later."

"Later." Kelly waved to Burt as her cell phone rang from her coat pocket.

Jennifer's voice came breathless on the line. "Kelly, you never will believe who showed up in my office this morning."

"Who?"

"Gothboy."

"Who's that?

"He's that weird Denver real estate agent, remember? I told you about him before, when you were trying to buy the canyon ranch. He made a lowball offer on it. He works with clients who're always looking to pick up properties cheap."

"Oh, yeah. Now I remember. What'd he want?"

Jennifer's voice dropped. "He was asking about ranch properties that were available in the canyons, and guess which one he was especially interested in?"

Kelly felt a little shiver run up her spine. "You're kidding."

"Nope, I'm not. In fact, he kept asking questions about the previous owners and how long they had the place, and how long you've owned it. When I asked him why he was so interested in that ranch, he looked away then said he'd heard all sorts of rumors about it in Denver. He'd heard there were 'problems.' Seems he's got these buyers in Colorado Springs who're on the lookout for distressed properties. And he figured this place sounded like one. I tell you, Kelly, it gave me goose bumps just listening to him. I've only seen him at a distance at real estate functions. He's creepy as hell in person." She gave an audible shiver.

"What do you think he's up to, Jen? Do you think he's legit? I mean, do you think he's really scoping out places for his clients?"

"I don't know, Kelly. Let me talk to some agents in Denver then get back to you. I've heard stories about this guy over the years. I tell you, he sure spooked me just standing here in my office. He's really over the top with that Goth look. I swear he uses more eyeliner than I do. His hair is as black as a raven's wing. And his wardrobe is straight out of the movies, complete with a long black trench coat. In this weather, yet. He must be freezing his butt off."

That comment made Kelly smile despite herself. "Well, if he went up into the canyon, he'd certainly be easy to spot against the snow, wouldn't he?"

"It's not funny, Kelly. He was weird, the way he focused in on your ranch, asking all those questions, his eyes boring into me."

"Just because a guy looks and acts weird doesn't mean he's dangerous."

"Well, I'm not taking any chances. Not after that fire in your barn. Somebody is out to drive you off that ranch, Kelly. Who knows? Maybe Gothboy is working for those clients to get that ranch for some special deal. There were other parcels sold close by. Let me check the rumor mill to see if anyone's heard of a mega development planned for the canyon. Someone is willing to resort to violence to get that ranch."

"Now, you're starting to scare *me*."

"Good. I've got your attention. Let me work my networks and get back to you, okay? 'Bye."

Kelly clicked off, the unsettled feeling still there. She spotted a familiar truck pulling into the shop driveway and felt herself relax a little. Jayleen. Now there was a no-nonsense person to bounce these crazy ideas off of. She hadn't filled Jayleen in on the fire yet, and she'd be curious as to the savvy rancher's opinion. Jayleen didn't spook easily, either.

Jayleen gave a wave as she jumped to the icy driveway. "Hey, Kelly, I was looking for you. Finally got all my tax stuff together, so I thought I'd bring it in." She handed an oblong portfolio to Kelly.

"Thanks, Jayleen, I'll get on it in a few days. How's the road going into the canyon? I'd like to drive up there tomorrow to take a look around."

"It's the usual after a storm, still snow-covered in patches." She glanced at the sky. "With all the sun, it'll melt for sure. But tonight will be below zero, so it'll be ice again tomorrow morning. You should wait until afternoon to be safe. Especially with your little car." She glanced at Rosa and Carl, still marching back and forth. "What's all this? Carl getting a workout?"

Kelly noticed Carl's "sits" were getting sharper and quicker. "I'm paying Rosa to train Carl so he can come into the shop with me while I'm there. Hopefully, he'll learn enough to behave and not cause trouble."

Jayleen threw back her head and let out a hearty laugh. "Whooee! Now, *that* I've gotta see. I'd say you have a fighting chance as long as you keep Carl in the middle of the yarn. But don't take him anywhere near Pete's café. Once Carl learns there's food nearby, it's all over."

# Eleven

**Steering** away from the edges of the canyon road, Kelly maneuvered her car over the icy patches. This was the worst she'd seen the road all winter. Didn't the county plow it yesterday? Then she remembered the gusty winds that roared through town last night, leaving snowdrifts three feet high against the side of her house facing the golf course.

Her cell phone's ringing broke through Kelly's concentration, and she debated taking her attention—and one hand—off the wheel. Habit won out over caution, and she flipped the phone open. She had to buy a headset.

"Where are you, Kelly? I tried calling twice before," Jennifer demanded.

"Probably a lost signal. I'm heading up into the canyon to the ranch. I want to check out that fire damage for myself. Boy, it's nasty up here. Jayleen said they plowed the roads, but they're still snow-covered." She felt the car slide and corrected as the road continued to climb higher into the canyon.

"Remember all that wind in town last night? Well, that's nothing compared to the wind in those canyons. Gusts can reach gale force. You may not even get into the ranch. The driveway may be drifted over."

"Oh, I'm sure it'll be okay. Bobby would have been through with the truck this morning."

"If you say so. Listen, I've got to take some buyers out in a few minutes, but I wanted to let you know what I found out about Gothboy. My sources tell me he's developed quite a business in buying up so-called distressed properties for bargain prices. Then, he works deals with people who wouldn't be able to qualify for a regular loan. You know, bad credit and all. He's using sleazy lenders, too. Anyway, I heard he's had some problems with the licensing commission. A couple of disciplinary actions, but nothing bad enough to lose his license. Plus, I heard rumors that he's got a real shady past."

"Like what?"

Jennifer lowered her voice. "I heard he used to work for collection agencies and repossessing cars. Word is he also used to hire himself out for assignments for private debt collection. Kind of like an 'enforcer.' He was brought in to beat up guys if they didn't pay on time."

Kelly felt a chill run up her spine. "Does this charming individual have a name? Surely he doesn't go by 'Gothboy.' "

"His name is J. D. Franklin. Everyone calls him J.D. to his face, and Gothboy behind his back."

"Better not let him hear you. He doesn't sound like the forgiving type."

Jennifer laughed softly. "I'll be careful. Meanwhile, my buzzer is going off on this guy. He's used to working the edges quasi-legally and getting away with it. Maybe he's straying further over the line. Maybe Franklin's got some clients who're willing to do anything to get that property, and he's working for them."

"Do you really think that's possible, Jen?"

"Anything's possible when money's involved. And this guy sounds like he's willing to do whatever is necessary. I'm still checking into other land sales near the ranch to see if there's a connection. Oh, and get this . . . I found out Franklin has been in town for several weeks now. Another agent has seen him at a couple of bars. Apparently he has a girlfriend in Fort Connor. If he was in town, then maybe he's behind all the vandalism."

The old familiar cold returned to Kelly's gut. It was never far away. Was that possible? Creepy Gothboy skulking around the canyon. Targeting her.

"Whoa, Jen, you should tell all this to Burt."

"I will, but I want to get more information first. I sense Franklin's hiding something about that property, and I want to find out what it is. Talk to you later. Gotta go." She clicked off.

Kelly steered around the curve and saw the ranch in the distance. Slowing as she approached the entrance, Kelly was about to turn into the driveway until she took a good look at it.

The driveway was gone. It was completely blown over with snowdrifts, at least three feet high. She stared at the snow. How was she supposed to drive through that? Where were Bobby's truck tracks? Peering at the blanket of white, Kelly thought she detected a broken path through the snow.

Noticing a flattened patch just off the road, Kelly figured Bobby must have parked his truck and walked up the drive. If he couldn't make it up that driveway, she sure as heck couldn't.

Waiting for a car to pass, Kelly backed out and edged off the canyon road and parked along the side. She'd have to have a talk with that snowplow guy she hired. Didn't he bother to check the roads after a windstorm? She'd have to hire someone else.

Grabbing a borrowed knitted hat and her gloves, Kelly closed and locked the car, glad she'd worn her extrathermal outwear because she'd be slogging through knee-high drifts to get to the barn.

Kelly stared at the pastures and the evergreens, all blanketed in white, as she set out to follow Bobby's path leading up the driveway. The morning's clear skies had brought back the sun, and the Rockies sparkled in the distance. Somehow, looking at those mountains made her aggravation go away. She always felt peaceful when she was up here staring at the mountains.

The cold, crisp air crackled sharp in her nostrils as her breathing settled into workout rhythm. Icy cold air sliced into her lungs, sharp and clean. The sunshine was so bright, reflecting off the snow-covered pastures, it caused her to squint. She should have worn her sunglasses.

Kelly marked the distance from the road to the barnyard. Halfway there. No alpaca in sight. They were probably still inside the barn or the corral where the snow wasn't as deep.

The glint of something black at the corner of her eye caused Kelly to stop in her tracks. *What was that?* Her pulse started to race as she scanned the surrounding trees, searching. Was someone there? Or was it her imagination? The image of black-garbed Gothboy hiding behind the trees, spying on her, darted through her head.

Suddenly ebony wings flashed through the sunlight as a raven took flight from a snow-laden evergreen branch. Kelly watched the large bird as it flew high across the pasture.

*See? It was a bird. Nobody's hiding in the trees. Get a grip.*

Reaching the barnyard, Kelly noticed some of the alpaca peeking at her from the corral. "Too deep for you guys?" Kelly called out to the animals as she slogged through the fluffy Colorado powder heading to the barn.

The pungent smell of hay tickled her nostrils as she stepped inside. Already aware of Kelly's arrival, the alpaca clustered around the corral fence, watching her. Kelly scanned the interior of the barn, searching for traces of the fire. She found a patch of blackened hay and dirt at the far end.

"It's too bad you guys can't talk," Kelly told the attentive alpaca, who were observing her carefully. "You could tell me who did this." Kelly kicked at the blackened spot.

She walked over to the corral fence and rubbed the noses of those alpaca that were brave enough to venture close. Only a few came forward. They all watched her carefully, but most kept their distance. Kelly wondered if they missed their first owner. Geri Norbert had been willing to kill to keep these beautiful animals and her ranch.

"Am I still a stranger?" she asked the bravest of the herd, who kept pushing his face up for attention. "I hope not for long. Maybe this spring I'll get to spend more time with you." She gave the big gray male a farewell pat. "But right now, I've gotta go, before that road ices over."

As she turned to leave, Kelly noticed a red metal can on a nearby shelf and a kerosene lantern hanging from a nail on the adjacent post. Maybe it *was* a squatter, like Burt suggested, she thought as she closed the barn door and headed toward the driveway. After all, the place had been vacant since last summer. Jennifer had told her about people trying to sneak into empty canyon homes, taking up residence when they could get away with it. Maybe they started a fire to keep warm.

Trudging back to the canyon road, Kelly let all those conflicting thoughts bounce around inside her head while she trekked through the snow. Jennifer's suspicions, Burt's rationalizations, the bad feeling inside her gut. Was the truth somewhere in the middle? Reaching the road at last, Kelly unlocked her car and jumped inside, revving the engine as soon as she turned the key.

*Come on, warm up,* she urged the heater. Shivering, Kelly pulled onto the road and aimed her car down the canyon. Back home to Fort Connor. Home to hot coffee. She shook her travel mug. Empty. *Rats.* She could really use some coffee now. Even hot chocolate would do as long as it was hot.

Kelly briefly wondered again if she was cut out to live up here in the canyon. It was definitely colder. A helluva lot snowier, too, she thought as she steered around a gentle curve, the road ahead angling down. What would it be like to drive these icy roads all winter? she wondered. Would she be able to come into town every day? Would she want to?

The car picked up speed. What if she was snowbound up here with a blizzard? Would she go nuts with only Carl to keep her company? No friends across the way like it was now. Maybe she could keep the cottage and stay in town during the winter. Maybe she'd only go up to the canyon on the weekends. No, that wouldn't work. Who'd feed the animals?

Her car swerved around a curve in the road, and Kelly jerked the wheel to steady it, braking to slow down. But the car didn't slow. It kept picking up speed as the canyon road wound down the mountain. Kelly pushed hard on the brake this time. Nothing. The car kept picking up speed, faster.

*What was wrong with her brakes?* Kelly pumped the brakes now, again and again, but nothing happened. Her car kept picking up speed as the canyon road descended. A truck suddenly appeared in the opposite lane, and Kelly fought the wheel to avoid him and keep from heading into the ravine alongside, where trees and boulders dropped off into deep crevasses.

*Oh-my-God!* She panicked. Her brakes were gone, and she was going over sixty miles an hour! She had to do something fast. She grabbed the gearshift and jammed it into low gear. There was a sharp screech of metal, and the car slowed. But it didn't stop. Down, down, down, it hurtled.

Steering around a curve, Kelly's heart sank. Up ahead was the steepest decline of all—twisting, turning, winding curves. Her car started picking up speed again, faster and faster.

She'd never make it down the canyon. She'd crash and die. Unless . . . unless she crashed before she got to the bottom. Before the car picked up any more speed. She'd be going over ninety miles an hour by the time she reached bottom. She wouldn't have a chance.

Spotting the boulders up ahead around the curve, Kelly froze for an instant. *Good God.* Could she make it around that curve? If she didn't, the boulders would kill her for sure!

Suddenly she saw them. Thick bushes along the side of the road. *Quick, over there!* said the little voice in her head. *Now! Crash now!*

Kelly listened and jerked the wheel to the right, aiming straight for the bushes.

It happened in a flash. Kelly was in the brambles, then—*wham!* All of a sudden she was swallowed by a huge white marshmallow. And then she went to sleep.

"**Oh,** my God, Kelly! What happened?" Megan cried as she peeked around the white curtain dividing the hospital emergency exam rooms.

Kelly looked at her friend's horrified expression. Megan's face was almost as white as the curtain. Even though it hurt to make the gesture, Kelly beckoned Megan inside the cubicle to join the rest of her friends who circled her examining table bedside. "It's okay, Megan. My brakes failed coming down the canyon. Thank God for air bags."

"She's lying, Megan," Jennifer retorted from the corner. "She has a concussion and a broken ankle."

"She's damn lucky to be alive," Steve said, standing beside Kelly. "Lots of people have crashed on that canyon road and died."

Kelly had to agree. She *was* lucky. Every muscle in her body ached, her head felt like it was about to explode, and her left ankle, well . . . she hadn't felt anything that painful since she'd slid into third base at college and collided with the baseman, cracking three ribs.

"Yeah, well, I thought I'd be one of them. That's why I headed for the trees halfway down." The side of her head throbbed again. *Damn.* Even talking hurt.

"That's probably what saved you," said the orthopedic resident who stood at the foot of the narrow table, carefully wrapping plaster-soaked gauze strips around Kelly's ankle.

Kelly stared at her throbbing left ankle. It was fat and getting fatter as the stocky young man kept wrapping the strips. *Damn.* A cast. She'd never had a cast. Not in all her years of sports and athletic injuries. Never until now. *Double damn.* She'd be clunking around for weeks. She tried to scowl at the injury, but that made her head hurt even more.

*A fair trade for your life, don't you think?* the little voice inside reminded her. Ohhhh, yeah, she admitted to herself, giving silent thanks once again.

Megan ventured into the small enclosure, which was filled already. "I bet your car is—"

"Totaled, yes," Burt interrupted from where he stood beside Jennifer, frowning. Worried frowning, too. Kelly recognized that expression and felt guilty at being the cause of it.

She glanced around the circle of concerned friends' faces. Not a smile to be seen. Steve, Jennifer, Burt, Megan, even outspoken Lisa, who normally would be all over Kelly, fussing, sat silently chewing her lip.

"It's been towed to the dealership," Steve added. "Since it's Saturday night, they probably won't be able to look at it until Monday. But I figure it's gotta be a total loss, Kelly. I mean, the ER guys told me you crashed right through the bushes and into the tree along the ravine." He shook his head. "Damn."

"Okay, I think we're just about done here," the doctor announced, wrapping the last strip around Kelly's ankle. Her huge ankle. "I'll go write up a prescription for some painkillers. You're going to need them when the anesthetic wears off for this foot."

"Thanks, doc, but it's my head that's killing me right now," she said, rubbing her left temple.

"Well, these will help your head, too," he said, scooting back the metal stool as he rose. "Your head is going to pound for a while yet. Oh, and let me grab some crutches from supply while I'm at it."

Kelly flinched, even though it hurt like the devil. "Not crutches. . . ."

Lisa, who hadn't spoken a word since getting there, leaped to her feet and pointed at Kelly. "Not another word!" she ordered, her face a thundercloud. "If I see you without those crutches, I swear to God, I'll beat you with them myself!"

Kelly had to laugh, even though it hurt so much tears came to her eyes. All her friends were laughing.

"Uhhh, I don't think that's the right response, Lisa, but you made your point," Steve said.

"Looks like you're going to have lots of help during your recovery," the young doctor said with a twinkle in his eye. "The pain will let up after a few days when the swelling starts to go down. But your right ankle looks sprained as well. So you won't be getting around much for a while. I'll be back in a minute," he said, before disappearing around the curtain.

"I can stay with you for the next few nights, Kelly," Megan offered. "I don't want you to be alone. And you're gonna be pretty uncomfortable."

"You don't have to do that," Kelly countered. "I'm sure I'll be okay."

Lisa fixed Kelly with her professional physical therapist's expression. "You've never had a broken ankle, have you? Well, I have, and it hurts like hell the first couple of days. Face it, you're going to need our help."

Now she was beginning to feel like an invalid, and Kelly didn't like it, not one little bit. "I'll be okay, really," she demurred.

Lisa arched a brow. "Wait'll you try to stand up."

Kelly glanced about the circle of friends and saw them all nod in silent agreement. *Well, damn.* She guessed she really was an invalid. A temporary invalid, at least.

Just then, the young doctor slipped around the curtain again, holding a slip of paper in one hand and crutches in the other. Kelly tried not to scowl. It hurt too much.

# Twelve

"Sit down here, Kelly. We've fixed an extra chair with a pillow for your leg," Mimi said, gesturing toward the knitting table.

Kelly wanted to respond, but it was all she could do to make her way through the adjoining yarn room without yelping in pain. After two days, her broken left ankle had finally stopped throbbing and the pain had diminished to a dull ache. But her severely bruised and nearly sprained right ankle was supporting all her weight and sent spasms of pain shooting up her leg in protest.

"Thanks, Mimi," Kelly managed after she'd finally clumped her way around various yarn tables and bins. She sank into the proffered chair, grateful to be off her crutches.

Who would have thought the journey from her cottage to the shop would be so exhausting? Kelly was breathless with exertion, which shocked her. She was an athlete, for Pete's sake. She thought her stamina would make recuperation a breeze. So far, it had been an ordeal. Simply getting to and from the bathroom was a major project. Everywhere she went, she clumped around and bumped into things, and she hurt like hell. When would it stop?

"Here, you go, Kelly," Megan said, plopping Kelly's knitting bag and laptop on the table. "I know you want to do some client work, but my advice would be to take it easy. Stick to the knitting, okay?"

Boy, she must really have turned into an invalid. She couldn't even carry her knitting bag. "Thanks, Megan. Go back home and get to work. You've nurse-maided me long enough."

Megan grinned. "Well, I leave you in good hands. Mimi will mother you, and Lisa will kick your butt if you don't do what she says. That's the perfect combination. I'll be back later in the afternoon and take you home. I saw a pizza in your freezer."

Kelly waved goodbye, just in time to see one of the café's waitresses place a mug of Eduardo's coffee in front of her. "You're a lifesaver, Julie, thanks."

"Anytime, Kelly. I'll keep refilling it, compliments of Pete."

Everyone was babying her. She couldn't do anything for herself. She needed help getting dressed, getting around, going up and down steps—everything. Showering would have been funny—complete with her left foot wrapped in a plastic bag—if it hadn't been so frustrating.

"Wow, free coffee. I should break something more often," she said, mustering a wry smile as she took a sip.

"Now you settle in with your scarf, and I'll keep checking on you," Mimi said, patting Kelly on the shoulder. "Oh, by the way, Connie returned from her winter vacation yesterday. She had a fantastic trip and says she's still operating on a Caribbean rhythm. So don't be surprised if she starts to samba while she's working around the shop."

*Samba, huh? I'd be happy to walk straight,* Kelly thought as she retrieved the raspberry and pink yarn from her bag. Now that she was incapacitated, she could finally finish the scarf. At least she'd have something to show for her recuperation.

Kelly picked up the needles and started the knit stitch. After several moments of focused attention, Kelly relaxed into a comfortable knitting rhythm. She noticed the knitting also took her concentration off her aching ankle.

Her thoughts must have been on rhythm, because Connie sashayed into the main room then, singing some Spanish tune and swinging her hips, her arms filled with balls of yarn. Kelly grinned. She didn't know if it was a samba or not, but Connie had made her laugh. Always a good thing.

"Hey, Connie, I hear you had a great time in the Caribbean. It sure looks like it."

"Oh, boy, did I," Connie said while refilling yarn bins with the colorful bundles. She half-danced her way around the table until she glimpsed Kelly's casted foot resting on the chair. "Oh, Kelly, I'm so sorry you had an accident. That must have been frightening. Driving down the canyon with no brakes."

"Crashing down is more like it," Kelly quipped. "But I'm lucky to come out of it alive."

Connie pulled out a chair beside Kelly's resting leg. "I swear, I'm afraid to go away again. I come back and find out horrible things have happened." A look of concern shadowed her face. "Like poor Tracy. How could someone kill her? She was such a quiet, friendly girl. It's simply incomprehensible. And to think, I was probably the last person to see her alive."

"Were you here that night, Connie? How late did you stay?" Kelly asked, curiosity stopping her stitches.

"Probably until around six. I was finishing up lots of stuff because my husband and I were leaving on vacation first thing Saturday morning. Tracy arrived earlier, as she had each afternoon that week, and started working on dyeing her fibers." Connie bit her lip. "She was trying so hard to match that Aztec Blue she liked. Poor thing. I remember she came upstairs to ask me some questions before I left. She was so conscientious."

Kelly let her knitting drop to her lap. "Connie, do you remember anything else from that evening before you left? Did anyone come to see Tracy? Did she talk about anyone? Did she get a phone call?"

Connie stared at the bookshelves, her brows worrying each other. "Now that you mention it, I do remember a phone call. Her cell phone started wiggling and buzzing on the counter and playing this funny circus music. I started laughing."

Kelly sat up straighter, her injured extremities forgotten. She'd wondered if Tracy had a cell phone, but Burt had never mentioned one. Kelly had often thought it strange that a college student wouldn't have a cell phone. Why hadn't Burt said anything?

"Did she say who called?"

Connie smiled maternally. "I figured it was her boyfriend, because she was all flushed while she was talking. I even teased her about it. She must have been going to meet him because I heard her say she'd see him 'later.'" Connie's smile disappeared. "Poor thing. She never got there. Those vicious animals killed her first."

Kelly stared at Connie, her thoughts picking up speed. So, Tracy *did* have a boyfriend. A boyfriend she planned to see later that evening. Her cell phone would have a record of the call.

"Is Burt coming in today, Connie? You need to tell him about Tracy's phone conversation. It may be important."

Connie shrugged. "Sure, if you think Burt would be interested."

"Interested in what?" Burt's voice asked as he entered the room. "Good to see you back in the shop,

Kelly. A little worse for wear, maybe." He leaned on a yarn bin and winked at her.

"Hey, Burt, Connie was with Tracy that Friday night in the shop. She says Tracy got a phone call from her *boyfriend* on her *cell phone*." Kelly emphasized the words.

Burt arched a brow at Connie. "I was going to say 'Welcome back, Connie,' but I guess Kelly has whizzed right past greetings. Were you here that night with Tracy?"

"Until at least six or so. Then I had to go home and pack. I'm not sure if I know anything that's important."

"How come you never mentioned the cell phone, Burt? The cops could track the boyfriend's phone, find out who he is, find out—"

"I never mentioned it because they never found a cell phone. They didn't know if she had one or not. Dan said they looked all over the shop and downstairs in the basement just in case. Those guys probably grabbed it when they were trashing the shop. Tracy's backpack was found tossed behind the counter, and her wallet was empty."

"Damn," Kelly said softly, unable to hide her disappointment. The tantalizing clue had been so close, only to disappear.

"Connie, why don't you come into Pete's with me and get some coffee, so we can talk," Burt suggested. "I'll tell Mimi you're busy for a few minutes." Glancing at Kelly, he added, "You'll be glad to know the department is working its way through that north side bunch. Some of those guys are talking. Others aren't saying much. They're scared. One of the head guys is a pretty bad customer. He's already done time for assault."

That got Kelly's attention. "Whoa, that's scary, Burt."

"You're right. I'll keep you posted," he said as he and Connie left.

Picking up the half-finished scarf where she left off, Kelly let Connie's comments sift through her head. That call had to be from Tracy's mysterious no-name boyfriend. Why else would she have been blushing? And Tracy planned to meet him later . . . or . . . maybe he came over to the shop instead. Was that why Tracy left the front door unlocked? It *had* to be.

Kelly's heart beat faster now than when she'd clumped her way across the driveway earlier. If only she could hop out of this chair and race into the café and tell Burt what she was thinking. She glanced around the shop, but no one was around. *Rats.* What she needed right now was a pair of legs.

The sound of the front bell's jingle was followed by Lisa's swift steps into the room. "Ahhhh, good girl, Kelly. I see you made it across the driveway, and you're working on your scarf, too. Excellent," Lisa rattled off as she dropped her things on the other side of the table.

Kelly was about to ask Lisa to run into the café when Julie appeared with a fresh mug of coffee. Talk about special service. "Whoa, Julie. You're a sweetheart.

Listen, Burt's in the café with Connie. Would you tell him I need to speak with him after he's finished? It's about Tracy."

"Sure thing, Kelly," Julie said.

"What's this about Tracy?" Lisa interrogated, looking up from the turquoise and gray yarn in her lap. "Wait a minute, don't tell me. You're sleuthing again, aren't you? I swear, Kelly, what does it take to get through to you? You've had a serious accident, for heaven's sake. You need to take it easy." Lisa glared at her.

"I *am* taking it easy. Check it out." Kelly pointed to her leg propped on the chair. "I can barely get to the bathroom, much less get into trouble."

Clearly dissatisfied with Kelly's reply, Lisa gave a disgusted snort. "Then what was all that about Tracy a minute ago? You're still poking into things. Sleuthing around."

"Hey, I can still ask questions, can't I?" Kelly affected a wounded tone. "What's wrong with that? And if I learn something that could help solve Tracy's murder, you bet I'm going to tell Burt. Tracy's death has too many loose ends to suit me."

Kelly picked up her knitting where she left off, but her concentration was still with Tracy and the cell phone and the mysterious boyfriend.

"You're impossible, you know that?" Lisa accused, not looking up from the sweater that dangled from her needles.

"I know. That's one of my better character traits,"

Kelly said with a smile, then dodged the ball of yarn that sailed past her head.

Six feet away. Three more crutch steps to her chair. Kelly gritted her teeth as she continued her agonizingly slow progress back to the knitting table. Her nearly sprained right ankle sent another stab of pain shooting up her leg. Protesting. How would she get across the driveway if she could barely make it from the bathroom? She wondered. She sank heavily into the chair.

"Wow, I'm beat," she admitted to Megan, who was watching her with a worried frown.

"Have you had that painkiller yet?" Megan asked as she helped Kelly lift her leg onto the chair.

"I don't like those pills. They make me loopy. Like I'm drunk," she protested, despite the fact that both of her ankles—broken and sprained—throbbed unmercifully.

Megan grabbed Kelly's bag and retrieved the pill bottle. "Too bad. You need these, Kelly. I can see how much it hurts from the look on your face. Take these right now." She shook two pills into her hand and held them out. "No excuses."

"Okay, okay," Kelly acquiesced and tossed down the pills with the rest of her coffee. "Boy, you're getting more and more like Lisa."

"Yeah, yeah, yeah," Megan teased, imitating Lisa's frequent reply.

"Hey, Kelly, how's that foot doing?" Steve's voice sounded behind her.

*Oh, great.* She'd just taken the loopy pills. In a few minutes she'd start talking stupid and acting funny. In front of Steve, yet. She didn't mind acting stupid in front of Megan. Megan just laughed. Like she had last night when Kelly started singing along with the television commercials.

"Good thing you showed up now, Steve," Megan said as she settled on the other side of the table and picked up her knitting. "Kelly just took her pain pills, so she only has a few minutes of coherent thought. After that, she'll start singing and then fall asleep."

"Gee, thanks, Megan."

"Just telling the truth," Megan said with a grin.

Steve pulled up a chair beside Kelly. To her surprise, he picked up her hand and held it between both of his. "In that case, I'd better talk fast while you can still understand what I'm saying." He looked into her eyes. Kelly was startled to see the concern there. "Kelly, I just came from the dealership that has your car—"

"I bet it's totaled, right?" Kelly cut in anxiously.

"Yeah, it is. And it wasn't an accident, either."

"What do you mean?"

"Your brakes were cut. As soon as the mechanic called me, I went over to see for myself. No doubt about it, Kelly. Someone cut your brakes before you drove out of the canyon. Probably while you were checking the ranch."

Kelly heard Megan's sharp intake of breath across the table. Meanwhile, she tried to process what Steve had said.

"Wh-what? Someone wanted me to crash? Who would do that?"

"I don't know, Kelly, but until the police find out, you've got to be extra careful. I've already talked with Burt, and he's alerting the police."

"Oh, my God, Kelly," Megan gasped. "That . . . that person who tried to kill Carl is after *you* now!"

Kelly stared at Steve, then Megan. Were they serious?

"Meanwhile, we're going to make sure you're not alone at any time. You can work here in the shop during the day, and Megan or Lisa or Jennifer can help you in the morning and evening. I'll handle guard duty at night. I've got my sleeping bag in the truck."

Kelly stared, still not comprehending all that she was hearing. Someone cut her brakes in the canyon. Someone wanted her to crash. Someone wanted to kill her?

"Wh-what . . . what do you mean 'guard duty'?"

Megan leaned over the table, face sheet-white, blue eyes huge, but her voice was firm. "Kelly, someone's after *you* now! You can't be left alone. We have to protect you." Turning to Steve, she continued. "I'll work out a schedule with the others for dinner, Steve, and we'll take turns staying with Kelly until you can take over at night. I know you have to work late. We can come early in the mornings, too."

Kelly listened to Megan and Steve plan out the next few days of her life—schedules for meals, sleeping, getting dressed in the morning. Their conversation swirled around her, and she wanted to jump in and protest all these arrangements, but her thoughts were having trouble traveling from her head to her mouth. The loopy pills were starting to work, and bringing their fog with them.

"Hey . . . wait a minute. . . . I don't need someone to . . . to guard me at night," she managed to protest.

"Yeah, you do," Steve said, reaching over to brush a lock of dark hair from her face. "No arguments, sweetheart." He placed a finger against her lips.

The warmth of Steve's hand and the loopy pills started to mess up her mind. Now she *really* couldn't think straight. Did Steve just call her sweetheart? He'd never called her that before. Kelly tried to remember, but her memory cells weren't responding. They'd gone off-line already. Loopy pills at work.

"I think we're losing her, Megan," Steve said with a crooked smile.

"Ohhh, yeah, she's going fast."

"I'm still here . . ." Kelly said through the fog.

"Listen, Kelly, before you check out entirely, Burt wants to know if you saw any cars parked near the ranch when you went up there."

Kelly blinked through the rapidly thickening fog. "Cars? Just my car . . . I parked . . ."

"Yeah, up at the ranch. But did you see anyone parked on the road?"

"Me . . . I parked on the road . . . driveway snowed in."

"The driveway was snowed in? It wasn't plowed?"

Kelly shook her head slowly. "Nope . . . footprints in snow . . . so I walked . . . deep snow . . . real deep."

"And you didn't see anybody around?"

She shook her head again. "Nobody . . . nobody there . . . no cars . . . no trucks, either."

The fog had taken over entirely now, leaving behind that delightful euphoria. She couldn't even feel the pain in her ankles. Heck, she couldn't even feel her ankles. Did she *have* ankles? Just the sound of Steve's voice close by and his warm hand on hers.

Steve was there. What did he say? He was going to guard her? Watch over her. *That's good.* She'd like that. She'd like that a lot.

Kelly smiled crookedly at Steve. "You're staying the night with me?"

Steve grinned. "Yep. I'll be watching over you."

"That's good. . . ." Kelly reached out her hand to Steve's cheek. "I've wanted you to stay over . . . lots of times . . . but I just didn't say it."

Steve captured her hand against his cheek. She could feel the stubble on his chin. He smiled into her eyes. "Yeah, I know. I figured you'd get around to it when you were ready."

"I'm ready."

Steve laughed softly. "Not tonight, tiger. Not while you have that cast on your foot."

"What cast?"

*Cast?* How could she have a cast? She didn't even have feet, did she?

The sound of Megan's snickering across the table didn't bother Kelly. She glanced at her friend and saw Megan holding her hand across her mouth, shoulders shaking with nearly silent laughter. It didn't even register on Kelly's distorted radar screen. She was oblivious.

"But I'll take that as a formal invitation, okay?" Then Steve kissed her palm.

*Oh, boy.* That felt really, really good. "Do that again," she whispered.

"Uhhhh, better not," Steve said, laughing as he released her hand. "We'd better get you back while you're still awake." He leaned over and brushed his lips against hers before he rose.

*Rats.* Just when it was starting to get interesting. But Steve was coming home with her. Warm Steve. Good. She liked that.

Kelly glanced up and spotted Burt leaning on the doorway into the yarn room, smiling at her. "Hey, Burt, where did you come from?" she chirped.

"Ohh, I've been here a few minutes. Making sure you're all right. It looks like you're in good hands."

"Steve's coming."

"That's good, Kelly."

"He's staying the night."

"It's about time," Burt said, chuckling.

Both Steve and Megan ducked their heads, laughing. Kelly joined in. Everyone else was laughing. Why shouldn't she?

"Steve's going to tuck me in tonight," she announced. Was that a giggle? She never giggled.

"*I'm* going to tuck you in, Kelly," Megan said authoritatively as she helped Kelly on with her jacket. "Steve does the guarding. I do the bedtime shift."

*Well, damn.* That wasn't going to be any fun at all. "No, I want Steve," she protested.

"You got me, Kelly," he said as he helped her to her feet. "Now we're going to get you home."

Suddenly upright, Kelly felt the room spin, and she reached out. "Whoa . . . everything's moving." Steve caught her and quickly lifted her into his arms.

"Here, I'll get the door," Burt offered, heading to the front.

Kelly waved at Burt as Steve carried her out, Megan following behind. "No cars, Burt. No cars at all . . ." she called over Steve's shoulder.

# Thirteen

"Is the café still open? I thought Pete closed at three o'clock." Kelly maneuvered her crutch carefully around the yarn tables.

"He said he was staying open especially for you," Megan replied as she followed behind. "Pete made his bourbon pecan pie. He said it will help your ankle heal faster."

Kelly gave a short laugh as she carefully put weight on her abused right ankle. It sent a short spasm of pain up her leg. Not as bad as yesterday, though. It wasn't much, but it must be progess, Kelly decided.

"Help me gain weight, you mean. I swear, I'm going to weigh a ton by the time I get rid of this cast and can start to run again." She slowly made her way down the hallway to the café.

"I told Steve about the pie, and he'll be over, too," Megan added with a devilish grin.

Fragments of memories darted in and out of Kelly's mind, fleeting, elusive. "Boy, I must have said something really dumb to Steve last night, because you've been teasing me all day."

"You weren't dumb, you were cute. And honest," Megan said, as they entered the back alcove of Pete's café.

Honest. *Oh, great.* No telling what she said. *Damn.* She wished she could remember. Glancing around as she entered, Kelly noticed Jayleen and Curt Stackhouse sitting at a small corner table. It looked like they were sampling the pie already. "Hey, Jayleen, Curt. Is that pie any good?"

"Delicious as always," Curt replied from behind his raised coffee cup. "How're you doing, Kelly girl? Looks like you're moving pretty slow."

"Afraid so," Kelly said as she negotiated her way to a nearby table.

Jayleen watched her with a worried frown. "Damn girl, you are in bad shape. I sure would like to catch whoever messed up your car. Wouldn't you, Curt? We'd show him a thing or two."

"Damn right," Curt said in a low voice. "We used to deal with bad hombres in our own way years ago. Frontier justice."

Kelly had to smile. "Now, don't you two go rounding

up a posse, okay? That canyon road is too slippery to be chasing bad guys." She leaned to the side so Pete could pour her a huge ceramic mug of Eduardo's coffee. He placed the pie on the table with a flourish. "Thanks, Pete, that looks delicious. You didn't have to stay late for me. Pie could have waited until tomorrow."

"There were a lot of folks waiting for this pie, Kelly," Pete said, his round face spreading with his familiar grin. "I've had calls all morning."

"I can believe it," Kelly said, lifting a forkful to her mouth. The heavenly combination of brown sugar, pecans, and syrup melted on her tongue. Delicious didn't even describe it. "Ummm, yummy," she said when speech returned.

"Where's that pie, Pete? I smelled it all the way across town," Jennifer said as she walked in. Shedding her winter coat, Jennifer retrieved a slice while Pete poured her a cup of coffee. "Ahhhh, sugar. I need this. It's been a rough afternoon." She settled at the table with Megan and Kelly and dove into the pie.

"Boy, you weren't kidding, Pete. That pie will be gone in a few minutes with us—"

"Hey, what's this I hear about pecan pie being dished up?" Marty demanded as he rounded the café corner. "Whoa, now you're talking." Marty headed straight for the pie counter and snatched two slices.

"Uh-oh. Here comes trouble," Jayleen teased. "I hope you made a lot of pies, Pete."

"You're looking right spiffy, nephew. You been arguing a case in court?" Curt asked the lanky redhead.

"Yep, in court all day. That's why I've gotta up keep my strength," Marty said as he pulled out a chair next to Megan, then tossed off his black overcoat.

"Well, sugar does it for me," Jennifer said, licking pie remnants from her lips. "Pete, I swear you've outdone yourself this time. I may have to arm-wrestle Marty for the last slice."

Marty uttered a sound of enjoyment as he savored the pie. "Give it up, Jennifer. You wouldn't have a chance," he said before he took another huge bite.

"Don't be so sure. I fight dirty," Jennifer threatened as she polished off the last morsel on her plate.

"I believe that," Steve said as he entered the café. "Whoa, Marty's here. I better grab some pie before it's gone." He strode over to Kelly's table and gave her a quick kiss. "How're you doing?"

"Better. My right ankle doesn't hurt as much."

"That's good, because it's the only thing holding you up," he said with a grin as he headed toward the counter.

Kelly finished off her last bite of pie and toyed with the thought of asking for another piece. This pie was too good, and it was late afternoon. The dangerous time for hungries. She'd better wait until someone else got seconds.

"Uh-oh, looks like Marty beat us here," Greg announced as he and Lisa appeared around the corner. "Quick, Lisa, go sit next to Marty so you can trip him if he makes a run for the pie. Steve and I will stand guard."

Marty grinned before demolishing the last morsel on his plate. "Speaking of seconds, I'm ready, Pete."

"Dude, no way are you getting seconds until I have firsts."

"Relax, guys," Pete said, chuckling as he handed Greg and Lisa the pecan delicacy. "I made four pies. There's plenty for everyone."

Greg dove in as he stood guard, clearly enjoying the pie, while Lisa settled at the table beside Jayleen and Curt.

"I hate to be the one to squeal, but Marty's already had seconds. He started out with two slices," Jennifer said after licking her fork. "So you're already behind, Greg."

Kelly glanced around at her friends as they all laughed and joked and exchanged insults with Marty, who deftly fended them off with a nonchalant smile. All the while, Kelly noticed that Megan looked as relaxed sitting next to Marty as she did sitting across the knitting table.

Meanwhile, Kelly's little buzzer inside went off. There was no way everyone would suddenly show up to sample Pete's pie at the same time. What was up? She searched for possible reasons but her memory had a few blank spots thanks to the pain pills from last night. Maybe that was it. Megan had been acting funny all day and teasing her. She knew she'd acted dumb, but . . .

"Well, well, the gang's all here," Burt announced as he and Mimi entered from the shop doorway. "I see

Marty licking his fork. Any pie left, Pete?" He and Mimi settled at a nearby table. Mimi cast a sly glance at Kelly before accepting Pete's offer of pie.

*Okay, that's it. Everybody but Carl is here.* No way this was accidental. Pete's pie was good, but . . .

Kelly drained the last of her coffee and held out her mug for Pete to refill as she leaned back in her chair. "Steve, I know those loopy pills made me stupid last night, but what the heck did I say to you to cause a 'gathering of the clans'?"

All conversation ceased with the exception of Burt's chuckle. "Sharp as ever, Kelly."

Steve leaned against the wall as he lifted another pecan-filled forkful. "You didn't say anything I didn't already know, Kelly." He winked then devoured the morsel.

"We're here to talk about something else, Kelly. Something important," Burt told her, his smile fading.

Kelly glanced around the cozy alcove. No smiles to be seen anymore. A second ago everyone was laughing, and now . . .

She knew what this was about.

"Ahhhh . . . you mean the car crash. Somebody cutting my brakes, and all. Believe me, folks, I *have* been thinking about it. All day, in fact. You'll be glad to know that a police officer took my statement this morning. Unfortunately, I don't remember seeing anyone around the ranch so there's not much for the police to go on—"

"There's *nothing* for the police to go on, Kelly. No

leads at all," Burt interrupted in a firm voice. "No one saw a car parked near yours or anyone walking around in the canyon. I've already checked with the deputy sheriff who patrols up there. Whoever did it may have followed you from town, then saw you leave the car unattended and grabbed his chance. With all the snow piled around, no one would have seen him crawl beneath your car."

Kelly felt a ripple of cold run across her skin, picturing the harsh scenario Burt had painted. It was still hard for her to believe that someone would try to kill her.

"So you agree that this is all about the ranch," she said in a quiet voice.

Burt nodded. "Yes, I do, Kelly. I didn't believe it at first, but now I'm convinced. Someone wants that ranch bad enough to try and kill you. Jennifer has filled us in on the details of the earlier buyers and everything that happened to them. The threats start with vandalism first, then get more serious. I agree that whoever did this poisoned Carl. Maybe he was hoping you'd dump the property like the other owners did when the threats hit home. And when you didn't, well, the threats turned deadly."

Kelly looked into Burt's careworn face. He was as serious as she'd ever seen him. She looked away, staring into her coffee instead. "You know, it was hard for me to believe at first. I mean, trashing houses and attacking dogs is bad enough. But trying to kill someone . . ." She shook her head. "But I've been thinking about it all day, and I agree. It's gotta be the same guy, and it's all about the ranch." She wasn't sure, but Kelly thought she heard an audible sigh emanate from the group surrounding her.

"That's why you have to sell it," Steve said, his voice cutting through the quiet.

Kelly's head jerked up at that. She stared into Steve's steady dark gaze and saw the truth of what he said. Even so, she rebelled. "Sell it? Hell, no, I don't want to sell the ranch."

This time the collective groan that went around the room was audible.

"Damn, Kelly, be sensible!"

"Kelly, let the bastard have it."

"The ranch isn't worth risking your life."

"What if this psycho strikes again?"

Kelly listened to her friends' pleas, still staring into her coffee, but every one of them hit home. And they resonated within. That was the thing. Everything her friends said echoed what her own little voice inside had been whispering all day. Most times, she listened to that little voice. But sometimes . . . sometimes she ignored it. Kelly remembered that every time she did, she regretted it.

"Kelly girl, I know how much that land means to you," Curt said, his voice gentle but firm. "But you have to face facts. You've never flinched from any decisions you've had to make. I've watched you analyze the facts, then decide. Selling the ranch is just another decision. Don't let personal feelings get in the way.

Pretend one of your clients came to you with this problem. You'd tell him or her to sell. Simple as that. Am I right?"

*Damn.* Curt hit home on that one. She glanced back to her coffee, which was probably stone cold by now. "I know you're right, Curt," she said with a sigh. "But I don't like being forced to sell. I feel like I'd be running scared."

That comment caused an even louder uproar than before.

"You got it. Run like hell."

"This isn't a game, Kelly!"

"That guy's a psycho. Who knows what he'll do next?"

"We want you alive, Kelly. Let it go."

Kelly drained her coffee, trying to find the right words to answer her friends. She couldn't find them. They were right.

Jayleen spoke up then. "Kelly, I know what you're feeling. The mountain gets ahold of you and won't let go. For some of us, we've just gotta live up there. But don't you worry. That canyon has plenty of gorgeous places left for you to find. I promise, I'll start asking around. Meanwhile, you gotta get rid of that property. The quicker the better. I swear, after listening to Jennifer, I'm convinced that place is cursed. It must be. Damned if I know what's happening, but there's some baaaad juju hangin' over that ranch."

As usual, Jayleen had been able to pierce through all the reasons and feelings that fogged Kelly's mind and blow them away in one breath. *Cursed.* Kelly didn't believe in curses. But she did believe that some people were capable of doing terrible things. She'd seen it happen often enough. That much was real.

She looked at Jayleen, then around the circle of her friends, who were clearly awaiting her response. "Bad juju, huh?" she said with a wry smile. "Well, damn. I guess that settles it."

This time, loud expressions of relief echoed around the room.

"Thank God you're listening to reason."

"It's the right thing to do, Kelly."

"Right, hell. It's the smart thing to do."

"No piece of land is worth your life."

She had to agree. Jayleen was right. The canyon was filled with gorgeous views from the bottom to the top. She'd find another place. She knew she would.

Jennifer reached into her briefcase beneath the table and pulled out a sheaf of papers. Even from where she was sitting, Kelly recognized a contract. A real estate contract to sell property. Jennifer waved the papers at the circle.

"Okay, everyone, keep the coffee and pie coming, so we can get Kelly to sign this listing contract before she changes her mind."

# Fourteen

**Kelly** reached over the laptop and snatched her ringing cell phone. Flipping it open, she continued to tab through the spreadsheet columns, entering client revenues and expenses. Jennifer's voice came quickly.

"Thought you'd like to know, we've got the ranch officially entered into the multilist. I'm sorry it's taken several days, but I needed to hear input from other agents at the office. And my broker, of course."

"I understand, Jen. I've been busy catching up on my client accounts anyway."

"Now that it's listed, I'm hoping we'll generate some interest, but don't hold your breath. It's still winter."

Kelly looked through the knitting shop windows to the blustery wind-driven snow outside. The tall evergreens surrounding the shop's driveway swayed, branches laden. Another winter storm. It was nearly the end of February, and no end in sight. At this rate, March would really come in like a lion.

"That's for sure. It's miserable outside. Carl and I are hunkered down here at the knitting table." She glanced to her dog, lying beneath the table asleep. "Of course, I'm working; Carl is sound asleep."

"Give him a pat for me."

"I will. Say, what listing price did you and your broker decide on? I know you wanted to stay at market value, but I'll bet he thought otherwise. Considering, you know . . ."

Jennifer sighed. "Yeah, he thinks we should offer below market and pray we can get that. I dunno, Kelly. Gossip travels fast in this town. Other real estate agents have no doubt heard about the problems, so we may have to accept a lower price."

Kelly felt the anxiety lobe of her brain coming to life. Here she was, up to her ears in medical bills for herself and for Carl, and she would probably have to take a lower price than she had paid for the property. Damn. It wasn't fair.

"I understand, Jen. We'll take what we can get. I'll just have to brainstorm with Curt on how to raise extra cash between now and summer. He says the drilling company won't start any gas wells until springtime at the earliest." She looked outside. "It doesn't look like spring's coming anytime soon," she said gloomily.

"And springtime always comes later in Wyoming."

"Why am I not surprised."

"I called up Franklin, alias Gothboy, to let him know the ranch was back on the market, and he really was excited. Told me again about his clients who were interested in Fort Connor mountain properties. Of course, that made my antennae buzz again, so I asked him if his clients were investors. He said no, they were private individuals. So I'm hoping he'll make one of his ridiculously low offers."

"Why's that? Just so we can turn him down?"

"Well, that, too. But I want to know who the buyer is. The purchase offer will have all the pertinent information. I'm curious who these 'private individuals' are."

Kelly heard a tone in Jennifer's voice. "Why?"

"I want to check 'em out. See what I can find out on the Web. See if they're legit. Or if they're really a part of some development group or something. Oops, another call coming in. Talk to you later."

Kelly slid her little phone onto the table and returned to the spreadsheet. Thinking about the ranch churned her up inside. Numbers were soothing, calming. What better way to get her mind off her worries? The knitting lobe of her brain spoke up then, reminding her there was a much better way to relax and it was way more fun, too. She could return to the scarf buried in her knitting bag.

She paused in the midst of the spreadsheet, considering. Although the yarn was sorely tempting, she was almost caught up with her client accounting. Knitting would have to wait. Numbers were calling right now. In fact, they were nagging.

**Kelly** clumped around the yarn bins to the knitting table, slowly but surely. She was finally getting a rhythm going with the crutches. Swing the crutches, swing the cast, step with the right foot. Swing, swing, step. She might not be speedy, but she got there. Now it only took five minutes to get from the table to the restroom. Progress. Of course, it helped that her sprained right ankle was recuperating quickly. Her one good leg was all she had to stand on.

As she rounded the corner Kelly was surprised to see Burt sitting in the chair next to hers, patting Carl. Carl, of course, had forgotten any semblance of discipline and was trying to climb onto Burt, his long pink tongue slurping Burt's face. Carl never fully understood that he was not a lap dog.

"Down, Carl! Get off Burt, for Pete's sake," Kelly ordered. "You'll get him all dirty with those big feet of yours."

Carl ignored her completely, and continued trying to crawl into Burt's lap, still slurping his chin. Burt kept laughing, clearly not minding being slurped, which only encouraged Carl more.

"Carl, down! Off! Whatever—"

"Carl, *sit*!" Rosa's commanding voice resounded as

she strode to the table, giving what Kelly recognized as the hand signal to sit.

Carl glanced at Rosa and backed up, still wiggling, clearly wanting to slurp Burt again. Wiggling won out, and Carl lunged for Burt's lap. The better to reach his chin. Burt simply laughed and rubbed Carl's head.

Kelly sighed. "I guess he's forgotten his commands, Rosa."

"Oh, he knows them, all right. He just doesn't want to obey," Rosa said as she swiftly walked around the table. Grabbing Carl's leash, she gave one quick tug on his training collar. "Carl, *sit,*" she commanded in a firm voice.

This time Carl obeyed. He didn't want to, that was plain to see. He whined and looked from Kelly to Rosa to Burt with brown-eyed doggie pleas. But, he stayed in his "sit."

"Wow, Rosa. I gotta hand it to you. Talk about the voice of authority," Kelly said in admiration. "I wish he'd pay attention to me like that."

"It's not me, Kelly, it's the attitude," Rosa said. "Carl's gotta know you're boss. Then he'll obey. Right, Carl?" She gave him a big head rub. "Good boy, yes, you are. Good sit."

Carl gazed up at Rosa, clearly enjoying her praise.

"Good dog, Carl," Burt said, reaching over and scratching Carl's ear. That was more than Carl could bear, however, and he broke his sit, heading for Burt.

He didn't get far. Rosa gave another quick jerk of the leash. "*Sit!*" Once again, Carl obeyed.

"Good boy. Now let's get you away from temptation. *Down!*" Rosa commanded with accompanying hand gesture, palm facing the floor.

Clearly reluctant, Carl hesitated but obeyed, glancing up at Rosa, hoping for a reprieve. *Oh, to jump and slurp again.*

Not this time. Rosa held her palm up, facing Carl. "*Stay.*" Carl slumped his chin on his paws, exhaling a big sigh. A dog's life.

Kelly laughed. "Attitude, huh? I thought I had enough of that already."

"I'll say," Burt agreed.

Rosa handed the leash to Kelly. "Remember, Kelly, you're Alpha Dog. You're the boss. I'll check on you later."

"I am Alpha, I am Alpha Dog," Kelly repeated, trying to keep a straight face, which was hard because Burt was laughing. She sank into the chair, still repeating the phrase for her own amusement and Burt's. "I am Alpha Dog. I am mighty. I am strong. I am temporarily crippled, but don't let that fool you. I am Alpha."

"Lord, Kelly," Burt said, wiping tears from his eyes when he finally caught his breath. "I haven't laughed that hard in weeks. It sure feels good."

"Well, we haven't had much to laugh about lately, have we?" she said as she retrieved her almost-finished scarf. She could bind off and tuck the ends today if she had enough time. Maybe she could start the hat project this week.

"No, no, we haven't," Burt agreed, leaning back into the chair. "I guess that's why I stopped by. To update you on what's happening at the department and the investigation into Tracy's death."

Kelly looked up from her knitting. Burt hadn't mentioned anything in over a week. "I've been wondering how that's been going."

"I wish I could report that Dan and the guys are getting closer to finding out who killed her, but unfortunately, that's not the case. Those guys Dan has been bringing in for two weeks have told us about every break-in and car theft in the city. Of course, nobody admits to being anywhere near the shop that night. And the guy they beat up on the north side still refuses to talk. Without an eyewitness, we've got nothing." Burt shook his head. "So, detectives have hit a wall for now. Without any new leads, they've got nowhere else to go."

Kelly frowned as she worked the stitches. "And nothing has turned up on that boyfriend?"

"Not really. One of the girls in the same apartment building said she saw Tracy get into a car with a guy one night. All she remembers was he was wearing a black jacket."

This time Kelly scowled at the yarn and felt the stitches tighten. Oops, she reminded herself. *Don't take it out on the innocent yarn. You know what happens. You'll strangle the wool.* Kelly remembered and loosened her stitches to let the wool breathe once more. She could almost feel the yarn sigh.

"That is so frustrating. Connie heard Tracy say she was meeting him that night. I'll bet he came over to the shop. That must be why she left the door unlocked. So this boyfriend has got to be the one who killed her, Burt! If those other guys were nowhere near the shop, then he must be the one, don't you think?"

Burt exhaled a long sigh before answering. "Don't forget, Kelly, those other guys could be lying. But Dan will continue to look into the boyfriend lead anyway. I have to admit this no-name boyfriend is looming larger on my radar screen."

Kelly knitted without speaking for a minute or so. "You know, this guy is going to get away with murder if we don't find him."

*"We?"* Burt said, brow arching. "Might I remind you, Kelly, your junior detective status is temporarily on hold. You're not sleuthing, do you hear me?"

Kelly snorted. "Whether it's sleuthing or not, you know I'm going to help anyway I can. Even if I can't go looking around, I can still ask questions and tell you if I learn anything."

"Questions are good, as long as you ask them on your cell phone. From the knitting shop, okay?"

"Does it look like I'm going anywhere?" Kelly retorted.

"Just so we're on the same page."

"Yes, sir," she said in an obedient tone.

Burt looked surprised at the uncharacteristic response. "Don't worry, Kelly. Killers always leave loose ends dangling somewhere. We simply have to find them, and we will. They won't get away, I promise."

Sort of like dangling yarn tails waiting to be tucked between the stitches and hidden, Kelly thought as she started to bind off the stitches on the last row. "I hope you're right, but let's be honest. What if you do discover a 'loose end' and find this guy? How would you ever prove he did it? There was nothing left at the scene that could identify him."

"Well . . . that isn't entirely correct," Burt hedged. "They did find something they could use, but they didn't want it to become public knowledge."

Kelly's ears perked up and the knitting dropped to her lap. "What did they find? I swear, I'll never tell a soul."

"Remember how I said they couldn't find any fingerprints from strangers at the scene, just shop personnel? Dan figured the killer wore gloves. However, he must have taken one off, because investigators found one good thumbprint on the laundry tub near the faucet. A bright blue thumbprint, no less. They think the killer must have taken off his glove to run cold water on his hand. Remember, Mimi said the dye water was hot. The hot water must have seeped under the glove and his hand must have hurt like hell."

"A fingerprint? Burt, that's great! Now you've really got something. Has the print matched any database yet?"

Burt shook his head. "Not yet. But we haven't matched

all those guys yet. There are a couple from out of town in that crew. And it looks like they've gone underground."·

"What about the guy with the assault record?"

"Nope, his prints didn't match."

Kelly picked up her knitting and pondered the information while she finished binding off the last row. "It's a start, Burt. I've got a feeling more of those loose ends are going to turn up now. Maybe they'll get a lead on that boyfriend and check his prints."

"I hope you're right, Kelly. They're looking everywhere," Burt said as he rose from his chair. "By the way, they also heard something on your case. The deputy sheriff for Larimer County who patrols the mountain areas called in. He helped the department last December, remember? He was the one who reported the parked car that was seen in the canyon at the time of Derek Cooper's murder."

"You bet I remember," Kelly said. "He provided the crucial piece of evidence."

Burt nodded. "Yeah, Don's a good cop, and he's still doing his job. He heard that the department was looking for anything out of the ordinary or any suspicious people wandering around your property, so he started asking questions of everyone who lives in the vicinity around your ranch."

Kelly's head popped up. "Did they see anyone lurking about?"

"Nope, nobody. But your nearest neighbor on the south told Don that he'd seen a small black car frequently parked off the road that runs between your property and his. He said the car has been parked there off and on ever since last fall. The deputy said that section of road is surrounded by trees, and your land isn't even fenced there. Apparently the car was off the road and parked in the trees."

Kelly frowned. "The car was parked on my property?"

"Apparently so. But not all the time, the guy said. It shows up every now and then. Of course, he never thought to take down the license number. But he did give a good description. It's an old-model black Toyota."

"That really narrows it down. The roads are full of them."

"Well, Don's going to keep his eyes open in case he spots it in the area. This one is kind of distinctive. Apparently there's a dent in the trunk, a broken rear taillight, and a Broncos sticker on the back."

"I don't know, Burt, it could just be someone who parties late then finds a place to sleep it off. That canyon road is bad enough in the winter when you're sober. I can attest to that."

"We'll see. Don's a good cop. If he's curious about that car, then so am I. Particularly since it's been parked on the edge of your land in the trees. You could never see it from the ranch."

Kelly's skin prickled at that. "Do you think that car has something to do with the psycho who's after the ranch?"

Burt slipped on his winter jacket and zipped it to his chin. Wind still whipped the evergreen branches beside the shop window. "I don't know, Kelly. But if there's a connection, Deputy Don will find it. You can bet on it."

# Fifteen

**Kelly** carefully placed her crutches into the muddy gravel that lined the path from her cottage to the driveway. Grateful that it was merely messy, not slippery, Kelly slowly made her way across the driveway—a mixture of mud, gravel, and sand. Once she reached the sidewalk, she'd be okay. Ever since her accident, Burt had regularly spread crutch-grabbing sand along all the walkways leading to the shop's front door.

"Kelly, what on earth are you doing out here?" Megan's voice called from the parked cars. "You'll slip and fall and break something else."

"It's okay, I won't slip," Kelly said when Megan hurried to meet her as she clumped along the walkway. "Burt has so much sand here, we could play volleyball."

Megan reached out to help Kelly anyway. "How come you didn't wait for me to take you over like I've been doing? You shouldn't be out here all by yourself," Megan scolded as she held the door open.

"I wanted to see if I could do it," Kelly said as she balanced and wiped mud from her "walking" foot. "My right ankle is much better. I won't be needing you to hurry over here every morning, Megan. You've got your own work to do. I can manage, see?"

Megan followed Kelly to the knitting table. "I swear, Kelly, you're always pushing the limits. It's only been a week and a half since your accident, and you're going outside in the snow and mud."

"Actually, it's mostly mud. Ever since that last storm, the temps have started rising. Everything's melting."

Megan pointed to the still snowy golf course reflecting the morning sunshine. "That's not snow?"

"Well, I don't plan to hike across the golf course," Kelly teased. "Don't worry, Megan. I know my limits."

Megan gave her an incredulous stare. "You have to be kidding, Kelly. You're *always* pushing the edges. You know you do."

Kelly slipped off her coat and settled awkwardly into a chair, then gave Megan a smile. "I can't help it, Megan. I'm disobedient by nature, I guess."

Megan sniffed. "I'll say. Where's Carl?"

"Rosa already took him for his training walk this morning. We thought we'd let him sleep at home today and keep those big muddy feet over there and not tracking about the shop. Rosa's going to work him again at lunch."

"Well, at least I can bring your briefcase over," Megan said as she dropped her knitting bag. "Oh, and your knitting. Aren't you finished with that scarf yet?"

"Yep, and I'm ready to begin that hat. But I'm going to need help."

"Don't worry, I'll get you started," Megan said as she left.

It was midmorning and customers milled around the shop, browsing in yarn bins, fondling fibers. Without her laptop or her knitting to distract her, Kelly watched the browsers.

Thanks to the "Lambspun Elves," springtime colors had chased the Valentine reds away overnight. Now, lavender, pink, yellow, and robin's egg blue spilled from the yarn bins and scattered across tables. Jellybean colors.

"Good morning, Kelly," Mimi greeted in a voice that sounded more and more like it used to. "Would it be okay if you put your computer at the end of the table today? I'm teaching a class on dyeing, and we'll be setting up several small tubs." Mimi gathered items from the center of the library table.

Surprised that Mimi could teach a dye class without using the large laundry tubs, Kelly readily agreed. "Sure, Mimi, no problem. I didn't know you could teach dyeing in a small tub. I thought you needed those big ones downstairs."

Mimi's bright smile disappeared. "We'll only do a

small batch of fiber. But they'll learn how to mix the dyes—that's the important part. In fact, if you're trying to create a new color, you should work in smaller batches anyway." She scooped up more table items. "If you're not too busy working, you'll probably enjoy this, Kelly. Feel free to ask questions."

"Oh, you know me, Mimi. I'm always full of questions." Kelly wondered if the real reason Mimi was demonstrating dye techniques in small batches was because she still didn't want to venture into the basement.

Memories of Tracy hanging over the laundry tub surged from the back of Kelly's mind—vivid and horrifying. Blonde hair tinted Aztec Blue, floating on the water. Kelly shook them away, but they left a chill behind.

Mimi headed toward the doorway, then paused and turned toward Kelly again. Kelly recognized Mimi's worried look. "You haven't had anything else happen around the cottage or at the ranch, have you? Burt doesn't tell me anything anymore."

Kelly shook her head and gave Mimi a reassuring smile. "Nope. As soon as I put the ranch on the market, all the problems stopped."

Mimi chewed her lip. "I hope and pray that it's over, Kelly. What with poor Tracy's murder and your nearly being killed in that car crash, I'm petrified that some other horrible thing will happen."

"Don't worry, Mimi. It's over."

"I hope you're right, Kelly," she said softly before she hurried through the doorway.

Connie entered the room, carrying several pink plastic tubs stacked together, and began setting up places around the table while Kelly shifted to another chair.

Megan returned then and plopped Kelly's knitting bag and her briefcase on the table. "Is Mimi having a class or something?"

"Yeah, Mimi canceled the other scheduled dye classes after Tracy died," Connie said in a lowered voice. "She's still afraid to go downstairs. Problem is we've run out of some of our custom-dyed fibers, and customers are being told to wait." Connie shook her head. "We're going to have to start dyeing downstairs again, even if Mimi doesn't do it."

"I can't blame her," Megan said. "I had to go downstairs last week to fetch the last bag of Sandstone Red for Rosa. She was swamped at the register. And I swear, it gave me the creeps just being down there. Knowing what happened to Tracy, I couldn't get back upstairs fast enough." She gave an exaggerated shiver.

"You know, maybe Rosa and I should go down there and clean the whole place out," Connie said, hands on hips. "It's so full of stuff stored here and there in every crack and cranny, it takes forever to find anything. I'm going to suggest it to Burt. Maybe he can get Mimi to agree. The basement needs a thorough cleaning. That might do the trick. We'll fix it up so Mimi won't even recognize it downstairs."

"You'd have to get Pete's cooperation, though. He uses the other half of the basement for café storage," Megan pointed out.

Noticing Mimi in the doorway talking to a customer, Kelly added, "I think that's a great idea, Connie. And I'll bet Burt will pay you and Rosa handsomely to do it, too."

"Kelly, why don't you relax and watch Mimi's class while I search through the hat patterns? I want to find just the right one for you."

"Make sure you pick one that's nice and easy, okay?" Kelly said. "You know me."

"Ohhhh, yeah," Megan said as she headed into the next room.

"All right, everyone, find a tub and settle in," Mimi announced as she led several women into the room. "Here are some handouts so you can follow along while I demonstrate."

Kelly was anxious to settle in herself and watch the custom dye class, but her cell phone rang. Anxiously digging it out of her briefcase, Kelly apologized to the class as she turned away. Jennifer's voice came on the line.

"Just thought you'd like to know. J. D. Franklin faxed through an offer on the ranch this morning."

"Below market like you expected?" Kelly asked quietly.

"Oh, yeah. Way below. Fifty thousand below."

Kelly flinched. *Ouch!* She couldn't absorb a loss that large. "Ooooh, that's ugly. What are you going to do?"

"I'm going to let it sit for now, then we'll talk. I

want to see if anything else comes across my desk. But so far, no one seems interested. Meanwhile, I've got the buyer's name and address. Now I can do some digging."

"Who is it?"

"Uh, it looks like one person. Carolyn Becker."

"Just a minute," Kelly said as she pulled her Day-Timer from her briefcase and grabbed a pen. Keeping her voice down so as not to disturb the students, she said, "Let me write that down."

"Carolyn Becker, 15432 County Road 11, Colorado Springs. Sounds like Mimi is teaching in the background. You go back to listening while I see what I can find on this Carolyn Becker. Talk to you later."

Kelly slipped her little phone into her briefcase as she returned her concentration to the dye class about to begin.


"**Okay,** now cast on sixty-six stitches just like you would normally," Megan said.

Kelly stared at the pattern's brief instructions, then at the small circular needles in her hands. Only sixteen inches from wooden tip to wooden tip. They looked tiny compared to the circular needles she'd used for her sweater-in-the-round.

"Are you sure I won't need longer needles? Won't I need more room?"

Megan chuckled. "Oh, no. These are exactly right.

If you used longer needles, that hat would grow huge. Trust me, these are perfect."

"Okaaaay," Kelly acquiesced as she began measuring the soft red yarn, preparing to cast on. Bright red to match her scarf. She'd learned to trust her friends' knitting advice. They were always—infuriatingly—right.

"I need some coffee. Do you want some?" Megan asked as she left the table.

Kelly checked her mug. "No, I'm good."

Winding the red yarn around her fingers, Kelly began the intriguing method she'd adopted. It wasn't the easiest way to cast on stitches, but it worked for her. For some reason, she could remember these intricate movements.

She glanced to the other end of the table where Mimi held a hair dryer on the robin's egg blue fibers spread out on paper.

"That's a luscious shade of blue, Mimi," Kelly said.

Mimi didn't answer, clearly unable to hear over the dryer's noise.

Drying the class's custom-dyed fibers by hand was not Mimi's normal procedure. Kelly already knew that. Mimi had told them the fibers were dried overnight while they lay stretched out next to big fans. Downstairs in the basement.

Connie was right. The basement needed to be totally cleared out and cleaned so Mimi could go downstairs again. Otherwise, loyal customers might look elsewhere for their custom-dyed fibers. Mimi had to get back into the game, so the shop could return to normal.

From the corner of her eye, Kelly caught a sudden movement and saw her cell phone blinking. She dropped her knitting and grabbed the phone.

"Kelly, this is—hey, what's that noise?" Burt asked.

"Mimi's drying fibers from her dye class."

"Boy, it's a good thing Connie and Rosa are going to clean that basement. I'm hoping Mimi will be able to go downstairs again. If not, the rest of us will have to start dyeing fibers. Customers are calling in every day."

The noise from the other end of the table stopped. "Oh, Kelly, I'm sorry. You should have waved at me," Mimi said.

"Don't worry, Mimi. Burt understands," Kelly said with a grin.

Mimi's face lit up. "It's Burt? Then tell him I've got his favorite pot roast simmering right now. Dinner at six thirty." She fluffed out the robin's egg blue before leaving the room.

"Did you get that?" Kelly heard Burt chuckle.

"Oh, yeah. My stomach's growling now. But before I head over there, I wanted to tell you the reason I called. I just heard from Don. You know, the deputy sheriff who works the canyons?"

"Oh, yeah. Deputy Don," Kelly said as she reached for her coffee mug.

"Remember a few days ago, when I told you he'd learned about a black Toyota parked near your ranch and he was going to keep an eye out?"

"Yeah, did he spot it?"

"He sure did. It was parked on some vacant land next to an auto repair shop. Dent in the trunk, broken right taillight, and a Broncos sticker. Don ran a check on the license number, and you'll never guess who's the registered owner of the black Toyota."

"Okay, I'll bite. Who?"

"Geri Norbert."

Kelly paused for a second. "What? How can that be? She's in that treatment facility waiting to go to prison. What would her car be doing in the canyon?"

"That's what I'm wondering, and so is Don. He called me as soon as her name came up. Believe me, Deputy Don knows where Geri Norbert is, and what she did to get there."

"You know, Burt, I never saw Geri in a black Toyota. She always drove that old beat-up pickup. Maybe it's another Geri Norbert."

"Don already checked that. Car registration shows the same address in Colorado Springs that Geri Norbert gave police for her former residence. Apparently she lived with her sister in the Springs area before she moved to Fort Connor."

The little buzzer inside Kelly's head went off. "What's that address, Burt?"

"It's 15432 County Road 11, Colorado Springs."

Kelly sat still for a second, recognizing the address. She reached for her Day-Timer and reread the address Jennifer had given her earlier. The address of the woman who wanted to buy her ranch. Geri Norbert's former ranch. It was a match. Kelly's pulse speeded up.

"Kelly? Are you there?"

"Yeah, Burt, I'm here. I was just checking the address that I'd written down in my Day-Timer earlier today. Jennifer told me we received an offer from a buyer in Colorado Springs. One Carolyn Becker, who lives, interestingly enough, at 15432 County Road 11, Colorado Springs."

This time, Burt went quiet. "Now, that is interesting," he said when he spoke.

"Isn't it, now? There's no way that could be a coincidence, Burt. The woman has got to be Geri Norbert's sister."

"It would seem so. Listen, let me give Jennifer a call and have her fax a copy of the cover page of that purchase offer to the detectives. They can check the names on it with Geri Norbert's records, and see if this Carolyn Becker is listed as a relative. Meanwhile, I'll let Don know about this, so he can start snooping around some more."

"Do you think Geri Norbert's family is buying the ranch for her?" Kelly asked, feeling slightly unsettled.

"I don't know, Kelly. But I don't believe in coincidences like this, either."

"That doesn't make sense, though. She'd be in prison a long time, right?"

"Not necessarily. It all depends on the judge's sentencing. He may be lenient, and she could be out in a few years and on probation. Who knows?"

The unsettled feeling in Kelly's stomach switched to uneasy. "But even if Geri's family is simply trying to regain her ranch, that wouldn't explain the car, would it?"

"No, it wouldn't. In fact, I think the detectives will want to ask Geri Norbert a few questions. Maybe she sold the car to someone in the canyon. That would explain it. If so, Deputy Don could check them out."

Somewhat reassured, Kelly nodded. "Yeah, I guess."

"Listen, Kelly, let me make some of these phone calls before it gets too late. I'll let you know when I hear anything, okay?"

Kelly listened to Burt click off, then flipped her own phone closed. Still unsettled, Kelly returned to casting on stitches. Realizing she'd lost count, Kelly carefully counted the neat stitches she had so far. Twenty-six. Forty more to go. She wound the yarn around her fingers and began casting on once more.

Twenty-seven. Twenty-eight. The rhythmic movements were calming, settling. Kelly's thoughts slowed down, too, becoming more orderly. One by one, her earlier concerns claimed her attention.

Geri Norbert's family wanted her property. That was clear. And they wanted it cheap, too. Wanting Geri's ranch back in their ownership, she could understand. But their offer was almost insultingly low. Jennifer's comments about J. D. Franklin rose to the surface. He always made unbelievably low offers. That was his habit. Maybe the low offer was his idea, not Geri's family's.

An image of a black car parked in the trees surfaced next, and uneasiness began to nibble once again. *But what about that car?* What was it doing there? Did that car belong to the psycho who tried to kill her? Was there a connection?

Kelly counted the stitches again. Fifty-two. Almost done. She cast on the last stitches and counted again to make sure. Sixty-six. Meanwhile, the uneasiness kept nibbling. Suddenly, a familiar face appeared in her thoughts, and Kelly dropped her knitting and reached for her phone again.

After punching in Jayleen's number, she waited for an answer. Voice mail came on instead. "Jayleen, this is Kelly. Give me a call, will you? I need to talk to you. A car registered to Geri Norbert has been seen up in the canyon parked on the edge of my ranch. In the trees. Call me, please."

**Jayleen** rested a booted leg on her knee as she sipped from one of Kelly's ceramic mugs. Leaning back in the dining room chair across from Kelly, she frowned. "Lord, Kelly, I don't know what to make of all this you're tellin' me. It makes no sense. Geri's in prison, or soon will be."

"Well, according to Burt, she may get a light sentence. Maybe that's why her family wants to buy back her land."

Jayleen shook her head. "If she gets away with only a few years in a mental health facility after killing those two women, then there is no justice in this world."

Kelly agreed silently. "And you're sure you never saw Geri Norbert with a black Toyota?"

"Never. The five years I knew her, she only drove that old blue pickup."

Kelly stared into her coffee. "Well, maybe she did sell it to someone else. But even so, why would someone park it on the edge of my land? Unless the car belongs to the guy who's been out to get me."

"I tell you, Kelly, I can't help but think the same thing."

"Do you think Geri's family is behind all this? You know, all the vandalism and attacks against me and the other people who bought the ranch?"

Jayleen stared at the floor. Carl was sleeping at their feet. "I don't know, Kelly, maybe they are. It just sounds so crazy."

Kelly nodded. It did sound crazy. Maybe she was crazy to even think it. Maybe the car belonged to some local who simply parked it there a few times. Maybe . . .

A quick knock on the front door brought Carl to his feet with an authoritative "woof!" Steve appeared, and that was all Carl needed to break discipline and race headlong to the door. Steve was here! That meant play-time. *Oh, boy, oh, boy!*

"Hey, big fella," Steve said, rubbing Carl's head. "No! No jump. Have you folks eaten yet? I brought some pizza."

"No, thanks, Steve, I've gotta mosey back up into the canyon," Jayleen said as she rose and headed toward the door. "I can't wait for springtime and more daylight. I'm sick and tired of this darkness." She stared out the window.

Steve gave Kelly a quick kiss before placing the white box on the dining room table. "It's pepperoni and cheese. I was starving after that last meeting in Old Town, so I ate a couple of pieces already. Down, Carl. No jump."

Carl, of course, was paying no heed to Steve's orders and continued to leap and dance about.

"Hand me his leash," Kelly said. "Let's see if this Alpha Dog thing really works."

Steve grabbed the leash and handed it over, then snatched another slice of pizza. Carl saw the pizza and lost it.

*Okaaaay,* Kelly thought, *let's give this a try.* She immediately switched into On-the-Field Command Voice, suitable for instructing players of any sport. The Voice of Authority.

"Carl, *sit!*" she instructed, copying Rosa's no-nonsense manner. She gave a quick tug on the training collar.

Carl glanced over his shoulder and started to jump

again. This time, Kelly repeated the command, complete with quick jerk and release of his collar. Carl sat. Clearly, he didn't want to, but he sat.

"Good dog, *Carl*!" Kelly exclaimed, delighted in his performance. Rubbing his shiny head, she enthused. "What a *good* dog. Such a *good* dog. Yes, you are. Now, *stay*!" She held up her hand in the signal. Carl looked disappointed.

"Well, I'll be damned," Steve said, as he started another slice.

"Good work, Kelly," Jayleen said as she opened the door. "If Carl learns to mind his manners, my chili will be safe."

"I am Alpha Dog. I am pack leader. I am the one to be obeyed," Kelly intoned in a deep theatrical voice.

Steve snickered. "If I see any packs, I'll be sure to send 'em your way. Take it easy going up into the canyon, Jayleen. One accident in the group is enough."

"Oh, I will," Jayleen said as she paused in the doorway. She gave Steve a devilish smile. "You bring dinner over every night, do you?"

"Sometimes. Sometimes we go out. But I'm here every night for guard duty." Steve reached for a soda can and drained it.

Jayleen leaned up against the doorjamb, her grin spreading. "You sleepin' on the sofa, are you?"

Kelly knew where this was heading and decided to play along. "Unfortunately, yes."

"That cast could do some serious damage," Steve said with a wicked grin.

Jayleen laughed softly. "How much longer have you gotta wear that thing?"

"Another four weeks." Kelly deliberately rolled her eyes.

"Well, I've got a hammer in my truck if you get desperate, folks," she said as she left.

"*Good night,* Jayleen," Kelly called after her.

# Sixteen

**Kelly** sipped Eduardo's coffee and looked through the café windows at the mountains in the distance. The foothills, as the locals called them. The Front Range of the Rockies, doorway to gorgeous scenery. From here, Kelly could see the glazed mountain peaks beyond, glistening white in the sun. The high country. Snowy high country, too. Nearly forty feet accumulated this winter, so far, and the season wasn't over yet. March was always the snowiest month in Colorado. At least the reservoirs should be full.

Kelly remembered the cycles of drought and wet from her childhood. She'd heard they'd been going on for centuries. But Kelly also knew these past few years had brought droughts that lasted longer than ever before.

Blazing hot temperatures in July, into the triple digits. That, she didn't remember.

"You think I should counter Carolyn Becker's offer?" she asked Jennifer, who sat across the table from her.

"Yes, I do. Now that we know Geri Norbert's family is involved in this, I want to give the cops more time to poke around."

"How do we do that?"

"This counteroffer will slow things down, especially since we're giving them a week to respond. My guess is they'll think about it for a whole week, then make a counter of their own."

"How do you know they won't accept my offer?"

"I don't. But we've only gone down ten thousand dollars on the asking price. I sense they want to get this property cheap, so they'll offer a little bit higher than last time but not much. But the important thing is we'll give the cops more time to check into these people and see what's going on."

Kelly stared at the pages of legal-sized documents spread on the table. "Sounds like a plan, Jen. Where do I sign?"

"Hey, Kelly, what are you doing working in here?" Connie asked as she approached the cozy corner table in the café where Kelly sat with laptop and briefcase.

"I haven't been able to pull myself away since breakfast," Kelly said. "You on break from the shop? Have a seat."

Connie shook her head. "Nope. Rosa and I are devoting the entire day to the basement. Mimi's handling the front. She actually told us she was 'relieved' we were cleaning down there. You can tell Mimi wants to get back to normal, too."

"All day? Wow, how's it going so far?"

"Actually, we've gotten all the fibers stacked and sorted and back on the shelves. Clean shelves, too. We scrubbed down the walls, the shelves, everything. We've finished with the main storage room. Now we're working our way back toward the dye tubs and those spooky nooks and crannies."

"Boy, I wish I could go down to see the progress," Kelly said, pointing to her cast. "But stairs are still a challenge. Thank goodness both the shop and the cottage are all on one floor."

"Thanks, Julie," Connie said to the waitress who refilled her coffee mug. "You know, when I had a cast like that, I used to go down the stairs on my butt. I live in a two-story so I had to find a quick way. Try sitting and sliding down the stairs. It's not elegant, but it works, and it's fast."

Kelly laughed at the picture forming in her mind. "Okay, I'll give it a try. But I think I'll wait until you guys clean the stairs first."

"That's a good idea. I'll let you know when we finish."

Glimpsing Mimi hurrying through the café, heading their way, Kelly called out, "Hey, Mimi, what's up?"

Mimi rushed to the table. "Kelly, someone just came in," she said in a soft voice. "She says she's Tracy's sister. And she wants to ask some questions about . . . about Tracy and her death." Mimi's expression turned pleading. "Could you please talk to her, Kelly? For me? I just don't think I can do it. She wants to talk to someone who was here when Tracy was found."

"Of course I'll talk to her, Mimi," Kelly said, reaching out to give her a reassuring pat on the arm. Just like Mimi would usually do for everyone else. "Why don't you send her in here? It's cozy and quiet in this corner."

The worry lines on Mimi's face relaxed away. "Thank you, Kelly. Thank you so much." She turned and sped from the café. Connie followed, giving Kelly a thumbs-up.

Meanwhile, Kelly closed out of her accounting spreadsheet and cleared the piles of papers she'd spread on the table. Glancing up, she saw a tall, stylishly dressed blonde walking her way. The woman appeared to be in her thirties. Tracy's older sister, obviously. Since Kelly couldn't quickly spring to her feet, she waved the woman over. "I'm Kelly Flynn," she said, offering her hand. "Please have a seat."

"Thanks for taking the time," the woman said as she sat. "I'm Tracy's older sister, Claire Putnam, and I've been out of the country for six months. My job as a researcher takes me into some pretty remote areas abroad. I only learned about Tracy's death two weeks ago. I didn't know what to think. . . . I was devastated. I came back as soon as I could, but it took nearly a week to get home to Colorado." Claire stared at the windows. "And when I did, I couldn't believe what I heard. My baby sister drowned in a tub of dye? I mean, that's horrible enough, but to learn that she was *murdered*? My God! Who would do such a thing? Tracy was a sweetheart, a total innocent, she was . . . she was . . . so trusting. . . ." Her voice trailed off.

Kelly's heart squeezed, watching Claire's raw grief flash across her face. "I understand your feelings, Claire. We couldn't comprehend it, either. Tracy was such a sweet girl. Her death was totally senseless . . . as well as tragic."

Claire peered at Kelly. "The police believe some vandals killed Tracy. Do you think that's what happened, Kelly?"

Kelly hesitated, not knowing exactly how to respond. Maybe she should keep her suspicions to herself. "I don't know, Claire. It doesn't make sense to me, either. Apparently Tracy was downstairs dyeing fibers at the tub when some guys came into the shop and started trashing the place. Maybe they found her downstairs and panicked. I don't know." Kelly stared into her coffee, uncomfortable with the version she'd recounted.

"Hitting her on the head, I can understand," Claire

said, looking out the window again. "But the police say she was held under the water until she drowned. That's . . . that's horrible! Why would anyone do that?"

Kelly held back the words that wanted to escape. "Maybe those guys were high on drugs or something. Who knows? Some criminals have no conscience. They're sociopaths."

Claire glanced back to Kelly. "I asked the detective if they had been able to question this man Tracy was dating. And the detective acted surprised, like he didn't know about him. Tracy only mentioned him once, and unfortunately she didn't tell me his last name. She called him 'Jimmy.' Did she ever talk to anyone here about a boyfriend?"

Kelly stared back into Claire's eyes. *At last.* The mysterious boyfriend had a name. Or part of a name. Finally there was a lead. Her pulse sped up. "Tracy told one of my friends that she was seeing a guy but didn't mention his name."

"Damn," Claire swore softly. "I've wracked my brain and cannot bring out a last name. Didn't anyone at the university—her classmates or her friends—ever hear Tracy talk about him?"

Kelly shook her head. "Apparently not, according to the police. They've interviewed her friends twice. She must have kept him a secret for some reason."

"But, why, for God's sake?" Claire's hand jerked out in obvious frustration. "If we could find that guy, maybe we could learn something."

"Did Tracy say where she met him?"

Claire closed her eyes. "Uhhhh, yeah . . . I think she said she met him at her office."

*Whoa.* Kelly wasn't expecting that. "You mean the real estate office?"

Claire nodded. "I believe so. That's the only place she worked."

Kelly's heart skipped a beat. If Tracy met this Jimmy at the real estate office, surely someone would have seen them together. Was he a client? Another agent? "Think, Claire. Did Tracy say anything else about this guy?" Kelly coaxed.

Claire closed her eyes again, clearly trying to remember. "Just little things. How crazy she was about him . . . and he was crazy about her, I guess. . . . He was real passionate . . . but moody. I remember she said he would drift away, kind of . . . and they would argue, but they'd always make up. . . . You know, stuff like that."

Kelly mulled over Claire's description. Passionate but moody. That could be a volatile combination.

"It's so discouraging," Claire said sadly. "My baby sister has been killed for no reason. My parents are heartbroken. And I want to do something to help, but . . . but it seems like there's nothing I can do."

Kelly instinctively reached out and placed her hand on Claire's. "You've done more than you know, Claire. You've provided information on this boyfriend. Did you tell the police where Tracy met Jimmy?"

"Yes, I did. They said they'd check it out." She gazed out into the café. "I need to know that I've done something to help the police catch my sister's killer. Otherwise I won't be able to sleep at night. I have to return to my parents' tomorrow, and I want to be able to tell them something that will bring them comfort."

Kelly held Claire's gaze for a moment. "Why don't you tell them that the police promised us they won't rest until they've found Tracy's killer."

Kelly swung her crutches forward, hurrying to return to the café table. Her cell phone was ringing away. Damn crutches, she fumed as she tried to move faster than usual. Two weeks down. Four more weeks to go. *Arrrrgh!*

Reaching the table at last, she snatched her phone and flipped it open. Burt was still there.

"Hey, Kelly, I'm glad I caught you. Got some more updates you'll like to hear."

"Thanks, Burt. Did you get my message about Tracy's sister? Have the detectives found out anything about this Jimmy? Have they interviewed the people in the real estate office again? Did anyone see Tracy with this guy?"

"Kelly, Kelly . . . slow down," Burt said. "According to Dan, they're still interviewing the agents. Some agents don't spend much time in the office, so it's taking a while to reach them all."

"Anything so far?"

"Not yet, Kelly. Some agents barely remember Tracy, let alone whom she talked to."

"Damn, Burt," Kelly swore softly. "I was hoping for a breakthrough."

"Give them time, Kelly. The police will find a lead somewhere. Now, back to your case. They did confirm that Carolyn Becker is Geri Norbert's sister. Her name was listed in the family records."

"I figured as much. So, now it's confirmed. Geri Norbert's family wants to buy my ranch. Did they learn anything from Geri Norbert about the car? You said they were going to interview her."

"Yeah, they did. Geri told them she sold the car to some guy in Colorado Springs last year and was surprised to learn it was still registered in her name. She said she drove down from Fort Connor to the Springs and signed over the title to him for five hundred dollars."

Kelly pondered what Burt said. She had personal experience with Geri Norbert's devious nature. Geri was a skilled liar. Kelly could attest to that. "Do you believe her, Burt?"

"I wasn't there to hear her, Kelly. Dan says she appeared to be telling the truth, but you can never tell with some people."

"Geri's a master liar, Burt. She comes across as genuine and totally honest and sincere. But then that other side of hers surfaces, and look out. Would there be any record of the sale other than the title? Did she advertise in the newspaper or something?"

"Nope, she said she put a sign with her phone number in the front window, then parked the car alongside the road. Risky way to find buyers, but people do it. Apparently the guy called her, and she went down to meet him. That's it. No record."

"No record, how convenient," Kelly mused out loud. "Boy, we're getting nowhere."

"Not necessarily, Kelly. Most investigative work is slow going. There are lots of little pieces of information that don't seem to mean anything at first, but finally you find enough to start piecing together the puzzle."

Kelly mulled over that comment, as pieces of information started forming into questions in her mind. "You know, Burt, Jayleen told me the other night she'd never seen Geri drive that black Toyota, so Geri must have kept it down in Colorado Springs until she sold it. Why, then, would that car, sold to some no-name buyer, suddenly show up in Bellevue Canyon, parked on the edge of my ranch? The same ranch that used to belong to Geri Norbert. That's a helluva coincidence, don'tcha think?"

Burt took a moment to answer. "I told you before, Kelly. I don't believe in coincidences."

"Neither do I, Burt. Both Jayleen and I suspect that Geri Norbert's family may be behind all these attacks on me and the other people who tried owning the ranch."

"We have no proof, Kelly, simply suspicions. But if there is a connection, you can bet we'll find it."

Kelly released a frustrated sigh. "I hope so, Burt."

"Hey, I do have something new to report. Deputy Don up in the canyon is still on the job. He paid a visit to the auto repair shop owner whose property is next to the vacant land where the Toyota was parked. The owner told Don that the Toyota is parked there most of the time, but every now and then, it's replaced with a gray pickup truck. Claims he never sees the driver. Apparently the vehicles are switched at night when he's not there. He only notices it when he comes into the shop in the morning. He says it's been happening for several weeks, ever since the snows started. That would make it December."

"Curiouser and curiouser," Kelly pondered out loud this time. "I swear, Burt, I feel like we've fallen down the rabbit hole with Alice on this one. Does that make any sense to you?"

"None whatsoever, Kelly," he said with a chuckle. "But at least we've got a new lead on the Toyota owner. Deputy Don told the auto shop guy to keep a watch out for that gray pickup and write down the license number the next time it shows up. So the information is still trickling in, Kelly. Bit by bit, like I said."

Kelly was quiet for a moment, sorting through what Burt was saying. "There's only one reason I can think of that someone would take the trouble to switch vehicles in the middle of the night, Burt. And that would be if they have something to hide."

Burt paused. "I'm inclined to agree with you."

"Curiouser and curiouser," Kelly said.


**Kelly** reached over her laptop for the jangling cell phone.

"Kelly, it's me." Jennifer's voice was breathless. "You'll never guess what I found out."

"Tell me."

"Our resident diva, Maya, just returned from Hawaii, and we went for coffee so I could update her on everything that's happened in the office. She's been away a month. Naturally, I told her about Tracy, and she was horrified." Jennifer paused to suck in wind.

Kelly settled into her café chair and sipped her coffee. "I imagine she was," she prodded, hoping this story had a point. She was right in the middle of her client accounts.

"When I told her that police were asking questions about this mysterious boyfriend Tracy met at the office, Maya said she remembered seeing Gothboy—I mean, Franklin—talking to Tracy one afternoon. According to Maya, he was real intense, too. Like hitting on her."

Kelly sat bolt upright. "You're kidding! When was this? Does Maya remember?"

"Oh, yeah. It was last November. Maya had just closed a sale with one of his clients. That's why she remembers him hanging around the office."

"Jennifer, you've gotta tell Burt right away. Maya's the only one who saw Tracy with someone. No one else in the office remembers anything."

"That's my next call. Can you believe that? Gothboy Franklin may be Tracy's secret boyfriend." Jennifer's voice rose with excitement.

"What's Franklin's first name?"

"Uhhh, let me check. I think I told you, everyone calls him J.D. to his face and Gothboy behind his back. Wait a minute, here's the Colorado book. Every licensed agent should be here."

Kelly heard the sound of pages being turned. "Isn't that online?"

"Trust me, it's faster this way. See, here it is. 'Franklin, J. D.' " Jennifer went quiet.

"Well, what's 'J.D.' stand for? Does it say?"

"Oh, yeah," Jennifer said softly. "James David Franklin."

This time, Kelly went quiet. "Oh, my God . . ." she breathed at last. "We've found Jimmy."

**Kelly** took a deep drink of coffee as she looked out into the empty café. Pete had already closed for the day but had thoughtfully left a carafe of his rich brew beside Kelly's elbow. She looked across the café table to Burt. His reaction to Jennifer's information on J. D. Franklin was more subdued than Kelly expected. Was that just a professional cop's cool?

"Why aren't you more excited, Burt? Jennifer and I are really psyched. We found Jimmy! *Tracy's* Jimmy. Passionate, moody, maybe volatile Jimmy. This is the first real lead we've had in the case."

Burt smiled at her enthusiasm. "I am pleased, Kelly, and Dan will be, too. But let's not jump to conclusions. All we've got for sure is that Franklin's first name is James, and he was seen talking to Tracy at the office."

"Burt, that's *huge*! We had nothing on the boyfriend before. He was simply someone named 'Jimmy.' Now, we've *got* something!" she exulted, allowing excitement into her voice again.

"Believe me, Kelly, if there's a connection, the guys will find it. After what Jennifer said about Franklin's background, Dan's bound to turn up lots of people who're willing to talk about him. Let's see what turns up."

"All right, Burt, let's see what turns up," Kelly repeated, allowing herself to be reassured. "Just make sure you keep me updated, okay?"

Burt chuckled. "Don't worry, Kelly. I always do."

# Seventeen

*"Heel!"* Rosa commanded, and Carl immediately fell into step on Rosa's left side as they paraded down the slushy driveway. Rosa made a quick about-face, and with only a little prodding, Carl kept up with her.

Carl appeared to be enjoying the workout, Kelly noticed, still amazed at Naughty Carl's transformation into Sometimes Obedient Carl. At least that's who he was with Kelly. When Rosa was anywhere around, he was Always Obedient Carl.

And it was all done to please. Rosa's only reward was lavish praise and attention and head rubs, which Carl clearly reveled in, gazing at Rosa attentively.

Rosa and Carl came to a halt right in front of Kelly. As soon as Rosa stopped walking, Carl sat. Even in the wet slush. *Amazing.* Rosa turned to him enthusiastically. "Good dog, *Carl*! Such a good dog you are. Yes, you are. Good sit. Good sit. Now, *stay*." She held up her hand and came to stand beside Kelly, who was watching from the edge of the Lambspun shop sidewalk.

Kelly's cast had mud splatters on it already from traversing across the fast-melting snow and slush mixture that mired the driveway between her cottage and the shop. Was this a taste of springtime to come? It was already the first week of March, which meant springtime would soon start to tease them with warmer temperatures. And if Kelly remembered her Colorado weather correctly, the teasing would quickly be followed by a frigid blast blowing across the mountains to remind everyone that winter was still in charge. Most of Colorado's blizzards occurred in March.

"He's doing great, Kelly," Rosa said. "I've enjoyed working with him. He's a quick learner."

"You've worked wonders, Rosa. I could never have done this myself without your training, even without crutches. You know, I'm going to need you to keep working with him until this cast comes off."

"I'll be glad to, Kelly," Rosa said with a smile. "Today's lesson is a little shorter, because I've got to get back to the basement." She nodded toward the shop. "Connie and I have been working on the basement whenever we get the chance, and we've finally got all the rooms in the Lambspun area cleared out and cleaned.

We must have thrown out a ton of trash. Mimi said if we didn't know what it was, we could toss it out."

"I can't wait to see what you've done down there. Connie told me I should try coming down the stairs on my butt and take a look. I just might do that," Kelly said with a laugh.

"Wait'll we finish. We're starting on the café side of the basement today. Pete was so impressed with what we've done for Mimi, he's paying us to do his side of the basement now."

Kelly remembered how cluttered the café side was, with refrigerators and shelves packed high with boxes and bags of stored food. "Boy, that will really make a difference. By the time you guys finish, we won't recognize the basement."

"That's the general idea," Rosa said with a laugh as she stepped beside Carl again. He looked up at her expectantly. "Okay, Carl, let's take you back home. See you later, Kelly."

And with a slap to her left thigh, Rosa stepped off, Carl right beside her. Kelly watched in admiration for a minute then swung her crutches in the walking rhythm she'd developed and headed into the shop.

Hurrying around the yarn bins, Kelly found herself able to maneuver with only one crutch now. Much faster, too. She clumped quickly toward the knitting table, where her cell phone jangled. Kelly grabbed her phone as she sank into a chair. Burt's excited voice came on the line.

"Hey, Kelly, Deputy Don just called from the canyon with more news."

"Wait a minute, Burt. First, tell me what's turned up on J. D. Franklin."

Burt released a sigh. "Nothing so far, Kelly. I mean nothing substantial. Apparently the guy operates right on the edge in real estate, but he never steps over into anything illegal. And there're no witnesses to his former strong-arm tactics."

"What about his personal life, Burt? Has anyone else spotted him with Tracy?"

"Not yet. Dan says there're plenty of people who drink with him at the bars in town. According to some real estate agents, Franklin's been spending a lot of time in Fort Connor working on some development deal. No details, though."

"Damn, Burt. Tracy's murder investigation is going nowhere fast," Kelly complained.

"Not true, Kelly. The guys are working hard. But the process takes time. It's not like you see on television when the murder is solved in sixty minutes with time for commercials."

Kelly had to laugh. "Okay, okay, you've made your point. Patience is not my strong suit, that's all." She leaned back into her chair beside the knitting table. "So, what's up with Deputy Don?"

"That garage owner called and said the gray pickup reappeared yesterday, and he was able to get the license number. The guy and his wife went to a concert in Denver and returned late at night, and there was the truck. He spotted it as soon as they drove past the shop." Burt chuckled. "The guy told Don he jumped out of his car and wrote down the tag number in case it disappeared again. And sure enough, when he looked this morning, the truck was gone and there was the Toyota."

Kelly took a sip from her ever-present coffee mug. Customers browsed around and behind her, poking in bins, stroking fibers, browsing through books. "That is so weird, Burt."

"Oh, it gets better. Don traced the license right away, and the truck is registered to Robert J. Lester."

"Any idea who that is?"

"Not yet, but do you want to take a guess as to what this Lester's address is?"

Kelly sat up straight and set her mug aside. "You are kidding me."

"No, I'm not. It's 15432 County Road 11, Colorado Springs."

Kelly stared across the table into the billowy bunches of coral pink and lime green fibers draping the wall. *"What?"*

"That's what I said. Don, too."

"What the hell are they doing on that property? Running a commune or something? *Everybody's* living there."

"Well, it's got Deputy Don's nose itching off his face. He told me he's going to start checking out the canyon ranches for any sign of that pickup. He thinks it's time to ask some questions. Trouble is, everybody in the canyon has a pickup and lots of them are gray, so it may take a while. We'll see. Don says he feels 'lucky.' "

"Let's hope so, Burt. Have you told the detectives yet? Have they checked out this Lester guy?"

"Yep. Don had already alerted them. Apparently, this guy's driving record is clean. He's in his twenties. No arrest record. Nothing else turned up."

Kelly shook her head. "There we go again. Tantalizing little bits of information that don't add up. Who the hell is this Lester guy?" Kelly said, letting her frustration into her voice. Noticing customers' heads turning, she hunched over the table, trying to keep her voice down.

"Burt, it's looking more and more like Geri's family is behind all these incidents. Now here's another person with a truck tied to that same address. He must be involved, don't you think?"

"I think it's highly likely, Kelly. But, as I said before, there is no proof. This guy, whoever he is, has been real clever. He's never left behind anything that could be traced to him until now. But I have a feeling Deputy Don is going to catch sight of him sooner rather than later."

"Thinking about this guy roaming around the canyon gives me a real bad feeling, Burt. He's probably the one responsible for . . . you know." She glanced around. Even more people were milling about the yarn bins than before.

"Well, there is one good thing about having him roam around the canyon. Deputy Don will be sure to spot him."

Kelly listened to Burt's goodbyes, but that bad feeling in the pit of her stomach kept growing stronger.

# Eighteen

"**Whoa,** Rosa, what's all that?" Kelly asked as she half-hopped, half-walked through the main yarn room.

She was getting around much better with one crutch now. In fact, she'd even started putting weight on her casted foot. Testing the waters. It had twinged but not horribly. She had to make sure Lisa didn't spot her. Lisa would give her hell.

"These are bags of trash from Pete's storage," Rosa said as she struggled to carry three stuffed plastic trash bags at once. "You should have seen it down there. Stuff was crammed into closets, shoved behind shelves, piled in the corners. Oops!" One of the bags slipped from her grip and hit the floor.

"Here, let me help you," Kelly offered. "I can carry it outside to the Dumpster."

"Are you sure?" Rosa peered at Kelly. "Hey, you're only using one crutch. How're you doing with that?"

"Actually, it's easier now than with two, because my right ankle doesn't hurt anymore. I can put my whole weight on it, see?" Kelly balanced on her right foot. "I can even walk faster. Here, let me get the door."

"Thanks, Kelly. You're a real trouper. Listen, I gotta move my car, because it's parked too close to the Dumpster and the trash truck will be coming in a few minutes," Rosa said, heading down the walkway to the muddy driveway. "Whoa, there's the trash truck across the street. It'll be here in five minutes, so—"

*"Rosa!"* Connie called from the front door. "Your sister just called. Your little girl was hurt on the playground. She's taking her to the doctor and wants to talk to you first."

Rosa paled, the bags slipping from her hands. "Oh, my God, I'm coming. . . ." Glancing back to Kelly, she said, "Listen, Kelly, wave the trash truck away, would you?"

Kelly suddenly had a better idea. "Rosa, give me your keys. I'll take care of your car and the trash."

Clearly distracted, Rosa looked at Kelly. "You can't do that with your cast."

"The cast is on my left foot, not my driving foot. Throw me your keys and get to the phone," Kelly directed with an offhand gesture. Now that she could move around better, there was no reason she couldn't help, was there?

Rosa dug into her pocket and tossed the keys to Kelly as she sped into the shop. Kelly grabbed the bags of trash and made two trips across the muddy driveway to the Dumpster. She was clumsy, but she got it done.

The low whine of the approaching trash truck sounded closer, and Kelly hurried to move Rosa's car before the truck arrived. Unlocking the late-model Honda, Kelly was grateful the driver's seat was already pushed back. That meant more room for her cast.

Kelly balanced on the crutch while she plopped into the seat, then lifted her heavy left leg inside the car. Catching movement from the corner of her eye, she spotted a huge burgundy-colored trash truck turning into the driveway. Kelly tossed her crutch into the car and slammed the door. Fumbling briefly, she shoved the keys into the ignition and revved the engine, then quickly backed the sedan away from the Dumpster just as the truck was approaching. Jerking the car into drive, she pulled down the driveway and out of the way.

Nosing the car into another parking space, Kelly felt a surge of confidence run through her. *Yessss!* She was coming back. She was no longer helpless. At last! The hardest thing about her recuperation was not the pain, Kelly had discovered. It was the sense that she was a helpless invalid. Kelly had never experienced that feeling before, never in her entire life. It was completely foreign . . . and completely repugnant.

Grabbing her crutch, Kelly carefully exited the car, feeling unbelievably proud of herself, almost as though she'd climbed one of Colorado's Fourteeners— mountain peaks over fourteen thousand feet. Her accomplishment might not be high altitude, but it was heady enough for her.

Clumping back into the shop, Kelly spotted Rosa hurrying toward the door. "How's your little girl, Rosa?" she said, tossing the keys to her.

"We won't know until we take her to the pediatrician. It could be a concussion. I'll call when we know more," Rosa said as she rushed out the door.

Kelly headed toward the café. Victories, even small ones, deserved to be celebrated. *Coffee.* Stopping by the front room, Kelly saw Mimi and Connie conferring behind the counter. Surprisingly, no customers were standing in line.

"I sure hope Rosa's little girl is all right," Kelly said as she approached the attractively cluttered counter. Buttons, pins, and various accessories were displayed along the length of the smooth wooden surface.

Mimi looked up at Kelly, clearly distracted. "Yes . . . Rosa said she'll call us." Then she glanced back at Connie, who was holding a black and white winter ski jacket.

Kelly couldn't help noticing the concerned look on Connie's face and sensed it had nothing to do with Rosa's emergency call. "What's wrong? You two look kind of funny," she said with a half smile.

Mimi stared at the counter, her brow furrowed, and

Connie spoke in a hushed tone. "Rosa found this jacket when we were clearing out Pete's side of the basement. It had fallen beside the coatrack in his back room and was completely covered with trash. I recognized it immediately. It's Tracy's. She was wearing it that afternoon, the last time she came to the shop."

Mimi turned away from Connie—and the jacket—clearly disturbed by the reference to Tracy's last night alive. Connie hastened around the corner. "Don't worry, Mimi, I'll take it away. Burt can give it to the police."

"Here, give it to me," Kelly offered, reaching for the jacket. "You folks are busy in the shop. I'll take it to my cottage. Burt can pick it up there."

Mimi gave Kelly and Connie a quick smile. "Thanks, girls. I appreciate that. It . . . it brings back memories."

Kelly headed for the front door again. Boy, she was getting lots of practice walking outside today. Her crutch was splattered halfway up already with mud from her travels. As she clumped quickly around the yarn bins, Kelly felt positively elated. Speed. *Yes.* She was moving faster, she could tell. Why, at this rate, she could do without her crutch earlier than six weeks. Maybe.

"Whoa, look at you!" Megan exclaimed as she entered the shop and wiped mud from her boots. "Three weeks since the crash, and you're down to one crutch already. Don't worry, I won't tell Lisa."

"I'm a one-crutch wonder, all right. I helped Rosa

take trash to the Dumpster, and I even drove her car out of the way of the trash truck," Kelly bragged.

Megan's eyes popped wide. "*No!* How could you drive with your sprained ankle? That must have hurt like the devil."

Kelly shook her head. "Nope. Didn't hurt at all. I'm thinking that ankle wasn't sprained as badly as the doctor thought. Whatever, I'm grateful."

"Well, don't throw that crutch away yet." Megan pointed. "Whose coat is that?"

Kelly lowered her voice. "It's Tracy's. Rosa found it in the basement. I'm taking it to my place and out of Mimi's sight until Burt can give it to the cops." Suddenly remembering her conversation with Burt the other day, Kelly beckoned. "If you've got a minute, Megan, I could use your help on the computer."

"Sure, what do you need?" Megan said, following Kelly through the doorway.

"I need to check out someone on the Web, and you're a master at that. Some strange coincidences have shown up in the canyon. Cars and trucks moving around. Different owners. All living at the same address."

"Coincidence?" Megan asked with a puzzled tone.

"Yeah. The only thing is, neither Burt nor I believe in coincidences."

**Kelly** leaned away from her own laptop and peered at Megan's laptop screen. Megan was seated at the edge of Kelly's desk in the sunny dining room corner. *Dueling laptops.* A sign of the times. Can there be too much information? Apparently not.

"What site are you on?" she asked, pointing to Megan's screen.

"It's a controlled-access site for state agencies. Don't even ask. I'm checking how many Lesters show up there. Let's see, there's a William B. Lester. That's all."

*Rats.* She and Megan were striking out. Robert J. Lester didn't show up on anything other than the auto registration records. No property records of any kind. And so far there was only one property owner recorded for 15432 County Road 11 in Colorado Springs. Carolyn Becker.

"Darn it," Kelly complained. "I was hoping we'd find something more on this guy. We know Geri Norbert is secluded in a treatment facility, and her sister, Carolyn Becker, lives in Colorado Springs. Lester is the only one from that address who's been connected to the canyon. That truck and the Toyota don't park themselves at night. It's got to be him. I just wish we could find out something about him."

Megan nodded, her attention still on the screen. "I know it's frustrating, Kelly, but a lot of Web searches turn out this way. Some databases are restricted, too. So we can't access those." She checked her watch. "Oops, I've gotta get back to my own stuff. Let me work on this some more tonight, okay?"

Kelly checked her own watch and was shocked by

the time. Web searches ate up the clock. "Yikes, you're right. Gotta get back to my accounts. Hey, you're welcome to keep working right here, Megan. My coffee isn't as good as Eduardo's but thanks to you guys, my fridge is full of leftovers."

# Nineteen

"Fill 'er up, Eduardo. High octane, please," Kelly requested as she dangled her coffee mug over the counter. "Where's Jennifer? Isn't she working the morning shift in the café anymore?"

"I think she's out with her real estate clients," Eduardo said, pouring a dark stream into the mug. "Pete said she'll try to make it in for the lunch shift. Those clients have kept her busier than usual this winter."

An aromatic plume wafted toward Kelly and she inhaled the seductive, rich scent of strong coffee. "Mmm, thanks, Eduardo. Now I can return to those numbers that are giving me such trouble."

Eduardo shook his head, grinning. "Be careful with those numbers, Kelly. They're always changing."

"Isn't that the truth?" she said, noticing Burt enter the café from an outside door. "Hey, Burt, what's up? You got any more information on J. D. Franklin?"

Burt did not return her smile. "Nothing yet, Kelly. But I do have something else to tell you. Why don't we find a quiet table?"

No smile meant Burt had something serious to share, so Kelly gestured to a table at the end of the café. "Sure, I've already started working over here in the corner. I'm taking turns working at home and working over here. Trying to wean myself away from the shop's warm and fuzzies, I guess. It's kind of hard to concentrate on numbers with customers fondling yarns all around you."

She managed to move herself and the coffee across the café fairly speedily for a woman on a crutch. Balancing on her good foot, Kelly executed her "plop sit" into a chair.

"Looks like you're getting around pretty good now. You amaze me, Kelly," Burt said in admiration.

"That's me, Amazing Kelly. Kelly-on-a-Crutch." She grinned as Burt pulled up a chair beside her. "Now, what's up? I can tell it's something important from the expression on your face." She took a deep drink of Eduardo's brew and savored the tangy burn as it went down her throat.

"Yeah, it is. Don called me this morning. He spotted the gray pickup at one of the canyon ranches like he thought he would. He even drove up and asked the young man some questions."

Kelly sat bolt upright. "Really? That's fantastic! Way to go, Deputy Don!" She held up her mug in salute. "So, who the hell is this Lester?"

"He's the young ranch hand who works for you, Kelly. It's Bobby. Don had a printout of the license photo, and he said it's a match. Bobby is Robert J. Lester."

Kelly stared at Burt in disbelief. *"What?"*

"I know. I had the same reaction. So did Don. That's why he didn't let on he was suspicious. He asked Bobby if there'd been any fires set on the ranch since the last one and acted like he thought it was some squatter spending the night. Apparently Bobby was real friendly and calm. Didn't act suspicious at all. He told Don there'd been no more trouble at the ranch since he'd started keeping watch at night. He even gave Don your phone number in case he had more questions."

"But I've been writing checks to him as Bobby Smith for weeks."

Burt gave her a wry smile. "And all he had to do was go to your bank, show a fake ID, and cash the checks. No problem."

Her mind spinning a mile a minute, Kelly stared through the window behind Burt. Bright sunshine was steadily melting the snow-covered golf course. Spring wanted to come, badly.

*Bobby.* Bobby Smith. Robert J. Lester. One and the same. Images of Bobby smiling and talking, helping with the animals, taking care of the ranch, *her* ranch. Friendly Bobby. Smiling Bobby. Sincere Bobby. Helpful Bobby. There was never a clue that Bobby was anything other than what he appeared to be—a friendly, young Colorado cowboy who loved working on a ranch. Helpful, hardworking . . .

"Son of a—" Kelly bit off the stream of her dad's favorite Navy curses. Meanwhile, each and every colorful invective ricocheted through her head. "That *bastard*!" she hissed. "It's been him all along. Sneaking around, trashing my place, spying on me. He nearly killed Carl, and he damn near killed *me*! Dammit, Burt! I want to be there when Don arrests him! Let's go get him *now*!" She grabbed for her crutch.

"Hold on there, Kelly," Burt said, reaching out to stop her. "We can't charge Bobby with anything. It's not against the law to own a truck and a car in the canyon, even if you do move them around at night and park on someone else's property. There's no proof that Bobby did anything. Nothing can be traced to him."

"Of course it's him!" she argued. "He was using that Toyota so I wouldn't see him spying on me. Dammit! That's why I didn't see him anywhere around when I drove up to the ranch. I'll bet he parked that Toyota in the trees and was waiting for me to show up. *Bastard*!"

"Still, there's no connection between Bobby and anything that happened in the canyon, let alone here in town. Not the vandalism, not the killing of that woman's dog, not Carl's poisoning, not even the cutting of your brakes. Nothing. So far, he's been clever as hell."

Anger shot up Kelly's spine like a righteous fire. "But that's not *right*!" she said louder, causing heads to turn at the other end of the café. "He can't get away with that, can he? He deliberately cut those brakes, Burt. I could be *dead*! That's attempted murder, isn't it?"

Burt shook his head with a rueful smile. "There's no proof he did it, Kelly. Even if there was, it wouldn't prove attempted murder. He could say he simply wanted to scare you enough to dump the property."

Kelly scowled through the window. Scowled at the sunshine. Scowled at the snow melting on the golf course and the dead patches of grass showing through. "Damn it, Burt, there's got to be something we can do."

"Don't worry, Kelly. The cops will find a connection. They always do. Bobby's left other loose ends dangling somewhere, and the police will find them. Maybe Deputy Don will, who knows? He's taking this case to heart."

Another wave of Navy invective washed over Kelly, pushing for release. "*Bastard!*" she muttered before taking a deep drink, trying to quench her anger with coffee. But even coffee could not quench this fire. "And there's nothing on him in police records? This guy went straight from upright citizen to trashing houses, killing dogs, and threatening me?"

"Well, not quite. We have found evidence of juvenile records. Nothing serious, though. But at least that points to a history of troublemaking. Apparently, he's kept his nose clean since then. No charges of any kind. A couple of speeding tickets is all."

Kelly snorted. "*Troublemaking.* I'll say. Trying to kill people, you mean."

A familiar tune sounded, and Kelly recognized Burt's cell phone. "I'll talk to you later, Kelly. Don't worry, Bobby will slip up, and they'll get him," Burt said as he rose from the chair.

Kelly watched Burt head outside into the sunshine, cell phone to his ear. *"Slip up," huh?* She'd like to help that bastard slip up.

"**What** the heck are you doing, Kelly?" Jennifer's voice called across the driveway.

Kelly didn't stop her pacing to answer. Her clumping pacing, that is. Mud splattered up to the knees of her sweatpants, she'd been clumping along with one crutch from one end of the Lambspun driveway to the other for the last hour. And getting madder and madder by the minute.

"I'm trying to calm down, but it's not working," she told Jennifer when she approached. "You got my phone message?"

"Yes, I did," Jennifer said, slipping a hand into her bright green winter coat as she walked beside Kelly. "Your instructions were loud and clear. Emphasis on loud. I'll make sure I don't mention anything about Bobby at the office. But I'm afraid I won't call J. D. Franklin and tell him his buyers can shove their last offer up their butts."

"Why not?" Kelly snapped, still pacing. Jennifer stopped on the sidewalk, watching her.

"Professional courtesy and all that. Even I have

my standards," she said with a smile. "Besides, our delay strategy is working. Franklin called this morning and said his clients wanted to know—"

*"Screw them!"*

"—if you planned to accept their last offer by tonight's deadline or make a counteroffer of your own. So, I think we should continue to drag out the process." Jennifer stared off toward the empty golf course. "What I really wish is that the police would find someone who saw Franklin and Tracy together."

Kelly paused her angry walking for a moment. "So do I, Jennifer."

"Meanwhile, let's get back to real estate business. We'll wait until the last minute tonight to respond to their offer with another counter and give them a week to respond. We'll be inching away from the top price, while they inch away from the bottom. I sense they assume we'll eventually settle closer to their price, so they'll keep making counters. If you really get sick of dealing with them, simply ignore their last offer."

"That's all?"

Jennifer nodded. "As soon as they submit a counteroffer, your previous offer is null and void, like it never existed. Then all you have to do is let the deadline expire on their offer. So, what do you say? Let's give the police more time to dig up stuff on these people, okay?"

Kelly scowled at the mud. "They're scheming, devious, bastards, just like Geri Norbert. That whole family must have inherited lying, cheating, and stealing genes. I'd like to go down there—"

"And what? Beat them with your crutch? C'mon, Kelly. There's nothing you can do, because you can't prove anything. Has it occurred to you that all of this might be some gigantic coincidence?"

"I don't believe in coincidences and neither does Burt. Bobby and that family are behind all these incidents . . . these crimes!" Her hand jerked out in frustration. "Trashing my house and car, poisoning Carl, killing that woman's dog, and damn near killing *me*!" Kelly returned to her pacing, while Jennifer stared at the ground.

"I agree these people definitely want to buy Geri Norbert's ranch. Whether they're the same family or friends, who knows? And maybe they are the ones who've got a vendetta against you."

"Vendetta is right. They're out to get me, I swear."

"Maybe and maybe not. Face it, Kelly. There are other people out there who probably hold a grudge against you. Geri Norbert isn't the only person you helped put in jail."

Kelly stopped her pacing and turned to face Jennifer. Early afternoon sunshine streamed down, making even the mud sparkle. She was aware of the cold breeze against her cheeks, the smell of mud. "What do you mean?"

"I remember your saying Lieutenant Morrison reminded you that you've been responsible for leading the police to four different killers. If not for you, Kelly, those people would have gotten away with murder."

"What are you saying, Jen? That there are several

people in Fort Connor who hate me? Gee, thanks. That really makes me feel good."

"No, I'm not saying that . . . exactly. I just wish you'd be more careful. You scare me sometimes. You scare all of us. You get right in people's faces, Kelly. You make them say things, admit to things, trip them up. I've watched you. You're relentless." Jennifer stared off toward the golf course. "Maybe Bobby and that crew from Colorado Springs are behind all the trouble. They probably are, and I hope they'll slip up so the cops will catch them. But part of me is afraid you've pissed off somebody else, some psycho who's lurking around town."

Kelly tried to capture the image that Jennifer described, but it wouldn't come into focus. A psycho lurking in Fort Connor who was out to get her? Her analytical side spoke up. *Riiiight.*

She couldn't help but smile, even though she could tell Jennifer was serious. "A psycho, huh? Boy, Jen, I don't know if I can handle that or not. What with Jayleen's 'bad juju' and now you with some stray psycho, I might as well hide at home in my cottage and never come out."

"**Hey,** Megan, what's up?" Kelly said into her phone as she continued tabbing through the accounting spreadsheet on her computer.

"I've found something else about Robert J. Lester. My friend who works for the university was able to access enrollment records for previous years. It seems Lester was a student at the branch near Colorado Springs a couple of years ago. He took a course in ranch management but didn't finish. Dropped out. And he's not registered now."

"Well, well," Kelly said as she leaned back in her office chair. Carl padded across the dining room floor and rested his chin on her knee, waiting for a head rub.

"She also checked the name Bobby Smith, but nothing showed up."

Kelly gave an exasperated sigh. Then an idea suddenly pushed itself forward. "Hey, Megan, if you're online, could you check the main university directory, please? The one here in town. Check the separate departments and see which one teaches courses on ranch management."

"Sure, hold on a sec."

Kelly sipped the last of Eduardo's coffee and rubbed Carl's silky soft ears. Carl offered first one ear, then the next. Meanwhile, the sound of Megan's keyboard clicking away drifted over the phone.

"Okay, got it. There's a Department of Forestry, Rangeland, and Park Management. Now, what?"

"See what courses they have in ranch management this semester and who the professors are."

"Let's see . . . ranch management. There it is. Professor Baxter Brown is teaching this semester's course. May I ask why you want to know? It sounds like you're fishing for something."

Kelly scribbled the name on the edge of a client file.

"Thanks, Megan. I'm going to give Bobby a call and ask him how he likes his professor, this Baxter Brown. I'll say I met him or something."

"Why, Kelly?"

"Because I want to catch him in another lie. He told me he was taking a course in ranch management at the university this semester, and we've discovered he's not enrolled. We know that's a lie. I want to see what happens when I ask him how he likes the course. I'm betting he'll lie again. He's lied to me from the start."

"So, what does that prove?"

Kelly exhaled an exasperated sigh. "I don't know. Proof of another lie, I guess. That's something. We can't catch him doing anything else. That's what frustrates the living daylights out of me, Megan. It's not right."

"Kelly, that guy is trouble. I don't think you should be calling him. Why don't you—oops, that's my client calling. Talk to you later, Kelly." Megan clicked off.

Kelly stared at her phone, debating for a minute, before she searched the directory for Bobby's number. She punched it in and took a deep breath to calm down. Bobby answered on the third ring.

"Hey, Kelly, it's good to hear from you. Jayleen told me what happened. I sure am sorry you had that accident. Is your foot gettin' any better?" He sounded as friendly as ever.

*My foot's fine, you bastard.*

Kelly bit her tongue. "Yeah, my foot's actually doing great. Almost healed," she exaggerated. "It wasn't broken, just a real bad sprain." Now, *that* was a lie. Talk about Bobby. . . .

"Well, that's good to hear, it sure is. What can I do for ya? The animals are comin' along great, especially now that the snow's startin' to melt."

"That's good. I hope to come up there as soon as I can. No special reason for the call, just wanted to check in. I haven't talked to you since my car accident."

"Lord, Kelly, that was somethin' awful. You were downright lucky."

Kelly held her tongue, while Navy curses bounced around her brain. "Yes, I was. But I'm better now. By the way, I think I met your professor last night at a dinner party. Professor Brown. Baxter Brown? He said he taught ranch management at the university. That's the course you're taking, right?"

Bobby didn't miss a beat. "That's right. So, you met him, huh? He's a nice guy, isn't he? Talks over my head a lot." He chuckled in a good-natured way.

Kelly had to hand it to him. Bobby was one skilled liar. Smooth, affable, and unflappable. Positively scary.

"Yeah, he was real entertaining with his ranch stories," she lied. *If you can't lick 'em, join 'em.*

"Oh, yeah, he's got a million of those." Bobby's chuckle sounded again, low and friendly.

*That's it.* She had to get off the phone with this lying son of a sailor before she slipped and said something. "Hey, Bobby, talk to you later. I've got another call coming in."

" 'Bye, Kelly, take care of yourself, now."

Muttering under her breath, Kelly clicked off and tossed the phone into her briefcase. Pulling herself out of her chair, she half-walked, half-hobbled to the kitchen—without her crutch. She was carefully putting more and more weight on her casted foot. Right now, she needed to pace or clump or walk off her frustration after that conversation.

Searching for more coffee, she found nothing but an empty pot and settled on a cold soda from the fridge instead. As she hobbled back to the dining room, Kelly glimpsed Tracy's jacket on the sofa. *Damn!* She forgot to tell Burt about the jacket. She'd better call him now.

Kelly grabbed the jacket and hobbled back to her desk, where she dug her cell phone out of the briefcase again. She was about to dial when she noticed one side of the jacket was heavier than the other. There was probably something in the pocket, she figured, and set her phone aside while she searched. She withdrew a cell phone from the jacket's left pocket. Tracy Putnam's cell phone. Kelly caught her breath.

Tracy's jacket had been buried beneath trash on Pete's side of the basement. That's why the police didn't find her cell phone. Now they could trace her boyfriend, Jimmy. They could discover who he really was. There would be a record of his last call to Tracy the night she died. Or better yet, a message with his voice.

She had to see that number for herself. Then she'd call Jennifer and check if the number matched J. D. Franklin's. She couldn't wait for police to confirm it. She wanted to know *now*. Kelly switched on the phone.

Several arrows appeared on the screen, pointing to various functions. Each brand of phone was a little different from the others. *Why can't cell phones be uniform?* she wondered as she worked through several screens.

Finding the message inbox at last, she saw that it was empty. *Rats.* No messages from boyfriend Jimmy. Searching the menu again, Kelly found the directory and started scanning the names there. Not that many, actually. But at least these would provide another checklist for the police to interview. She continued scrolling through the alphabet until her eye caught the name she was looking for.

There it was. *Jimmy.* Her pulse speeded up. *All right! Now, we're in business,* she exulted. She'd call Jennifer right away and . . .

Kelly read the phone number listed for the mysterious Jimmy. It looked familiar. It should. It was the very same number she'd dialed only a few minutes ago. Bobby's number. Bobby was Jimmy.

Kelly's heart skipped a beat. Oh, my God! Bobby was the mysterious boyfriend. The mysterious Jimmy. Robert J. Lester. Was that Robert *James* Lester? It must be. That means . . . Bobby was the last one to talk to Tracy. He came to the shop that night and entered through the door Tracy left unlocked for him. Bobby killed Tracy. And he trashed the shop to make it look like vandals.

Images bounced around Kelly's brain now, her heart racing double-time as her imagination went into overdrive. Bobby was a liar, many times over. He'd lied to everyone. To her, to Jayleen, to everyone who hired him, and finally, to Tracy. But was he a killer?

*He nearly killed you. In the canyon when he cut your brakes. You could have died in that crash.*

But why would he kill Tracy? Did she discover his lies? Is that why he killed her? Was he dating her solely to get information about the ranch? Find out who the buyers were and where they lived? That had to be it. Smooth-talking Bobby probably picked out quiet, shy Tracy on purpose, then poured on the charm while he pumped her for information, using her. What a lying, devious, heartless son-of-a-bitch. Maybe Tracy discovered what he was doing and confronted him. Bobby must have killed her to protect himself.

Kelly tossed the jacket to a nearby chair, while she searched through Tracy's phone for "Received Calls." Sure enough, the last one was dated the night Tracy was killed. And the caller was "Jimmy."

"*Gotcha,* you bastard!" Kelly swore in triumph as she clicked out of the message menu.

Or, so she thought. Unfortunately, pressing "OK" did not close out the screen on this phone. Instead, it dialed the number listed. Bobby's number.

Watching the dancing symbols flash across the screen, Kelly realized what she'd done and quickly pressed the Off button. She drew in a deep breath and sent a quick prayer heavenward that the call hadn't gone through. Placing Tracy's phone carefully on her desk, Kelly picked up her own and punched in another familiar number. She needed to talk to Burt now. Listening to the rings, Kelly took a deep breath and tried to calm down.

Burt picked up Tracy's cell phone from Kelly's dining room table. "This is great, Kelly. Now our investigators have a *reason* to question Bobby. He'll have to answer for his whereabouts on the night of Tracy's death. I've gotta hand it to you, Kelly. Broken ankle, foot in a cast, nothing stops you, does it?" He gave her a grin.

Kelly didn't return it. That cold feeling in her gut was still there. "I wish I was as optimistic as you, Burt, but questioning Bobby will get you nowhere. He's a master liar, like his relative sitting over there in the mental health facility. I'm sure he's got an alibi all planned out. Hell, he probably got some drunk to claim he was drinking with him at a bar that night."

"Hey, don't be so skeptical. Those detectives know their jobs. They're professionals."

"Yeah, and Bobby's a *professional* liar," she shot back. "He lies right to your face and comes across as completely honest and sincere. He oozes cowboy charm and trustworthiness. And he's devious as hell. He's got an alibi, I'll bet. Wait and see. Those detectives will never trip him up, and they'll come away with nothing substantial." She frowned at the phone. "Like you've said before—without anything that connects him to Tracy's murder, you've got no grounds to charge him. I'll bet you can't even get his fingerprints, can you?"

Burt shook his head.

Kelly's arm jerked out in frustration. "You'd think since he was the last one talking to her, he'd become a 'person of interest,' or whatever you call them."

Burt gave a rueful smile. "Well, you're right about that. Since we've found absolutely no link between those north side guys doing the break-ins and the shop vandalism, the boyfriend-killer theory appears more likely. Now that we know Bobby was the last one to call Tracy that night, it's highly probable he also came over to the shop. But—"

"*But* you can't prove it, right?" Kelly finished in frustration.

"No, they can't, unfortunately. He could tell us they were simply talking on the phone or making a date for the next night or whatever."

"*See?*"

"We can't prove anything yet, Kelly. Give the detectives a chance. Bobby's bound to have left other loose ends somewhere. They'll find them. Wait and see."

Kelly gave a disgusted snort in reply. She'd never been good at waiting. She was too impatient. "Wait and watch him get away with murder, you mean."

Burt shook his head again, giving her a fatherly smile. "They'll get him eventually."

She exhaled a loud exasperated sigh. "It's the eventually part that gets me, Burt. Meanwhile, I have to sit and do nothing. You know that drives me crazy."

Burt laughed as he rose from his chair. "I know, Kelly. Listen, I'll take this to the department first thing in the morning. The guys will get right on it, I promise. Meanwhile, you'd better keep this new information to yourself, okay? Don't share it with the others until the detectives have checked it out. Believe me, I'll keep you posted."

"You got it," Kelly said as she pulled herself out of the chair and hobbled—without her crutch—to the door with Burt. "Oh, don't forget to let Deputy Don in on all this, okay? Without him, we'd still be clueless about Bobby's identity."

"Don't worry. Don will be right there with the Fort Connor team when they go into the canyon to interview Bobby. The county cops are definitely interested in this guy, too. I'll talk to you tomorrow, Kelly," he said as he left.

Kelly hobbled back to the dining room, her insides still churning with frustration. There was no way she could sit still tonight. She needed a distraction. Something to take her mind off all of this.

Staring through the patio door at Carl sniffing his empty doggie dish, Kelly realized what she needed. She grabbed her cell phone and punched in Steve's number. The Jazz Bistro would keep her mind occupied and ease her frustration. There was nothing like great food, an icy martini, and hot jazz to keep aggravation at bay.

# Twenty

"**Good** morning, Rosa, how's your little girl, Naomi?" Kelly asked as she hobbled through the yarn room, coffee mug in hand.

Rosa looked up from filling yarn bins with bright green froth. "She's doing fine, Kelly. Thanks for asking. The doctor said it was a bad cut on her head, not a concussion. She stayed at home yesterday, and I let her watch her favorite cartoon channel all day." Rosa laughed softly.

"Wow, Saint Patrick's Day must be coming." Kelly pointed to the stacked baskets spilling over with varying shades of green. Forest emerald, vibrant shamrock green, lime green, pale early-spring green, melon green, olive green, even chartreuse.

"Oh, yes. Spring is coming, and we're ready for it," Rosa declared as she left the room, empty basket in hand.

Kelly slowly headed toward the knitting table, still maneuvering without her crutch. She found the crutch helped outside and on uneven surfaces, but inside the cottage and here in the shop, she was now clumping along fine without it.

She set her mug on the table and plopped into a chair. It was midmorning and the shop only had a few customers wandering about. A perfect time for quiet knitting. Kelly needed some quiet this morning. Knitting peacefully always helped settle her thoughts. Maybe knitting would help settle this gnawing unease in her gut.

Pulling out the circular needles, she carefully examined the vivid scarlet yarn. Her hat was coming along nicely. She'd completed nearly five inches of neat, even stitches which—thanks to the magic of knitting in the round—had transformed into a smooth stockinette pattern. Without purling. Only four more inches to go, and she could switch to the feared double-point needles to finish the top of the hat. She'd probably need a lot of help for that.

Kelly slipped the needle beneath a stitch, wrapped the scarlet yarn, then slid the stitch from the left needle to the right. *Slip, wrap, slide.* The familiar cadence always helped her settle into a rhythm. Slip, wrap, slide. Slip, wrap, slide.

She was starting to feel the rhythm when her cell

phone rang. Anxious that it might be Burt, Kelly dropped her knitting quickly.

Bobby's voice came on the line, as friendly and down-home as usual. "Hey, Kelly, this is Bobby."

"Uhhh, hey, Bobby, what's up?" she managed, feeling her gut clench. She was talking to a murderer.

"I was hopin' you could do me a favor. My mom's just called from down in the Springs, and she needs my help real bad. My brother's off overseas in the army somewhere in the Middle East, so we're kind of looking out for his wife and kids while he's gone. I'm gonna hav'ta get some money and head down there this morning because the garage mechanic won't fix my sister-in-law's car without cash up front."

Kelly had to hand it to him. Bobby oozed sincerity. Looking out for a poor relative in Colorado Springs while her husband was fighting overseas. Pulling on the heartstrings. Patriotism and pity all combined in one pitch.

Maybe Carolyn Becker was Bobby's mother, and he was going to the Springs to celebrate with the rest of his scheming family. Their plan had worked. They'd "scared" Kelly into putting the ranch up for sale. Now they figured they'd get it for a bargain price. Or so they thought.

Kelly swallowed down the cynical response that rose to her lips and forced a reply. "That's too bad."

"I was wonderin' if you could come up and feed the animals this afternoon. I figure I'll be back by tonight, so I can close and lock 'em up in the barn. But it might be kinda late. I tried callin' Jayleen but couldn't get her."

Kelly hesitated. If Bobby was gone today, the cops couldn't question him until tomorrow. *Damn*.

"You said your foot was better, so I was hopin' you could come out, but if ya can't, I guess the herd can wait till tonight. I'll drive back as fast as I can."

Kelly paused, about to refuse. Why would she help him? Then suddenly a crazy idea surfaced, dancing in front of her eyes, and she found herself answering, "Uh, yeah, sure, Bobby. I'll drive up. I'll have to borrow someone's car, but I'll take care of it."

"If it's too much trouble for you . . ."

Another refusal started forming, but the crazy idea danced again, teasing her. Once more, Kelly jumped in—without thinking. "No, it's okay. It's fine. You take all the time you need with your mother. I'll close the barn doors, too. We don't want any predators coming in."

"Thanks, Kelly. I sure do appreciate it. I'll call you when I'm headin' back."

"You do that, Bobby. Drive safely." Kelly waited for him to click off before she closed her phone, her mind racing as fast as her pulse.

Bobby would be gone all day. Which meant she would have time to look around the ranch house. She could search for something, anything that could link Bobby to Tracy's death. Otherwise, Bobby would get away with murder. She *had* to find something. She owed it to Tracy.

Kelly grabbed her mug, ready to down more coffee, then realized the last thing she needed was more caffeine. Her heart was pounding already with the crazy ideas that were dancing through her head. She needed to calm down and think this through. She reached for her knitting again and took a deep breath, forcing her breathing to slow as she returned to her stitches.

Slip, wrap, slide. Slip, wrap, slide. Over and over, Kelly knitted, finishing one row, then another, while a war raged inside her head.

*Are you crazy?* the sensible side of her argued. *You've still got a cast on your foot. You have no business clomping through a barn in the mountains. And what about your other ankle? That's a thirty-minute drive up into the canyon. Your right ankle's not strong enough.*

That comment didn't faze Kelly's Crazy Idea side at all. She'd been getting around just fine this week, thank you very much. She would have the crutch with her. No problem.

Slip, wrap, slide. Slip, wrap, slide. *What about a car? Yours is totaled, or had you forgotten that?*

Crazy didn't miss a beat. Just like Bobby. She could ask to borrow Rosa's car. If she left now, she'd be back before shop closing time. No problem.

Slip, wrap, slide. Slip, wrap, slide. *What the hell do you expect to find in the ranch house? Do you think*

*Bobby has left something incriminating sitting there? Like a coat with Aztec Blue dye on it, or something? You're nuts if you think so. Bobby's far too clever for that.*

That thought caused a momentary pause while Kelly's racing ideas sorted themselves. She was good at finding clues. She'd find something. She *knew* she would. Papers showing his connection to the Colorado Springs people, phony IDs, something . . .

Slip, wrap, slide. Slip, wrap, slide. Knitting wasn't bringing the peacefulness this time. Calm didn't have a chance with Crazy Idea and friends crowding Kelly's mind. After another moment Instinct spoke up.

*Bobby's a liar. You know that. What if this is a lie, too? Something's not right about this, Kelly. Something's wrong. Don't go up there. Don't do it.*

That got her attention, and Kelly's needles paused while she took stock of what was happening outside the chaos in her mind. The uneasiness in her gut was no longer gnawing. It had taken a huge bite. Normally, Kelly listened to her gut. Listened to her instinct. Listened to that little voice that came from somewhere inside her. She hesitated.

Then the awful image of Tracy shimmered before her eyes. Tracy, facedown in the dye vat, her blonde hair floating on the water. Blue-blonde hair. Aztec Blue. Bobby did that to Tracy. He'd killed her, and now he was about to get away with murder.

Kelly felt a surge of anger shoot right up her spine. *The hell he would!* She'd find a way to trap that bastard. She knew she would. She owed it to Tracy. Kelly would get Bobby if it was the last thing she did.

She tossed the needles and yarn into her knitting bag as she grabbed her phone. Punching in Burt's number, she pulled herself out of the chair and headed toward the front, where she'd last seen Rosa. Burt's voice mail came on.

"Hey, Burt, Kelly here. Bobby just called and said he'd be in Colorado Springs all day helping out his mother. That must be Carolyn Becker. So you'd better tell the detectives to reschedule their visit to the ranch, okay? Talk to you later."

She clicked off, deliberately leaving out the part about her decision to go up to the ranch and search for evidence. Burt's constant answer was "wait for the detectives to do their jobs."

Waiting took too long to Kelly's way of thinking. The police were too slow. Today might be the only time Bobby would be away from the ranch for several hours. And he wouldn't be expecting someone to come searching.

The cold hand inside Kelly's gut gave another squeeze, but Kelly ignored that, too. Just like she ignored the warning voice inside her head. She'd made up her mind. She was going to find something that proved Bobby's guilt. She'd been able to find information on those other four killers. She'd do it again. She *knew* she would.

Rosa came through the archway of the main room, and Kelly gave her a bright smile. "Hey, Rosa, I was looking for you. Do you think I could borrow your car for a little while? I've got some business stuff I have to do right away."

"Are you sure you can drive okay?" Rosa said, clearly hesitant.

Kelly made an offhand gesture. "Absolutely. My right foot is even stronger now that I've been walking without my crutch. I'll be back before closing time. No problem."

Kelly drove the Honda to the end of the ranch driveway, grateful that the deepest snow had melted. She wanted to park as close to the barn as possible. That way she wouldn't be slogging through too much snow and slush. Grabbing her crutch, Kelly balanced on her good foot as she maneuvered out of the car.

Mud, slush, and gravel squished up the side of her booted right foot as she headed toward the barn. Glancing back at the car, she noticed that she'd parked between the barn and the ranch house and couldn't be seen from the road.

Two alpaca stared at her from the corral area, their huge brown eyes observing her strange hobbling gait. Then a third poked his head out. Then another. Since the snow had drifted higher near the pasture fence, none of the animals came to greet her.

Kelly decided to give the herd a final pat. Her alpaca, but not for much longer. She'd already decided to sell all of them to Jayleen's friend, so this could be the

last time she saw the animals. A slight twinge of remorse came and passed. Her dreams of owning a
mountain ranch were dying a slow death.

She hobbled inside the barn, and the smell of hay
drifted to her nostrils along with dirt and another
smell. Something oily. "Hey, guys, how're you doing?"
she said as she clumped through the hay to the wooden
fenced corral. "I guess this is goodbye, huh? You'll be
going off with another owner in a week or so."

The alpaca started to cluster around the fence, shoving their long necks toward her for attention. Their response spurred Kelly to get closer, so she unlocked the
gate and let them mill about the corner of the barn
with her. The more affectionate of the herd pushed
forward and crowded around her, looking for rubs and
attention, which Kelly supplied generously, returning
their affection. She placed her crutch against the corral
fence so she could pat them with both hands.

"I'm going to miss you guys," she said, rubbing the
soft gray nose of the most dominant male. He persisted
in standing in front of her, blocking the others' access.
"Will you miss me?"

"They won't miss you at all," a sarcastic male voice
answered.

Kelly jumped, her heart racing. *Bobby.* That was
Bobby's voice, but it sounded different. Not friendly
Bobby, not at all. She ducked her head around the al-
paca, trying to see toward the door.

Peering between two alpaca, she spotted him standing inside the barn door. But he didn't even look like

Bobby. Gone were the cowboy hat, boots, and jeans. They'd been replaced by white ski pants and jacket, goggles, and snow boots. Snow white.

"Bobby . . . wh-what are you doing here?" Kelly managed.

"Surprised you, huh?" he said, strolling into the barn. "I figured as much. I knew if I sprinkled enough bread crumbs out there, you'd come running. Like you always do. Sniffing around, looking for clues. Sleuthing, isn't that what your friends call it?"

Even Bobby's speech sounded different. No more cowboy drawl. No more friendly tone, either. This Bobby's voice was cold and harsh. The hand in Kelly's gut squeezed tighter.

"I figured you couldn't resist the chance to come up here and search the ranch house, right?" He walked to the middle of the barn and stopped. A couple of the alpaca bolted away from the corral corner.

Now that she could see him clearly, Kelly noticed Bobby was carrying a lantern in one hand and a gas can in the other. The gas can had an old-fashioned design, like the one that was found on the first buyer's torched construction site. The cold in her gut turned to ice.

"What . . . what are you talking about?" she forced out, her voice sounding strained, odd.

Bobby placed the gas can and lantern at his feet, then looked back at her with a cruel smile. "You think you're so clever, don't you, Kelly? Always figuring stuff out, right? Looking for clues. Well, I figured you out from the start. That's why I've been keeping a close watch on you."

Swallowing down the fear, Kelly found her voice. "It was you who trashed my house and car. You were behind everything."

His smile broadened. "Sure was. At first I thought you might pay attention, get the message, and let the ranch go. But no, not you." He wagged his head in a mocking fashion. "You dug in your heels, so I had to up the ante. But you still didn't pay attention. Not even when your dog nearly died."

A sudden flash of anger shot up Kelly's spine, thawing the ice. "You nearly killed him, you bastard!" she shot back.

Bobby laughed softly, clearly enjoying her anger. "See? I can play you like a violin, Kelly. I know just what to do to make you jump. Just like I made you grab a car and drive up here today. Right where I wanted you."

Kelly's anger died in a flash. Fear started to seep back in. Then that little voice from inside whispered, *Cell phone. Call Burt. Now!*

Kelly listened this time. It was the same voice that had saved her when she was careening down the canyon with no brakes. She slipped her hand into her jacket pocket and withdrew the phone. Obscuring her actions behind the large gray alpaca that stood in front of her, Kelly flipped the phone open and felt her way toward the directory.

Using the alpaca as a diversion, she glanced toward

the animal and stroked his thick winter coat. "Easy, boy," she said, as she sneaked a peek at the phone directory. Finding Burt's name, she punched in the number and prayed Burt would answer.

If she held the phone behind the alpaca, maybe Burt could pick up her conversation. Maybe Burt could figure out she was in trouble. Maybe she could divert Bobby's attention long enough for the cops to get to the ranch. Maybe . . .

"Did you just drive here now? I didn't see your truck," she said, hoping to draw him into conversation.

"Nope. After the deputy showed up asking questions the other day, I knew I'd better leave the truck parked in town. So I drove the Toyota to a dead-end road on the other side of the ridge right before dawn." He jerked his thumb in a northerly direction. "Then I came in through the forest."

That surprised her. Meanwhile, she spoke in a louder voice. "What? Through all those trees and snow?"

He grinned. "Snowshoes. Nobody even saw me in the early morning light. I lay low inside the ranch house. When I saw that deputy drive up here midmorning, nosing around, I figured you'd called and told them I was gone for the day. Or so you thought."

*Snowshoes.* Colorado cowboy modern. Kelly had to hand it to him. Bobby was razor sharp. He'd thought of everything.

"You trashed my place so it looked like vandals and poisoned Carl. What made you think I'd connect that to the ranch?"

"I figured your real estate friend would put it all together. She'd tell you what happened with those other buyers."

"That was you who scared off the other buyers, wasn't it? You torched that guy's building in town, and you snowshoed here and killed that woman's dog."

Bobby snickered. "Give the detective a gold star."

"Clever, Bobby, real clever," she said in a clear voice.

"We thought so."

"Who's 'we'? Is that your family in Colorado Springs who's trying to buy the ranch?"

Bobby nodded. "Yeah. They're doing the deal, but my mom and me figured it all out. We knew if we scared off enough buyers, the price would sink like a stone." He grinned. "And it has."

Kelly had to bite her tongue to keep the first response from her lips. "I figured you were all in this together. What with both the Toyota and the truck registered to the same Colorado Springs address as the buyer."

"Yeah, we could see you'd put it all together once the deputy came up here to question me."

"What made you think I'd eventually sell?"

"We figured your friends would do the convincing. Especially after your accident."

"I could have died in that crash."

Bobby shrugged. "I figured whether you lived or died, we'd still get the ranch."

Kelly held back the Navy curses that came to her lips. Bit them back. *Keep him talking,* the little voice said. She glanced to her phone while she stroked the alpaca's gray coat. Her phone screen still showed a live connection.

"I bet you were using Tracy to get information about the buyers and the ranch."

"Yep. That way I could keep track of who was coming and going." He gave Kelly a cocky grin. "Tracy told me everything."

"Why didn't Tracy tell her friends about you? Most girls talk about their boyfriends. How'd you get her to keep quiet?"

Bobby smirked. "I told her I was afraid of losing my job here at the ranch if anyone found out she was dating me and working at the real estate office. She bought it, of course. She was in love." He dragged out the word in a mocking fashion.

"Why did you kill her?" Kelly asked at last.

"Because she knew too much," Bobby said without a moment's hesitation.

And without an ounce of obvious remorse or feeling of any kind. It was as if Kelly had asked why he flunked a course. She was appalled by his response.

"She'd started asking questions. A lot of questions. Like why was I so curious about the buyers? Why was I always asking about the office? Why couldn't she tell her friends about me? She was getting to be a pain in the ass. Always ragging on me. I was getting ready to dump her when she told me she'd started taking a class at that yarn shop. I remembered you and Jayleen talking about the same class." He shook his head. "I couldn't take the chance that she'd let something slip, and you'd jump on it. She'd seen a bucket of red paint in the back of my truck and spotted paint on my jacket one night. She started asking questions. I couldn't take the chance she'd put it all together."

"I cannot believe you killed that sweet girl because you were afraid I'd find out you were trashing my house."

He shrugged. "I also knew I'd have to get rougher with you, and I didn't want her to get suspicious. She knew too much already. I'd let some other things slip when we were talking."

"But why kill her? Why not just dump her?"

"If I dumped her, she'd be mad and try to get back at me. I couldn't take that chance. My mom suggested I could make it look like an accident. Stage a break-in at the shop." The cruel smile returned, and Bobby's eyes narrowed. "It was easy. I hit her on the head, and she slumped right into the tub like I thought she would. Then I trashed the shop to make it look like vandals broke in. I figured it would look like one of them panicked when they saw her downstairs, so they knocked her out."

Kelly picked up the grisly tale to keep him talking. "So it would look like an accidental drowning, right?"

"Yeah, then she came to. So, I had to finish it."

*Finish it.* Bobby made it sound like he was cleaning up a spill. And his mother suggested he kill Tracy. Good Lord. Cold-blooded didn't come close.

Kelly stared at him while she stroked the big alpaca.

The animal was standing still, remarkably unperturbed by the intense human dialogue going back and forth. Two other alpaca surrounded Kelly in the corner. The rest had scattered back into the open corral.

Changing topics might keep Bobby talking. "If you and your mother think I'll let you steal my ranch, you're crazy," she said, deliberately showing aggravation.

Bobby's face quickly flushed with anger, and Kelly guessed she'd chosen the wrong topic. "*Your* ranch? That was never your ranch, you thieving bitch! That ranch was meant to be *mine*!"

Kelly watched the rage flash across Bobby's face, fury flaming from him, and her blood ran cold. She'd seen that rage, that fury once before. Where . . . ?

"My mom worked dead-end jobs for years to buy that place. Nobody helped her. Nobody. My dad was dead. She did it all herself. Working two jobs, even when she was sick. She put all her money into that ranch, and she was leaving it to *me*, dammit! Nobody else."

Suddenly the last pieces of the puzzle fell into place in Kelly's mind. Bobby was Geri Norbert's son. Those cold dark eyes. That cruel twist of the lips. Unmistakable.

*Good God!* Had Bobbby inherited some of his mother's other traits as well as her cruelty? He'd already shown he could kill as efficiently as his mother could. Bobby described drowning Tracy in a tub of hot water as dispassionately as Geri had described slitting her best friend's throat.

The icy cold squeezed Kelly's gut again as she watched Bobby glare at her. She was trapped in this corner of the barn. She couldn't get away. Even if she could, she wouldn't get very far with this cast on her foot. For the first time in Kelly's life she felt helpless. Like prey. What had she said this morning about predators? She was looking into the eyes of one right now, and it was not hard to guess his intent. Not with that gas can at his feet.

Her only hope was to keep distracting him as long as she could with questions. Meanwhile, she sent a prayer that Burt or Deputy Don or someone was driving up the canyon road right now.

"Geri Norbert's your mother, isn't she, Bobby?" she said in a gentle voice. *Keep him calm. Keep him talking.*

"Keep my mother out of it, bitch! It was your fault she was arrested," Bobby flared. "You tricked her into saying those things into a tape recorder. She didn't do anything wrong. It's all lies. People were trying to steal her ranch. Just like you and that real estate friend of yours. You two have been scheming to get the ranch and sell it to a developer so he'll pay you big kickbacks on the deal. Well, it's not gonna happen. This is *my* ranch, and I'm getting it back."

She stared at him. It was clear that Geri Norbert had built up one huge smoldering resentment toward Kelly. But it was also obvious that Geri had been feeding Bobby lies these past few months, and he believed them all.

"Bobby, you can't really believe that. Jennifer and I don't even know—"

"*Shut up!*" He cut her off with an angry gesture. "I'm tired of listening to you. You're just trying to sweet-talk me like you did my mom. Making her trust you, making like you were her friend, when all the time you were lying to her, tricking her. Well, you're not going to trick *me*. I've been able to outsmart you from the start. Once I discovered you'd found Tracy's phone, I figured it was time for you to go."

"How did you know I found the phone?"

His cruel smile returned. "Only you would try to call me." He reached down and grabbed the lantern and gas can from the barn floor.

Forcing down the panic that rose in her throat, Kelly spoke up in a loud voice. "You're going to burn the barn with me inside? Are you crazy?"

"Crazy like a fox, as my mom always says." He held up the gas can, and Kelly spotted a bandage on Bobby's right hand. "This way I can get rid of you and provide myself with an airtight alibi at the same time. You'll be toast by the time I reach my car. Nobody will even notice the smoke for a while. By the time they do, I'll be on the other side of the canyon and gone. I'll be in the Springs with my aunt Carolyn, who'll swear on a stack of Bibles I've been with her since morning."

"Bobby, be sensible. Nobody's going to believe that I stayed in a burning barn. Even with a cast on my foot, I'd run out. They're going to come looking for you. I told them I was coming to see you." Kelly prayed she could lie as convincingly as Bobby.

No such luck. Bobby's smile widened. "Stop lying, Kelly. I know you didn't tell anyone because they wouldn't have let you come. Not with that broken foot." He pointed at her cast. "Bad sprain, my ass. I knew you were lying on the phone. I could tell."

Panic closed in. Bobby could almost read her mind. In fact, he already had. Bobby had lured her here. He'd spread bread crumbs, and she had followed the trail. She'd deliberately ignored her instinct that warned her not to come. She walked right into his trap.

The big male alpaca snorted and shuffled in front of her. She grabbed his coat with one free hand. Without him, there was nothing between her and a cold-blooded killer. Fear clawed up her throat again.

"Nobody's going to believe it was an accident, Bobby."

"Sure they will," he said in an arrogant tone. "Same old Kelly, always snooping around, came up to the ranch looking for clues. Of course, you're pretty clumsy with that cast on your foot. So it's easy to believe that you tripped over something in the barn, bumped your head as you fell, and knocked yourself out. Fire started when you dropped the lantern, catching you on fire as you lay there unconscious." Bobby held up the lantern. "It happens to campers all the time. They get careless or clumsy and whoosh! They're on fire."

Kelly froze. Bobby had it all planned. Her death

would look like an accident. How could she get away? She couldn't run. Talking had run out. Time had run out. He was going to kill her.

Then the little voice whispered, *The lantern. Grab the lantern.*

Kelly didn't understand. How could she wrestle the lantern away from Bobby? He was bigger than she was and he wasn't crippled. What could she do?

Suddenly she glimpsed her crutch and started edging toward it. Maybe she could hit him with the crutch, and he'd drop the lantern. *And then what?* Kelly didn't know, but she grabbed the crutch anyway, trying to obscure her motion behind the alpaca.

Maybe she could frighten him into backing down. Tell him the cops were already on the way. She held her phone out for Bobby to see. "Give it up, Bobby. I've had the phone on all this time. The cops have been listening to us."

Bobby just smirked. "Stop lying, Kelly. Half the time we can't even get a signal up here. And if you did, it would sound like static in the barn. *You* give it up." With that, he bent to the ground again, pulled a lighter from his pocket, and lit the lantern, fanning the flame to life.

Kelly watched in horror as he unscrewed the top of the gas can. *Holy God.* He was going to douse her with kerosene. Burn her alive.

Something shifted inside Kelly. She didn't know what, but she could feel it. She pocketed her phone. She'd gone cold all over. She couldn't feel her cast. She couldn't feel anything. All Kelly could see was Bobby and the gas can and the lantern. And the flame.

"You really think I'm going to stand here and let you burn me alive?" she said in a low voice, a voice that came from somewhere else.

Bobby looked up at her and grinned. "No, I expect you to try and get away. But you won't get far. Not with that cast. Don't worry, Kelly. I'm gonna hit you on the head. You'll be unconscious when I set you on fire. You won't feel a thing. Probably." His smile turned dark.

Kelly had seen that same dark evil once before— glowering out at her from Geri Norbert's eyes. She'd faced it before. She'd face it again.

"I'm not going down easy, Bobby. No way."

"Good. I love a fight," he taunted as he approached, gas can in hand. "Go on, git," he yelled and smacked the alpaca standing in front of Kelly.

The animal bolted, and Kelly swung her crutch as hard as she could. *Wham!* She caught Bobby on the side of his head. Bobby let out a surprised cry, the lantern and gas can dropping from his hands as he fell to his knees.

Kelly swung the crutch again, knocking Bobby flat on the ground.

"You *bitch*! Wait'll I get my hands on you!" he yelped in pain.

Knowing she could never escape Bobby once he regained his footing, Kelly whacked him once more on the back of his head, then dropped the crutch and grabbed the gas can.

Moving from some inner direction, she poured a stream of kerosene in a swooping arc on the hay then threw the rest of it onto Bobby's face and shoulders as he tried to stand.

Bobby shrieked and fell to his knees again, pawing at his eyes. He grabbed some hay, trying to wipe his eyes while he screamed obscenities.

Kelly clumped over to the lantern and grabbed it. Heaving it over her head, she smashed it to the kerosene-soaked hay at her feet. The lantern's flame leaped to the hay and ignited it, sending a flame rippling in an arc surrounding Bobby.

Scrambling to the spot where Bobby first lit the lantern, Kelly searched for the lighter. Her hand fumbled through the straw until she found it at last. Grabbing a handful of straw, she stumbled back to the flaming corner. Fire encircled a screaming Bobby, who had staggered to his feet by now.

"You crazy bitch! I'm gonna *beat* you to death," he swore, blinking his raw, red eyes. His gaze darted around, clearly looking for a path through the flames to get to Kelly.

Kelly snapped open the lighter and set the straw afire. "Stay where you are, Bobby, or I'm gonna light you up like a firecracker, I swear to God I will!"

Bobby stood where he was, chest heaving, eyes darting between the fire at his feet and the torch in Kelly's hand.

Kelly fumbled in her pocket for the phone and

prayed that someone, anyone was on the line. "Hello, hello . . . anyone there?"

And then she heard it. In the distance. The unmistakable sound of a siren wailing up the canyon road. She glanced to Bobby and saw real fear for the first time.

# Twenty-One

"**Don't** do it, Bobby. There's nowhere to run," Kelly warned as the police siren's wail grew louder, echoing through the barn.

Bobby's eyes darted from the licking flames at his feet to the lighted torch in Kelly's hand, aimed right at his kerosene-soaked face.

"What's going on here?" a gruff male voice yelled from the barn door.

Kelly spun around and saw a county policeman stride into the barn, followed by a younger officer with Burt right behind.

Bobby clearly saw his chance and took it. He leaped over the fire ring and charged into Kelly, sending her sprawling backwards onto the barn floor. The lighted torch dropped from her grasp. Bobby raced to the back of the barn and crashed through the glass window.

"What the *hell*? Go get 'im, Bill!" the county cop directed the younger officer. The young blond man took off like a bullet, diving through the window, as he raced after Bobby.

Kelly scrambled to her knees, as Burt hurried up and helped her to her feet. "Kelly, did he hurt you?"

"No, I'm okay."

"Whoa, Don, let me help you," Burt said, as he joined Don in stamping out the ring of burning hay.

"Exactly what's been happening here, Ms. Flynn?" the older officer asked as he stomped out the last embers.

"Kelly, this is Deputy Don. I called him as soon as your phone call came in. Rosa told me you'd taken her car." He shook his head, face gray with worry. "Good God, Kelly, you took a chance coming here."

"Yeah, I know, Burt, and I fell right into his trap," Kelly said, brushing herself off.

"Start at the beginning, miss," Deputy Don instructed, peering over his shoulder at the window. "I want to hear your side before Bill hauls Lester back here."

"Bobby called me this morning. Said he was going to Colorado Springs to help his family and asked if I could come out and feed the animals." She closed her eyes and wagged her head. "And I took the bait, hook, line, and sinker. I figured I could search the ranch house while he was gone. Maybe find something to link him to Tracy Putnam's death. When he walked in on me, holding the gas can and a lantern, I knew he'd set me up."

"That was right risky, miss," the deputy admonished. "What was he planning to do? Burn down the barn with you in it?"

"Yeah, after he'd knocked me unconscious. He said everyone would think I'd tripped and fallen when I was poking around for clues." She stared off through the window. Sure enough, there was the young officer trudging through the snow, dragging a handcuffed Bobby beside him. "He'd left his car parked on a back road and snowshoed in so no one would see him. He planned to head down to the Springs afterward and swore his aunt would vouch he'd been there all day."

"Pretty clever," Deputy Don said, his eyebrows furrowing.

"Pretty damn diabolical," Burt muttered.

"I kept him talking as long as I could, hoping you guys would get here. That worked for a while, then he opened up the gas can and came at me. That's when I hit him with my crutch."

Deputy Don snorted, a smile peeking out. "You knocked him out with that thing?"

"No, but he dropped the gas can and lantern. I hit him again, then threw gas on him and set fire to the hay. It was the only thing I could think of to keep him away from me."

"Let me *go*! I didn't do anything! That crazy bitch tried to kill me! She was gonna set me on *fire*!" Bobby yelled as Officer Bill pushed him into the barn.

*"Settle down!"* Deputy Don commanded as he confronted Bobby. "Why don't you tell me what you're doing here with that gas can? How'd you get here? Where's your truck, Mr. Lester?"

"I snowshoed here. What's wrong with that? Why aren't you asking her any questions? She near killed me! She would have if you guys hadn't shown up."

"Is that the truth, now?" Don added sagely. "Well, that sounds real different than the version Ms. Flynn just told us. She said you were threatening to kill *her*."

Bobby sneered. "I told you, she's crazy! She thinks I'm out to get her or something."

Kelly couldn't hold herself back. "Check out his right hand. You'll see it's bandaged. That's from the burn he got when he held Tracy Putnam under the scalding hot dye water until she drowned."

"Shut up, you crazy bitch! I did no such thing."

"Hey, watch your mouth!" Don ordered, finger in Bobby's face. "Let's take a look at that hand."

Officer Bill removed Bobby's right handcuff and yanked his arm from behind his back. "Don't try to make a break for it. I caught you once, I'll catch you again."

"Yeah, yeah," Bobby said derisively. "So I've got a hurt hand. So what?"

"I'll bet if you check his skin, you'll find traces of

blue dye," Kelly said, leveling her gaze on Bobby. "I'll bet that hand was too tender for him to scrub all the dye away."

Bobby's smirk faded as Deputy Don pulled back the sleeve of Bobby's shirt, examining his wrist. "Well, well, seems like there's something dark under your skin, boy. We'll just have to take a closer look, won't we? I think you'll be coming in for some questioning."

"For *what*? I haven't done anything!" Bobby protested as Officer Bill secured the handcuffs and yanked him toward the barn door.

"Well, Ms. Flynn is charging you with assault, for starters," Don said as they headed outside. "We'll be bringing that gas can, too. It matches the description of one found last fall at a Fort Connor construction site that was torched. Another can was found up here at the ranch, too. In fact, I've got that one back at the department."

Kelly followed the police officers into the barnyard, Burt beside her. She glanced up at the cloudy gray sky. Bobby was right. No one would have noticed the smoke at first, especially since the barn was set behind the ranch house.

"I don't know what you're talking about," Bobby spewed. "I bought a can of kerosene, so what? I needed it for the lantern, for God's sake."

"Well, the Fort Connor police have some questions for you anyway, Mr. Lester. Especially after they check out your fingerprints. Seems Tracy Putnam's killer left a print at the scene of her murder," Don said as they walked toward the police cruiser.

Kelly wasn't sure, but she thought she saw Bobby's face pale. Then she caught a glimpse of a red truck barreling down the canyon road.

"Bobby and his family have been trying to get Geri Norbert's ranch back in their hands. That's what this is all about," Kelly blurted out, unable to hold back. "Bobby is Geri Norbert's son."

Bobby jerked around, despite Officer Bill's grip. "You shut your mouth, bitch! Leave my mother out of this!" he shouted, glaring at Kelly.

"Hey, I said watch your *mouth*, boy!" Deputy Don yelled, nose to nose with Bobby.

The sound of a huge engine roared up the ranch driveway. Sure enough, it was Steve. He jerked his truck to a stop and leaped out.

"Is that the guy? Is that the one?" he demanded as he strode up.

"Who the *hell* is this?" Don demanded, clearly unnerved by Steve's arrival and appearance.

Steve's face was dark with fury. He marched up to Bobby, then hauled off and punched him in the face. Bobby reeled out of Officer Bill's grasp and fell flat on the ground.

"You son of a bitch! If you ever get near Kelly again, I'll beat the crap out of you!"

*"Jesus bloody Christ!"* Deputy Don yelled as he stared at Steve. "Who the hell are *you*?"

Officer Bill bent to check the unconscious Bobby sprawled on the ground. "He's out cold, sir."

Kelly stood speechless. She'd never seen Steve mad. Annoyed, irritated, disappointed, worried, but never mad. Really, really mad. *Whoa.*

"Son, you're gonna have to come down to the station with us," Don said, approaching Steve.

"Wait!" Kelly cried, hobbling over to Steve. "Don't arrest him, Deputy. He's my boyfriend. He's just . . ."

"You okay, Kelly?" Steve said, shaking his right hand.

"I'm fine, I'm okay now," Kelly said, grabbing his arm.

Burt rushed up between a fuming Deputy Don and a rapidly cooling Steve. "Steve can explain, I'm sure he can, Don. I don't think an arrest is warranted." Burt gave Steve a stern look. "I'm sure Steve will keep himself in check."

Steve pointed to Bobby. "You guys better keep him in jail, okay?"

"Is that a threat, son?" Don asked, clearly exasperated. "I swear, you'd better get outta here before I change my mind. Go on, get!" He made a shooing gesture. "Ms. Flynn, we'll take your statement down at the station. Follow me, okay? Your boyfriend can wait in the truck."

Steve slid his arm around Kelly's waist. "Come on, Kelly. Let's do as the deputy says." A smile appeared. "Burt, you'd better drive Rosa's car back. She and Mimi are worried sick."

Burt followed behind them. "I'll call Mimi and tell her to send the word out. Let everybody know Kelly's okay."

"Hey . . . Kelly's boyfriend!" Officer Bill yelled. "Nice punch!"

# Twenty-Two

"**Come** on in, you two." Pete beckoned Kelly and Steve into the café later that evening. "Everybody's waiting."

"Whoa," Kelly said, as she shed her winter jacket and hobbled into the café's dining room. Pete wasn't kidding. All her friends were scattered around the tables, where they sat hunched over coffee cups. Burt was seated with his arm around Mimi.

Coffee had never smelled so good. And was that the irresistible aroma of pecan pie? A silent prayer of thanks rushed from Kelly into the heavens. It was good to be alive.

Megan sprang to her feet and raced over, throwing her arms around Kelly. "Oh, Kelly, we were so worried! Please, *please* don't do that again!"

Kelly embraced her friend as Lisa and Jennifer and Mimi hurried over to join them. Reaching their arms about Kelly, they swallowed her in hugs. She could barely breathe. When she could, she called to the guys who were hanging awkwardly at the edges. "Okay, everybody! Group hug! Group hug!"

The tension broken at last, everyone joined in, joking and laughing and teasing in a huge cluster.

"No tickling, Marty!" Megan cried.

"That wasn't me, it was Greg."

"Dude, touch me and you're a dead man."

That caused the group hive to shake with laughter, just as Curt and Jayleen charged into the room.

"What in Sam Hill are you folks doing?" Curt cried out. "Kelly, are you in there?"

"I'm here, Curt," Kelly called when she stopped laughing.

"Lord, girl, you sure gave us a scare," Jayleen said as she pulled out a chair. "What were you thinkin' when you drove up to that ranch?"

"She wasn't," Lisa declared sternly. "You know Kelly. Act first, think last. I swear to God, you're going to give us all a heart attack one day."

"I agree with you, Lisa," Mimi said. "And I've decided to take action."

"What are you going to do, Mimi, cut off Kelly's yarn credit?" Greg teased.

"Since we can't stop Kelly's sleuthing, I'm taking countermeasures, so I can survive the stress." Mimi lifted her chin. "I've enrolled in a tai chi class. I'm going to learn to relax. Burt's coming, too. He doesn't want another heart attack."

"Oh, wow, now I'm feeling way guilty," Kelly said, as she clumped to the chair Steve held out for her.

Curt pulled out a chair beside Jayleen and leveled a stern gaze at Kelly. "That may not be a bad thing, Kelly girl. Whatever it takes to change that risky behavior of yours. If a cast on your foot doesn't slow you down, I don't know what will."

"How about house arrest?" Jennifer suggested. "How does that work, Marty?"

Marty, hunched over the pie remains, looked up with a smile. "I'm afraid it doesn't apply to Kelly. She hasn't committed a crime."

"Well, if she gives us all heart attacks, it's a crime," Megan said.

Kelly held up her hands, surrendering to the group's goodwill. She could feel it wrap around her. Warmth had never felt so good. "Folks, I promise I will put the sleuthing on hold."

"Ha!" Lisa scoffed. "That'll be the day."

"I've heard that before."

"Burt, take away her junior detective license."

Kelly laughed and kept her hands in the air. "Promise."

"We'll hold you to that," Burt said, nodding.

Jennifer spoke up. "I guess this is as good a time as any to tell you, Kelly. We received another offer on your property. This one's from an out-of-town buyer. An investor. Unfortunately the offer is pretty low—"

"Sell it."

Jennifer stared at Kelly. "Kelly, it's still way below market. Thirty-five thousand below. There's no need for you to take that kind of loss, we can—"

"We're taking the offer. I don't ever want to see that ranch again. Bobby nearly killed me today. There's no way I could ever live up there, even if I burned down the barn and house myself and let Steve start from scratch. I would never forget. It's over. Jayleen was right. There's bad juju hanging over that place."

"Are you sure, Kelly?" Lisa asked. "You'll be short on your loan then."

"That's okay. Curt will help me find the money, won't you, Curt?" She smiled over at her silver-haired ranch adviser.

"Sure will, Kelly. Money's always the easiest thing to find, believe it or not."

"Okay . . ." Jennifer said with a sigh. "If that's what you want. I'll bring the papers over tomorrow for you to sign."

"Thank God you're gettin' rid of that place," Jayleen said. "You want to sell all those alpaca to my friend? I'll take care of it for you, Kelly."

"Sell every one except that big smoke gray male. Can't remember his name. He stood in front of me, like he was protecting me from Bobby."

"That sounds like Zuni. Yeah, he's the dominant one, all right."

"All the time I was trying to get Bobby to talk, I was hiding the phone behind Zuni so Bobby wouldn't see. If it wasn't for Zuni, I wouldn't be here right now. So I want to keep him. I'll board him with you, Jayleen, if it's okay."

"No charge, Kelly," Jayleen said with a wide smile. "My pleasure, believe me."

Pete stepped up then and announced, "Listen, if Kelly's selling the Bad JuJu Ranch, I say it's time to celebrate. Who's up for more pie and coffee? There's pecan and chocolate rum—"

"Stop right there, Pete," Kelly ordered, pointing straight at the good-natured café owner and friend. "You're not serving us. You're one of my good friends, and friends serve each other. So, put your butt in that chair and sit down."

Pete blinked, then his smile spread. "It's no problem, Kelly—"

"Butt in chair, now!" she commanded.

"That's her Alpha Dog voice, so you'd better obey, Pete," Steve said, laughing. "Otherwise, she'll come over there and jerk your neck like she does with Carl."

Everyone broke up laughing at that. Jennifer rose from her chair. "Lisa, Megan, come with me. I know where the goodies are. Marty, grab the coffeepot. We can trust you with that. Greg, grab cream and sugar. Steve, keep Alpha Dog in her chair while we set up."

Pete started to rise from his chair, so Kelly pointed at him again, dropping her voice into Alpha Dog range.

"*Stay!*" she ordered, then held up her hand, signaling the command.

Pete obeyed with a good-natured smile, while Kelly's friends hooted with laughter.

**Kelly** snuggled closer to Steve on the sofa. Across her living room, a favorite television program was continuing, characters indulging in their own banter.

"I meant what I said, you know," she said into Steve's chest, inhaling his warm scent. Sweat, wisp of aftershave, and pecan pie. He smelled good.

"About what?" Steve murmured into her hair, his arm wrapped around her shoulders, holding Kelly close.

"About the sleuthing. I'm taking a break."

"Uh-huh."

"No, really. I can't keep worrying people. I've driven Mimi and Burt into tai chi classes. Next thing I know, Lisa will be scheduling meditation between yarn sessions."

"Hmmmm. Not a bad idea. You could use a little meditation."

She gave him a playful squeeze. "What I need is to get out of this cast. It's starting to itch."

"Good sign. That means it's starting to heal."

"Oh, great. You mean I have to scratch for another two weeks?" She gave a shudder while Steve chuckled.

"You'll get the cast off right in time for softball season. Last week in March."

"Hey, you're right. Fantastic. How long do you think it'll take to get my foot back to normal? I don't want to lose my spot at first base."

Steve ran his fingers through her hair and kissed her forehead. "Not long. Why don't you ask Lisa to start working with you now, so you'll be ready for rehab when it comes off?"

The image of lovable but bossy Lisa being in charge of rehabilitating her ankle made Kelly groan. "Oh, no. I forgot about rehab. And with Lisa, yet."

Kelly flinched, while Steve laughed so hard Carl woke up.

# Collapsible Cloche

This delightful hat is stylish, easy to make, and the perfect "roll-up." The brim rolls to create a versatile edge to be worn with a big roll or smaller roll on a cold day when it needs to be pulled down to cover the ears. It rolls up in a purse or suitcase and comes back to shape, making it a great travel companion. Embellishments such as twisted ropes or braids can be added to make this a very personal cloche.

## FINISHED MEASUREMENTS IN INCHES:

| Sizes: | S | M | L |
|---|---|---|---|
| Head Circumference (inches) | 20 | 21 | 22 |

## MATERIALS:
Approximately 110 yards of bulky yarn or any combination of yarns to obtain gauge.

## NEEDLES:
US Size 11—16- or 20-inch circular needle (or size necessary to obtain gauge)
US Size 11—double-pointed needles (for crown shaping)

## ADDITIONAL SUPPLIES:
Tapestry needle
Stitch markers

# COLLAPSIBLE CLOCHE

**GAUGE:**
3 sts = 1"

**INSTRUCTIONS:**
Using the circular needle, CO 60 (63, 66) sts (or a multiple of 3 that produces the right size for you). Join in a circle, being careful not to twist sts. Mark the beginning of the round, and work in st st until the hat measures 9" or desired length from the beginning, depending how big you want your roll to be.

**CROWN SHAPING:**
Change to double-pointed needles and work decreases as follows:

**Rnd 1:** *K1, k2tog*. Repeat from * to * to the end of the round.

**Rnds 2–4:** Knit

**Rnd 5:** *K2tog*. Repeat from * to * to the end of the round.

**Rnd 6:** Knit

**Rnd 7–>:** *K2tog*. Repeat from * to * until 6 sts remain.

**FINISHING:**
With a tapestry needle, weave the 6 sts together and pass the yarn to the inside of the hat. Pull tight and weave in the end. Weave in the ends from the very beginning inside the roll.

*Pattern courtesy of Lambspun of Colorado, Fort Collins, Colorado. Pattern passed on to Lambspun by Laura Macagno-Shang.*

# Pete's Pecan Pie

This recipe for pecan pie is one of my family favorites. I've made it for family occasions for years—Thanksgiving, Christmas, and whenever we wanted a superrich, delicious dessert. Our family has always been big on pies. I developed this particular version by tinkering with several different recipes until I got the flavor I liked. You can make it with or without the addition of bourbon or rum. No matter which way you choose, it's yummy. Enjoy!

### BUTTER CRUST PASTRY
*Makes one unbaked 9-inch pie crust*

1½ level cups all-purpose flour
1½ teaspoons salt, as desired
1 stick regular butter, cold
4–5 tablespoons cold water

Measure flour into a mixing bowl and stir in salt. Mix well. Cut in cold butter with pastry blender or two knives. Mixture should be coarse and crumbly. Sprinkle in tablespoons of cold water gradually, mixing well with fork until all dry ingredients are moistened. Form pastry into a large ball. Lightly flour rolling surface (pastry cloth, wax paper, or other) and rolling pin. Roll ball into a circle wider than glass pie plate, so there is at least a 1–2 inch overhang. Fit crust into pie plate, trim overhang, and flute edge of crust as desired.

This recipe allows for an ample amount of pastry. Do not be concerned if pastry tears when trying to remove from rolling surface. Butter crust is light and delicate and tears easily, but is also easily repaired. Fit crust into pie plate and "seam" together the torn edges by dipping a finger into cold water and lightly brushing across the edges. Edges disappear when baked, and the fragile quality of the pastry when handling is responsible for the melt-in-your-mouth flakiness of the butter crust.

**PIE FILLING**
*Makes one 9-inch pie*

3 large eggs
2/3 cup dark brown sugar, packed
dash of salt
1 cup dark corn syrup
1/3 cup butter, melted (not margarine)
1–2 tablespoons bourbon or rum, if desired
1 1/2 cups pecan halves

Beat eggs thoroughly with brown sugar and salt. Add corn syrup and butter. Beat until well mixed, then add bourbon. Add pecans. Pour into unbaked pie shell.

Bake in a moderate (350 degree) oven for 50 minutes or until a knife inserted in center comes out clean. Cool on wire rack.